confederation
matador

confederation matador

by
J.F. Bone

Edited and illustrated by Polly and Kelly Freas
Starblaze Editions • Donning • Norfolk • 1978

For information, write:
The Donning Company/Publishers, Inc.
253 West Bute Street
Norfolk, Virginia 23510
Printed in the United States of America

Library of Congress Cataloging in Publication Data
Bone, Jesse Franklin, 1916-
    Confederation matador.
    I. Title.
PZ4.B7119Co [PS3552.0598] 813'.5'4 78-2196
ISBN 0-915442-53-1

confederation
matador

Chapter One:

At exactly 1000 hours I pressed my I.D. against the Seeing Eye in the doorframe of Room I Level 200 of 6th Fleet Base H.Q. on Garon. The door slid silently aside, its open rectangle framing an executive office which wasn't too different from the other executive offices in the steel and durilium catacomb buried deep beneath Garon's surface. There was a green carpet on the floor, a signed tridi portrait of Coordinator Chan on the wall behind the desk and a conference table extending from the front of the desk toward the door. The room was a little larger than usual, the console of the executive desk a little bigger and a little more complex; that was all.

But that was enough. Not even Flag officers had carpet on their floors, and Chan's usual portrait was a facsimile-signed 2-D conventional rather than a holograph. There was only one man in Fle Ba Six who rated these two variations from the Navy's by-the-numbers norm, and that man was Arturo Evars, Fleet Admiral and God Almighty to Line and Special Services alike. He was the reason my mouth was full of cotton and my spine so stiff that my toenails were quivering.

He sat behind the desk smiling a half-compassionate, half-cruel delicately introspective smile that touched only his lips. His eyes met mine and held. They were bright with withering intelligence and as remote as the stars they had looked upon in their long service to the Confederation. There was something about Evars' face and eyes that reminded me of images in the wayside shrines on

Dibrugarh, and I felt the same odd uneasiness that came when I looked at them too closely.

I choked down the cotton and said, "Special Service José Torres, sir, reporting to the Commandant as directed."

Evars' smile changed and became human, his eyes warmed, and his voice said, "You are prompt, Lieutenant Torres. Come in and sit down—no—not down there—up here next to me."

I did as I was told and marvelled that he didn't grow larger during that interminable walk up the length of the conference table. I took the indicated chair and sat down. The butterflies in my stomach slowly stopped flying and settled down. Evars grinned at me as my muscles loosened in the comfortable depths of the chair. At close range he wasn't quite as awe-inspiring as he was at a distance. There was a human warmth to his smile, and I responded to it even as my mind kept telling me that it was probably a ploy.

"That's better," he said. "There's no resiliency in a rigid object." He kept looking at me and I wondered what he was seeing.

"Senior Lieutenant José Torres, A-type Terranuevan, two Special Service schools, twenty standard years service, two citations for efficient missions, general service rating superior, qualified for independent operations," he said. "I am familiar with your official record, Lieutenant Torres."

"Yes sir," I said, as the shock wave raced along my nerves. He wasn't really a telepath, my mind insisted—merely a damn good muscle reader. To one versed in Sorovkin technique, I was probably as easy to read as a primer in my present mental and physical state.

"I am also familiar with your unofficial record," Evars continued, and I could feel my ears get red. There were things on that record which weren't good for any Fleet Admiral to know. "But I am not interested in selecting an aide," he said. "I did not ask you here to review your gambling, your duelling record, or your amatory exploits. I am not interested in your social graces or lack of them, or the reasons why the Selection Board passed you over in the last round of promotions. I want you for an independent mission. You are the only officer immediately available with the qualifications I believe are necessary. Most of your fellows are either too settled in career niches or too much in love with comfort and the organized life to do what must be done. They're good men, but they're not unusual. You are."

I looked attentive and kept my mouth shut.

Evars looked at me with mild approval. "Do you want the job?" he asked.

"Yes sir," I said.

"You don't know what it is."

"If you think it is necessary and that I'm the one to do it, that's enough," I said. I had some mental reservations, but I didn't let them show—once the shock had passed I'd managed to get my nervous system under control—and on the whole I was truthful. Evars probably knew more about me than I knew about myself, and if he thought I was the one for the job, I probably was.

"People like you are rare," Evars said. "Don't you have any questions?"

"Lots of them, sir, but I expect I'll get all the answers I need at Mission Briefing."

"You will, indeed," Evars said, "but it might be better if I gave you the picture. You might change your mind."

"No sir," I said, "I won't change my mind." But Evars didn't pick it up. He let my answer dangle until I was forced to add something more. "It's a good gamble, sir," I went on. "If I score on this mission there should be at least a promotion in it."

"At least," Evars agreed.

"And besides, sir," I said—getting a trifle bolder—"whatever happens, I'll be away from garrison duty."

Evars chuckled. He sounded almost human. "I needn't have worried," he said obliquely, "but for a moment—" he let it die and started on another track—"I expect you have a sense of duty. At least that's what your record says, but what I need from you goes beyond duty. It requires intelligence. I need information, insight, comprehension, judgment, and an ability to make a strategic decision. BuPers says you can do these things, and the Bureau of Personnel is seldom wrong."

I said nothing, and Evars looked pleased. "It's a ticklish assignment," he continued. "It requires a trained military mind but one which is not hidebound. Your work will probably determine Confederation policy. You see, we went past this planet on a sweep survey about a century ago. The survey ship noted that the planet was Class III and nearly Class IV—right on the edge of spaceflight; an industrial world with an expanding technology and an estimated population of some six hundred million, right on the verge of a classical population explosion. By now it should have been precisely at the stage when a world's technology is so advanced and its problems so acute that it can be contacted openly."

I nodded.

"Judging from everything the original survey could discover without putting a landing party planetside it's an old Imperial colony that had somehow gotten cut off from mainstream development. The survey indicated that it was a relic of the Second Empire that escaped the Barbarians. Except for a couple of hotspots there's no evidence of nuclear activity."

"Then what makes it worth a visit, sir?"

"The last survey reported a civilization level barely at Class III and a population of 200 million."

I whistled under my breath.

"We'd like to know what caused that. It's obviously the result of war, or a paranoid society. We ultimately want to go in there. Segovia's in the path of our expansion and the world would make an excellent Confederation base a few centuries from now. But we don't want to get into another Hagar." He stopped talking and looked at me.

I knew what he meant by his silence, and so I thought about Hagar. The name brought unpleasant memories. I did a year's tour on that world as a member of a DDT team that worked under cover of a consultant firm. The team was busy complicating Hagar's government by preparing scenarios that demanded bureaus, boards and committees to do governmental business with contractors and industry. It was part of the total scheme to bring Hagar into the Confederation by creating so many bureaucratic frustrations that they would have to turn to us for help. And in the process they would become amenable to civilizing influences since the bureaucracy would stifle both the capacity and the will to make trouble. It was a long range project and a living workshop for the Navy's Division of Dirty Tricks, and the group was proud of the results they had already obtained. They'd already managed to achieve acceptance of women in government and industry and were working on juvenile rights. It wouldn't be too long before the disruption became self-sustaining and would need no more outside help to accomplish its ends.

I couldn't feel sorry for Hagar. The planet and its inhabitants deserved everything they were getting. But it was all unnecessary. If Bur Pol hadn't been so eager to sell the Confederation to a virgin world in the path of Confederation growth without checking on what kind of a virgin it was, the trouble would not have occurred. Policy should have known that an Earth-type colony—an Earth-colony, mind you—would have some mighty peculiar quirks and some mighty tough citizens. Those ancient colonial worlds had to be hard, simply to survive, since Earth didn't supply them or back them during their formative years. Indeed, most Earth-type colonies were illegal, and were founded by groups who were eager to get away from Earth. It wasn't until the Second Empire that the Central Government took any genuine interest in colonials and as a result the societies on the early colony worlds were not gentle.

Hagar should have screamed danger with a loud clear voice.

Every village had a meeting house. The adult males bore arms. The entire population was uniformly dressed with distinct style differences between the sexes and age groups. Babies were all dressed alike. Prepubertals wore one type of uniform for boys and another for girls, postpubertals wore another kind of sex-related costume and married adults a third. There was not only a sexual dichotomy in clothing but also in societal rules and it was so strong that it was overpowering. Families were patrilineal and nuclear. Morality was harsh and uncompromising. The social codes were essentially religious and sounded gentle enough, with their references to "love thy neighbor," "do unto others," and "brother's keeper," but the way they were enforced should have warned even the most stupid that here was a hair-trigger paranoid culture that would explode into vicious righteousness it its folkways were disturbed in the slightest degree.

Yet Bur Pol ignored the signs, or the Hagarians dissembled so well that they gave no hint of their real nature or intentions. At any rate, Bur Pol swallowed the hook and Hagar became the Bureau's pride and joy, a place where Policy could do genuine missionary work and bring these backward savages into the folds of civilization. They went into Hagar with a full embassy and supporting staff. They brought experts and do-gooders, scientists, technicians, traders and tourists. It was the usual peaceful invasion that changes a normal world from isolationism to awareness of an interstellar society. Unfortunately Hagar was not normal. The natives took the whole influx with set jaws and fixed smiles and a feeling of hatred that grew with each violation of their social code. They wanted nothing from us except our technology, and the two decades they spent accommodating to our evils and perversities must have galled them unendurably.

Once they got what they wanted, they reverted to type, and became their normal antisocial xenophobic selves. They held a planet-wide meeting to determine what to do with the unclean strangers and followed the meeting with a planet-wide extermination campaign that left no stranger alive.

They closed their planet and started building spaceships. Then they went on a holy war that destroyed two primitive non-human worlds.

Then the Navy rounded them up, put them all back on Hagar, destroyed their spacecraft and placed a *cordon sanitaire* around the planet. That was two centuries ago and the cordon is still there. It has to be. The natives are still restless although there are signs that the DDT is bringing them into line with the live-and-let-live free-choice nonviolent philosophy of modern civilian society.

My reverie ended abruptly as Evars terminated the silence between us. "The name of the planet is Segovia," he said. "They speak a dialect similar to your native tongue."

Hmm—a classical world—I thought. It could be a problem.

"You won't be going into this completely blind," Evars went on. "The last survey ship made a detailed analysis and sent an intruder down to pick up samples. There should be enough data available for a penetration. You should be able to blend into the cultural pattern. What you do after that is entirely your affair as long as you fulfill the mission specifications."

The specs didn't call for much—just a detailed technological, political and sociological evaluation of an entire planet. However, I did have some advantages, being an A-class human. I figured that if everything went my way and I emulated the proverbial ant and worked like hell, I might get the job done in six months, But I knew from past experience that there was more grasshopper than ant in my character.

"Sir," I said, "How much time do I have?"

He shrugged. "Time is no object—within reason. There is no great rush. The Confederation is at peace and is stable, and we have no intention of moving in on the Segovians in the near future. However, we do want to know why they backslid. Take a year or two, and do a careful job if you need that much time. We won't come looking for you unless you yell for help. If you become a casualty your name will be entered on the Honor Roll. If you survive and succeed there's a two step promotion as a reward."

Two grades! Lieutenant Commander José Torres—humm—it sounded good. I'd risk my life for something like that—and then it dawned on me that this was precisely what I was going to do. But the thought of danger didn't bother me. "When do I start, sir?" I asked, managing to sound exactly like a glory hunting ensign fresh from the Academy.

He smiled. "Now," he said. "Report to Kalmard for briefing." He eyed me with the appraising look of a cattle buyer. "For assignments like this," he said, 'I like to see what I'm getting. You'll do. Good luck." He held out his right hand.

I recognized the gesture. It isn't often seen nowadays, but its origin is ancient. It goes clear back to pre-space Earth, past two interstellar empires and a horde of higgledy-piggledy Interregnum societies to the ancient times when two warriors extended hands to each other in a gesture of peace and mutual respect. The handshake was foreign to my culture but not to my instincts.

I took the proffered hand in my own. It was thin, dry, and strong, and the grip was firm and steady.

Chapter Two:

The car moved into the jagged hills south of the old Imperial base, and began a tortuous ascent of one of the narrow river-cut canyons that cut the mountain area into steeply eroded ridges. We rounded a hairpin turn and came to a halt before a barrier rod stretched between two massive concrete abutments.

A black-uniformed security officer blocked our path, and behind him a squad of Marines manning a semiportable projector gave muscle to his gesture to halt and dismount. The driver looked at me, locked the brakes and slid from her seat behind the steering wheel. I got out on the other side. We stood beside the car, shivering in the chill air while a detection squad went over us and our vehicle with microscopic thoroughness. The driver handed the security officer her trip ticket and I handed over a copy of my orders.

The security officer checked them against facsimile copies, nodded, and gestured to the Marines. "All right, sir," he said to me. "You may proceed." He gave me a soft salute and walked away. The barrier slide aside, the Marines depressed the muzzle of the semiportable and grounded the condensors. The driver returned to her seat, her face flushed from the exposure to the raw morning air.

Beyond the barrier was a bowl-shaped valley bustling with activity. Before us stretched a smooth field of yellow earth compacted to glassy hardness by the levellers that had formed it from the valley floor. Stubbed off tree trunks rimmed the area.

Temporary buildings set on glassite foundations stretched off to one side, dwarfed by the spherical bulk of a Navy tug that gleamed like a polished durilium marble in the center of the clearing, its generators humming softly as if furnished power to the various installations.

Beside the tug lay the pinch-waisted shining blue needle of a Second Empire scout ship, surrounded by technical service vehicles and overalled mechanics. Complete from nosecap to broad-finned tail, the little ship snuggled its blue indurium hull against the silver durilium of the tug, its rhomboid wings stiffly outthrust. It was a beautiful thing, I thought, the last word in warcraft a thousand years ago.

My driver stopped beside a low temporary building that bore a headquarters insignia and spoke the first words she had said on the entire trip. "Here we are, sir," she said, "Have a good tour." She gave me a crisp salute, took my gear bag out of the carry rack, and drove off.

I picked up my bag and walked into the building. The executive officer, a gray-haired, red-faced veteran wearing Commander's stripes, met me at the door.

"You're Lieutenant Torres?" he asked.

"Yes sir," I said.

"Just drop the bag here," he said. "Don't worry about signing in. You're not going to be here that long. Come with me. The Old Man wants to see you."

I went through a standard security incheck, orders, fingerprints, retinal patterns, and then guided by the obviously impatient executive officer entered the base commander's office.

"You took your time getting here, Torres," the Captain said. He was one of the keen hard types that Evars favored. I disliked him immediately, but that was because he was an Algonian, not because he was keen and hard.

"I had nothing to do with my travel, sir," I said.

"Your ship's as ready as we can make it," he said, "but you need a bit of work before we can close this mission."

"Is that Imperial my ship?" I asked.

He nodded.

"Atomics—I should have expected it," I said with mild bitterness.

The Captain grinned. "We'll furnish the lead underwear," he said, "but complain to Admiral Evars about the ship. He selected it personally." He shrugged. "Meanwhile, you go with Llewellyn here, and get your prep finished. And good luck to you." He made the ritual gesture of farewell and good fortune that characterizes the Algonian native. I felt better with the C.O.'s door closed behind me.

Algonians can't help being repellant to Terranuevans; it's something about their glands and subliminal body odor. I expect we affect them the same way. At least that's what Mike Bennetti said, and he should know since he's a BuPsych rate.

I went out with Llewellyn, who watched me with a smirk on his fat red face. "He's really a pretty good guy, Torres," he said.

"I wouldn't doubt it. It's just subspecies antipathy."

"Hell of a thing," the exec said as he led me down a corridor and ushered me into a standard prep room. "I'll be back when they're through with you."

The technicians gave me the works. They peeled me down to my skin, changed the color of my eyes from blue to brown and cut my hair into a different style. They shaved me and replaced my beard with a permanent depilatory.

"Segovian males do not have facial hair," a tech explained. It wasn't much comfort to me. I was proud of that Navy beard.

Then they dressed me from inside out in clothes which buttoned or closed with metallic fasteners. Not a seam tab in the entire mess. The calf-high boots, the skin tight stretch fabric trousers, the ruffled shirt, wide lapelled jacket and flat-crowned stiff hat and short hooded cape made me look like a figure out of a musical comedy, and I said as much.

"Can't help it, lieutenant. This is what those characters wear," the dress and costume tech said. "We researched this because we didn't believe it either. By rights you should carry a hand weapon in the belt, but we can't duplicate the armament and you can purchase it once you get there. You'll have plenty of money. There are two bags of raw gold and duplicate gold and silver coinage from the first survey sampling. You'll get along."

I walked out, feeling like a complete stranger, and returned to Llewellyn.

"I hardly recognized you," Llewellyn said as we left the headquarters building and walked towards the Navy tug.

"I don't even recognize myself," I said. "Can you tell me anything about that Imperial that I should know?" I asked as I pointed to the little blue ship. "I never saw one in working order."

"We found it last year," Llewellyn said, "orbiting one of the dead planets in the Alpharz system. It had apparently gone derelict and had been captured by one of the planets. We brought it back, intending to send it to the Historical Museum in Dibrugarh, but it never got any further than here. Special Services heard about it and requisitioned it. It was held in one of the warehouses until a couple of weeks ago, when it was brought up here."

"Why the secrecy?" I asked.

Llewellyn shrugged and muttered something about historical artifacts and cultural committees which I heard disbelievingly as I watched a tech rate come toward us on the double. She came to a panting halt before us; a chief petty officer in coveralls stained with lubricant, sealant, and carbonized fuel.

"Are you Lieutenant Torres?" she asked me.

"I'm Torres," I said, "and who are you?"

"Chief Engineering Rate Allord, sir," she said. "I'm the one responsible for getting your pushbuggy in running order."

"Are you reporting failure?"

"Oh, no sir—she runs as sweet as the day she was built. Those Imperials really knew how to build drives. There really wasn't much to do. We recalibrated the instruments, installed a Distorter in place of the old spindizzy, refueled and returned the engine and rewired the computer leads. It wasn't much. It's been a real pleasure to work on this job."

I grimaced—so that was that. Allord probably knew how to tune ion drives as well as any Imperial engineer.

"We put in better shielding and added ten feet to the hull to accommodate the Distorter," Allord said. "You can go about a hundred parsecs at a jump without a time lag, and the Imperial drive is just as good as our plasma jets for short range travel."

"Just so long as that atomic furnace doesn't castrate me, I'll be happy," I said.

Allord grinned. "You'll never know if it does, sir, but it won't. You're secure enough. And you'll like her better once you're aboard. She's a real beauty."

Llewellyn looked at me with amusement in his eyes. He was a Line officer and he knew how I felt about atomic drives.

Allord said, "You're supposed to come with me, sir. I'm supposed to bring you to Mr. Marklan."

"Who's Marklan?" I asked.

"The man who gives you your familiarization checkout."

"I hope he knows his business."

"Oh—he does, sir. He does indeed."

Chapter Three:

Marklan, a big bodied Alpharzian with a perpetual grin, looked at me with genuine admiration as I matched velocities with the tug. "You can fly," he said, "I thought there wasn't a pilot left in the service."

"It's not a bad can at all," I replied, thinking as I spoke that this was the nicest, most responsive vessel I had ever piloted except for an airball bounce ship. There was too much acceleration pressure, since the ship didn't have dampers and I don't like voice control computers. And incidentally, I learned why the scout was called "she." That computer had the sexiest contralto voice I had ever heard. It was sheer invitation to seduction. The originator of that voice was dead for at least a millenium, and had probably been fat and fiftyish with a wart on her nose, but her voice was everything a man needed to fantasize entire dream sequences. Still I didn't like it. Sex has its place, but it isn't in the control room of a fighting ship.

"So far as I'm concerned you check out hot and clean," Marklan remarked. He unwebbed, fastened his faceplace and kicked off to the hatch beside the axial spine. "She's your girl now, treat her well," his voice came through my headphones. "Watch your board." The hatch squeaked into its seals and a moment later I saw his silvery figure in the tank drifting across the gap between my vessel and the tug. The tiny figure disappeared into the huge tug's open airlock, the lock closed, and on my board appeared a string of spatial coordinates. I punched them into the computer's memory banks and a moment later the commo board glowed with the traditional "Good Luck" which changed as I watched to "Good Hunting."

The communications board glowed and letters formed on its surface. I snorted as I read the superscription, the file number, the classification code, the sender's data, the address and the index. There was a lot of hokum in the service, like this rigmarole that required a skipper to receive orders in space. The whole thing was a hangover from a time so distant that I didn't want to think of it. I scanned the commo, paying attention only to the four lines of Navyese.

1. PAC VO FLEBA6C EF IM L/C TORRES, J.C. CSN A 27431C TAIC SV K9-7432, & CONDCT ISC/M SEGOVIA FL CAT #6847

2. FT FAM CWO MARKLAN, A.L. CSN W 13942704 SOP XC ØLDG.

3. C FAM SBJ OFF WPAM.

4. TDN PCS PA1—4014, 2-1673, 8-4920 TDNA

EVARS CINC6

OFL: KALMARD BADJ

Translated it read: 1. Pursuant to authority contained in the verbal orders of the Sixth Fleet Base Commander, and effective immediately, Lieutenant Commander Torres, José Carlos, Confederation Navy Serial Number A27431C is to assume independent command of space vessel K9-7432, and conduct individual scouting mission of the planet SEGOVIA, Fleet catalog #6847.

2. Flight familiarization with Chief Warrant Officer Marklan, Andrew Longstreet, Confederation Navy Serial Number W13942704, will follow standard operating procedure except there will be no landings.

3. Upon completion of familiarization, subject officer will proceed on assigned mission.

4. The travel directed is necessary in the Confederation service. This will be a permanent change of station and authorized under procurement allowances 1-4014, 2-1673, 8-4920. Travel of dependents is not authorized.

EVARS

Official: Kalmard   Commander in Chief Sixth Fleet
          Base Adjutant

I grinned as I cleared the board.

"Computer," I said.

"Yes sir," it murmured passionately.

"Set first coordinates into the Distorter."

"Yes sir, shall I fire, sir?"

"Of course," I said. And space wavered, shifted, and steadied as the scout moved a dozen parsecs closer to my goal.

Two jumps later the scout ship flashed out of Distorter space halfway between the orbits of the third and fourth planets of the G-type sun that held them. The solar spectrum matched the chart data; so we were in the right spatial segment. Not bad, I thought, with mild self-congratulation, although it was really the computer's doing.

We were about half a million kilometers above the plane of the ecliptic and about twenty-three million ahead of the fourth planet which was where I should be going.

I had the computer lay a course for the planet and run in threespace drive although it protested that it could stop me just outside the atmosphere shell with a Distorter shift, and do it in a thousandth part of the time I'd use poking along on reaction drive, but I wasn't in a hurry and wanted to use the time to flesh out the bare bones of the survey report. Besides, I didn't trust the computer that much, for modern Distorter fields not only warped space but they also warped time, and I wasn't sure of the conversion circuits our people had installed to modernize my sexy thinking machine. The problems of objective and subjective time that had helped kill the Empire, were solved by the Distorter, which was, perhaps, the crowning achievement of human civilization, since it made communication feasible over interstellar spaces. Now if someone would develop an inertialess drive for operation in normal space, the time lapse problems of interstellar flight would be over. But operation of the Distorter over distances shorter than one Lume-minute was dangerous and I had no desire to abort this mission before it began. There was something odd about the fact that it took a couple of days to cross the ten thousand light year breadth of the Confederation, but a couple of weeks to cover the relatively short distance between breakout and destination. Like now, for instance—I had come better than six thousand light years in less than a standard day, but it would take almost two weeks to cover the less than two Lume-minutes that separated me from Segovia—leap along, creep along described it pretty well.

I swung the ship on her gyros until her nose was pointed directly at Segovia and centered the analyzer on the planet. Despite my caustic thoughts about the efficiency of the ship's computer, the Imperial job wasn't bad. It was at least as good as the ones we used and maybe better. It held accurately on the setting and required no adjustment.

I had the computer relay the radio noise to me via the pilot's helmet, and was delighted to learn that outside of a few flowery adornos and accent shifts, the speech was virtually the same as the dialect spoken on my homeworld, but I hadn't used Terranuevan for quite a while and I found my native tongue was a little rusty. I couldn't help shuddering at some of the flowery Segovian expressions, and felt that this language was a bit too rich for my cold Terranuevan blood. I would need to practice before it came trippingly to the tongue and I could handle it on a routine basis. I never said things like that, not even in Confed lingua. I checked the electromagnetic emissions from the world below. There were literally hundreds of occupied frequencies from the characteristic VHF and UHF emissions of videos to the lower range wavelengths of the radio range. I turned the ship's receiver to 1240 kilocycles which was the old Imperial Official band—reserved for government communiques, official announcements and state propaganda and enlightenment broadcasts. If the band was still official, it should give me a chance to evaluate the language in terms of its best usage, for whatever else the government stations may be, they are never uncouth, colloquial, or common insofar as words are concerned.

The channel wasn't governmental unless government on Segovia had gone commercial. That was possible, but hardly probable, and no conceivable government announcer would have the oleaginous voice that came from the headset extolling the virtues of a barium depilatory guaranteed to remove any and all hair—anywhere.

"Is your social status imperiled by primitive hirsutism?" the voice asked in hushed accents. "Are you conscious of end-of-the-week stubble? Do your legs, arms and chest have that smooth, manly, macho feeling? Are they totally devoid of bestial hair? If you have the slightest doubt about your grooming or appearance, you should try Maestro—the perfect depilatory for all occasions." The voice continued at some length extolling other products to control weight, improve muscle tone, enhance sexual potency and improve breath and body odors. I stood it as long as I could before changing frequencies. I could understand every word, but for some reason I was neither impressed nor convinced.

I found an odd musical effect which held my interest until it came to an abrupt end and a hoarse almost unintelligible voice replaced it. "Like cubes, man." the voice said "Yah—square on every side, but ear me machos—cubes have their good points—all eight of them. Like this skimmer by 'Moroso Gonzales and his bouncing brass called 'Fontanella'—here it goes—" and another odd orchestration of brass, strings and drums filled the headphones.

"Gah!" I said and turned it off. One thing was sure. I'd never be a radio fan, and if the video was of comparable quality, I'd never get red eyeball disease on this world. "Computer," I said.

"Yes, Don José," the voice murmured seductively, "What do you wish?"

"I wish you were more impersonal and less intimate," I said.

"I can't help it. It is in my construction and basic programming," the computer cooed. "But I've never had complaints from any of my other bosses."

"Forget it," I said. "You have the analysis of Segovia in your memory banks."

"Is that a question, sir?"

"Yes."

"I do, Don José." The computer made it sound like a response to a marriage vow.

"Then compare it with what you can detect on the planet surface and give me an evaluation as soon as possible."

"Aren't you going to program me?" the voice asked.

"Why should I? You have discrimination capability."

"Very well, my lord. But if I focus all my attention on the planet, you will have to keep watch. I can't analyze a problem of this magnitude and operate the ship at the same time."

"Noted," I said. "Proceed."

The complex of electronic and subetheric devices that formed the ship's search and analytic mechanisms went to work on Segovia. A language is not as simple as military orders, nor is a society as simple as a military unit or a fleet, nor are civilian customs and military traditions quite the same thing. Hence the ship, which could analyze a battle fleet in microseconds, ground away for hours that lengthened into days, while I enjoyed relative peace and quiet undisturbed by the passionate contralto voice of the computer.

At last the voice returned. "Mission complete to limit of my capabilities. Comparison Printout herewith." A thick spool of hairline wire extruded from the base of the analyzer.

"Am I expected to absorb that?" I asked.

"Negative—that is for Fleet Base analysis. I have prepared a short summary for you."

"Thank God," I said as a small spool followed the big one. "Take over," I said to the computer. 'I'm going to try to absorb this." I took a handful of food concentrate tablets and swallowed them. I was going to need energy for this ordeal. They'd keep me going while the auto-educator impressed data on my brain. When this was over, I'd know even more about Segovia than I already did—and I already knew quite a bit more than I really wanted to know. Mission Briefing on Garon had been more than generous. I took the educator helmet out of its rack, put it on my head, adjusted the contacts and flipped the switch....

I awoke feeling like I had been passed through a meat grinder. My body ached. My head was on fire. My eyes wouldn't focus. My muscles were cramped and I was hungry enough to enjoy emergency rations! I took a few analeptol tablets and when the pain subsided to a bearable ache I swallowed some emergency ration concentrate.

Presently—only mildly uncomfortable—I checked our position. The planet was in the forward screen looping across the plane in a crazy figure of eight orbit. It was the usual inverted relativity, I thought, as I coded for a stable orbit. The computer hummed, chirped, beeped, took a fix on the planet, and after a few bursts from the steering jets, the world settled down and hung quietly in the center of the forward screen.

I orbited, checking the ground for suitable landing sites, observing towns, farms and individuals. My costume, I decided, needed no change except for the hand weapon. I doubted whether a Kelly would be acceptable. The things I saw were projectile weapons, rather primitive but effective enough for killing purposes. I didn't worry about my capability of handling such a weapon since I was third or fourth fastest duelling draw on Garon, and while we shot only to stun, the use of a killing charge didn't change the technique. I was sure I could hold my own upon this world.

I noted that the cities were ghosts of their former selves. Vast suburban areas were abandoned and only the centers showed life. The country was fairly well settled except in the vicinity of some twenty circular areas enclosing a number of shining buildings. In the region immediately surrounding these structures there was no evidence of human life, although the structures themselves were rich with human traces.

I searched for signs of war. There were ruins and fire damage aplenty, but there were only three locations on the planet where residual traces of atomics could be found, and even there the radiation levels indicated that these areas had been established at least a century ago. Yet the absence of recent hostilities wasn't that reassuring. I decided to come down in some uninhabited spot and work my way slowly into the society until I discovered what had happened.

I was deep in the middle of computing a landing orbit when a bullhorn squawked behind the central panel and a whole bank of lights turned red.

"Evasive action!" I yelled in the command mode and reached for the control panel. I was slow by milliseconds. The computer spun the ship, fired a blast from the stern tubes, blew the starboard steering jets and fired another blast from the main drive. The lights blinked out, the noise stopped.

"What in hell was that?" I demanded.

"The larger satellite, Don José. Do you wish me to take evasive action when it approaches on the next revolution?"

"No. Change orbit to one closer to the surface of the planet."

"Yes, my lord."

I debated whether I should allow the computer discretionary powers over the ship and decided against it. "Take necessary evasive action from now on," I said, "but maintain your new orbit."

"Yes, my lord," the computer said. "You should have given me that instruction before."

"Shut up!" I snapped. Well, no harm had been done, but it showed that both the computer and I needed a better meeting of the minds, and that I needed time to organize the data I had acquired. I ran my fingers over the ornate Imperial script on the platinum plate embedded in the control panel. "Protect us, oh God," it read. "Thy space is so vast and we are so small." It was appropriate, I thought, especially for someone as alone as I. I couldn't help the thought that while it was typical of the Confederation to send out small investigative or contact parties, this mission was ridiculous. I had no business being alone. A one-man mission simply didn't cover enough territory or have backup capability if things went sour. Still, Confleet wouldn't use an A-class intelligence officer unless it was necessary, so there must be a reason behind this that I hadn't discovered. Maybe it had to be a one man operation. I shook my head. Anyway, I'd learn soon enough.

I picked a spot in the mountains near one of the circular areas and made a manual approach. Although the computer had behaved well enough, my faith in it hadn't increased. I like my machines to be seen but not heard, and a talking computer made me uncomfortable. Furthermore, its technical language banks were in Imperial dialect which was sufficiently different from both Terranuevan and Segovian to make immediate understanding somewhat less than a

90 percent probability.

The mission specs called for a concealed submerged landing site, but the choice of location was left to my discretion. I chose a deserted lake for the touchdown; a roughly circular body of water surrounded by the caldera of a collapsed volcano. I checked the lake with the organic detector on my first close orbit and drew a blank except for a few scattered life blips that weren't large enough to be human. It was a little surprising because a few kilometers away there was a large aggregation of them inside one of those circular perimeters that looked enough like a fortress to make me compute a low level approach that would keep the ship well away from its line of sight.

The landing went smoothly down to the final split second when I fired the braking jets. Something must have gone wrong with the ancient firing mechanism because the ship shuddered, stopped dead in mid-air, wobbled, and toppled flank down on the surface of the water. I was slammed sideways in my web and a piece of badly secured equipment broke from its fastenings and landed with pinpoint accuracy on my head.

The ship sank below the surface of the water, and by the time I recovered consciousness it was resting on the bottom of the lake in normal takeoff position, which the computer and the gyros had made it assume during its downward passage. I groaned. The ship's medical extensions had been at work on me with analgesics and restoratives but I still felt terrible. I had a throbbing headache and an egg-sized lump over my left temple.

The emergency lights were on and all around were the sounds of autoservice mechs as they checked circuits and components. To an extent unknown in modern ships, the Imperial military craft had self-repair facility. As long as its replacement bank held out, an Imperial war ship stayed spaceworthy. I listened until the noise died away except for the subliminal sounds of the computer.

"Computer," I said, "Report in general terms, omitting details, cause of landing failure. Damage report. Present condition."

"Proximate cause of landing failure," the computer said in an impersonal tone, "was pilot error. Secondary cause servo failure on vertical attitude steering jets. Pilot should have landed on automatic control. Human reflexes too slow to compensate." There was, I thought, a smug note in the passionless voice, as though the machine was saying "It serves you right, you slow-witted oaf."

"Impact force two point five seven gravities Earthscale," the computer continued. "No serious damage to ship or contents. No hull damage. Minor circuitry damage. Minor damage and replacement of interior fixtures, including crew. All damage and displacement corrected. List follows."

"Omit list. Continue report," I said.

"Pilot struck on left temporal region by improperly secured navigation component F-23. Approximately fifty kilograms per square centimeter impact damage along an area of forty two square centimeters incorporating the left parieto-temporal suture. Cerebral area code-"

"Omit details. Proceed." I interrupted.

"Pathology follows: Subcutaneous hematoma eighteen centimeters in diameter at impact area. Slight meningeal damage with some lymphoid effusion into subarachnoid space at area of impact. No hemorrhage contracoup. No detectable cerebral damage. EEG within normal limits. Pilot unconscious for eighteen point two one standard minutes. Routine analgesic analeptic therapy administered hypodermically. Prognosis good."

"Report acknowledged," I said. A fifty kilogram per square centimeter wallop was enough to fracture a man's skull. I must have a hard head, but hard or not, it still ached. I wished aloud that I had some aspirin.

"Why didn't you let me land the ship?" the computer asked as one of its handlers deposited two aspirin tablets into my left hand.

"I didn't trust you," I said as I swallowed the pills.

"You should. I was built to serve man, not to destroy him."

I had an irrational desire to justify my action, but somehow I managed to choke it back. "Fitness report on pilot and ship," I said.

"Ship operative," the computer replied. "Within human limits pilot also operative." I grinned. The machine had personality. "You will remain on auxiliary and standby power with a minimum screen up." I ordered. "If anyone except myself touches the screen you will alert all defensive armament. If interference continues or an attempt is made at entry you will repel boarders. If you cannot hold your screens you will place the ship in lunar orbit around farther moon. If you are prevented from reaching lunar orbit or are in danger of being overpowered you will distort back to Garon. If you are not further attacked, or if you can successfully defend yourself, you will remain in orbit until you receive my IFF recognition code signal on 21.4 megacycles. You will then open communication with the IFF signal and obey its instructions. Any questions?"

The computer beeped and chittered faintly. "No questions," it replied. "Instructions received and understood. Will comply. Out."

Silence fell upon the ship. The graveyard quiet shocked me a little. I shrugged. I'd have to return in a few years and recharge the ship's power supply if I wanted to keep the vessel in operating condition, but otherwise there was no sweat. Imperial indurium was one of the toughest synthetics man had ever made, tougher even than the Confederation's durilium, but considerably heavier and somewhat less resistant to Cth ablation and a little less opaque to cosmic radiation. But in resistance to ordinary corrosive processes, there was nothing that was its equal.

I unfastened my safety web, put on my helmet and entered the airlock. The inner door closed. There was a hiss of air and the outer door opened. Water rushed in, and surrounded by a horde of bubbles, I rose to the surface of the lake. Behind me the ship nestled blue and slim against the steep underwater cliff of the ringwall, the faintest of ghostly auras surrounding her lean slim-waisted shape.

Chapter Four:

I came to the surface of the lake in the shadow of a vertical sweep of ringwall, floated on my back and looked across the lake at the moon hanging above the dark serrations of the trees along the shoreline. Its light poured in a rippling gold cascade across the surface of the water. Beyond the trees a gap in the ringwall of the caldera blended with the darkness of the sky. I was conscious of the loom of those towering cliffs that enclosed most of the lake as I paddled down the moonlit path toward the tree-lined shore.

The water was cold, even through the insulation of the suit, but I left the heaters off and moved a bit more rapidly. The exertion made me dizzy. My head throbbed, but my body warmed. I had a gut feeling that no one should hurt as much as I did, but I'm sensitive to minor pains and a bit of a hypochondriac. Big hurt I can stand, it's the little ones that put me off, and as I moved most of the discomfort vanished.

As I reached the shore, the second of Segovia's satellites climbed swiftly into the heavens on the trail of the first, and swept past the slower and more distant moon. The shifting moonshadows on the trees and cliffs swayed as though they were alive as the speeding satellite soared past the zenith and dropped behind the escarpment, throwing brief knife-edged silhouettes of rock into black relief against the glowing disc.

I opened my faceplate as I came to my feet and waded ashore. The air was cool and aromatic. Its clean oxygen content was exhilarating. The ache in my head vanished. Someone ought to bottle this stuff and sell it to the Confederation, I thought. Places like Dibrugarh could use it.

Before the slow moon vanished I found a cave in the ringwall and cached my suit and the service Kelly. I buried them under the floor of the cave and covered my tracks as I backed out of the hole in the rock. I made a quick mental note of the location and the landmarks that would return me to the cave when the time came. I stuffed the second Kelly, an Alpharzian creation that didn't look at all like a weapon, into the waistband of my breeches and began to ascend the slope along the broken rim of the ringwall.

I found a game trail and followed its zigzag ascent, pausing every now and then to rest my complaining lungs and muscles. Those Distorter jumps must have taken longer than I thought, for I was in dreadful shape. I shouldn't be this decrepit, and despite the slightly low oxygen content of the air my lungs should handle the atmosphere readily enough. But I was exhausted by the time I took cover beneath a spreading bush to let my punished body rest. The noises of the night, stilled by my scramble up the slope, did not resume and I was conscious of the silence.

In the distance I heard a sputtering noise that was so palpably artificial that I froze. It rose to a crescendo and slowed to an intermittent popping a few meters away.

I have good night vision and I saw the two-wheeled vehicles and their riders quite plainly. They were dressed much as I, and I finally recognized the noise as a reciprocal, internal-combustion, hydrocarbon-burning, air-breathing engine; one of those noisy smelly stinkpots that poison the air of early Class III civilizations. I hadn't seen one since my visit to Arkane a few years ago. They were bulky, awkward, and inefficient—and positive evidence that this world's technology was low. Any civilization above middle III had better power sources than these smog generators.

I decided not to show myself since I had no idea why these nocturnal riders were here. They stopped their engines and began talking.

"Better let the bikes cool off a few minutes," one voice said. "That last climb was a bitch." The voice was light and clear and I had no trouble understanding.

"I don't know why I let you talk me into this," the second voice said. This one was heavier and deeper toned. "This is goon country. There's a Ring a few kilometers away. It's dangerous to be here at night."

"I tell you, I saw it, and whatever it was, it wasn't Alien."

"How could you tell?"

"It was coming at an angle. It had wings, and it sounded different. I watched it and it was heading for the lake. There's no Ring near the lake. It's south of the ringwall."

"A meteor maybe?"

"With wings and no glow?"

"A plane?"

"Who has planes nowadays? And it wasn't a convertible or a 'copter. There was no rotor noise."

"Okay, okay, but I'll bet you're dreaming. You've gotta be dreaming. That story about the Imperium finding us has been around so long that it's become a legend. Sure—there's men out there in the galaxy who could help us against the Aliens and the goons, and we keep praying for them. So we get wishful."

"We still should look," high voice said.

"Goons can get here as quickly as we did, and don't think they won't."

"So we keep the motors running and the drive in gear. If the goons come, those people in that ship will need help to get away. We can lure the beasties off."

"I wish you weren't so sure that was a ship," low voice said.

The two started their motors and rolled down the trail up which I had come. I watched them leave and wondered what a goon was. Probably something nasty if the voices were to be believed. The smaller faster moon rose again and hurtled across the sky. I should have parked the ship on that satellite, I thought. These people don't have space flight. But—I paused as the noise of the engines faded and the moon climbed into the sky. As it touched the zenith and began its plunge toward the ringwall a scream came from below. The sound, muted by distance, held such overtones of horror that my scalp crawled and sweat broke out on my forehead.

I put my hand on the Alpharzian Kelly and set it to maximum and full aperture. It was a jewelry piece, but it was deadly enough. At short range it packed the wallop of a service Kelly, and though it couldn't fire so long or so accurately as the bigger handgun, it could do a respectable amount of damage.

Hydrocarbon engines roared as wheel to wheel the two riders hurtled up the game trail and raced past, hunched over the steering bars of their vehicles. Behind them, moving swiftly through the dappled darkness came a huge grayish figure moving with great bounds on all fours. Yet fast as it was, the machines were faster, and vanished over the brow of the hill well ahead of their pursuer. The gray shape skidded to a stop on stiffened limbs, whirled, and leaped toward me. Its abrupt change of direction was so swiftly and smoothly executed that it was almost upon me before I realized what was happening.

But if my brain was slow, my reflexes were not. I am the third—maybe fourth—fastest duelling hand in Sixth Fleet, and an accurate shot. The Kelly came up and spouted a sizzling cone of energy into the leaping figure. There was a puff of smoke and a flat explosion as disrupted cells hissed and burst apart in the ravening energy of the blast.

The monstrous shape was hurled backward by the explosion, yet it still moved. It came crawling towards me.

I was appalled. That blast should have torn the thing in half, but it hadn't stopped it. I fired again, and the lower half of the thing disappeared, but the upper parts kept crawling toward me, the pits of eyesockets gleaming, the fanged jaws slavering, as the heavy forelegs dragged the shattered body toward me. I burned its head with a minimum aperture blast and it lay still. I came out of my cover, picked up a stick and prodded the charred body. The great gray arms moved, the clawed hand-like members clutched, the stick was twisted from my grasp and snapped in two. I shrank back. It was still dangerous. I looked down at the truncated shape. This had to be a goon. I shuddered with revulsion. It was alien to anything I knew, a horrid killing machine, yet in the aggregate it was familiar. Somehow there was a relationship between it and myself and the idea made me want to vomit. For it was not alive as I knew life. Its vitality was obscene, abnormal, almost incomprehensible. The idea that it was something made—something artificial, something designed to kill man was almost overpowering. I was certain that this thing was a construct. Nothing normal could behave as it had done.

Silence enveloped the area as I drew back from the charred mass that still clung to its imitation of life. I had better get out of here. There might be other monstrosities like this in the area, and the capacity of my weapon was limited. For an instant I thought of returning to the rocks where I had cached the space suit and getting the service Kelly. A larger blaster would be a comforting thing to have. I shook my head. No—that would really be tempting fate. It would be better to move away from the lake in the direction taken by the cyclists. They knew where safety lay.

My senses strained against the quiet. There was no sound. Even the breeze had died. The whole action couldn't have taken more than fifteen or twenty seconds.

It was obvious that this was not the best of all possible worlds. The silent environment was pointedly hostile. The star patterns were few and unfamiliar. Only the belt of the galactic lens relieved much of the sparse sky and even this was but a faint glow rather than the luminous brilliance to which I was accustomed. I was far out in an arm of the galaxy on a lonely world that was not my own and for a moment the feeling of aloneness was a fierce ache inside my chest and in the back of my eyes.

The fast moon raced downward toward the horizon while the larger and slower satellite continued to climb the sky. The shadows wavered and blurred in the double light, emphasizing the silence around me. I could feel my heartbeat and hear the blood sussurrating through the vessels in my ears. I strained to penetrate the silence. Man, I thought wryly, wasn't too well accepted on any planet but here he was isolated. Was it because I had killed the monster, or was it because this world had an inherent dislike for man?

My foot dislarged a pebble. It rolled down the path rattling with startling loudness. "Clumsy!" I thought. Behind me the goon twitched spasmodically and stiffened into a motionless mass as its tenacious flesh released its last hold on life. And then the stillness broke.

Softly into the silence came a faint stridulation. Some unnamed and unknown creature, braver or more reckless than the others gave forth a thin furry note that was picked up and returned by another, augmented by a third, and then—quickly—the voices of the night rose to a multitudinous chorus. My ears identified some of the sounds. Quite probably the creatures who made them were utterly foreign to my mental pictures but the sounds were familiar. The world was no longer hostile. It was merely strange.

I sighed. It was not I who was rejected. The knowledge was comforting.

I walked away from the dead thing and the night sounds did not cease with my movement. Gradually the forest gave way to scattered trees and then clearings. And as I walked I kept trying to plan my course of action. I would have to enter the human society in the not-too-distant future. Where I would enter it wasn't as much of a problem as how. A city was the logical place. There, numbers of people gave anonymity to an individual. I could begin at the lowest level of culture and work upward by degrees. There had to be slums. There had to be transients who lived in them; nameless, faceless, hopeless, and ambitionless. In this gray area I could blend with the stream of life and disappear into its murky depths to surface later as a member of the local culture. No human civilization had ever failed to produce its quota of misfits, intransigents, outcasts, and unemployables, and I could enter such a group with relative ease if I took reasonable precautions. Among the disenfranchised I would be but another member, and my oddities would be tolerated so long as I covered them with a camouflage of nonconformity.

The mountain trail joined a paved road whose cracked surface forked almost immediately into two branches. The one down which I had come was crossed by a wooden barricade as was the other fork. The road stretching ahead was unbarred. There was a sign in the center of each barrier.

The fast moon was up again and there was light enough to read. The script was florid, flanked by conventional skulls and bones. The individual letters were delicate with convoluted serifs, but the message was neither florid nor delicate.

"Warning!" it read, "Danger of death! Goons!"

There was an ancient signpost pointing down the unbarred roadway "Santayana 220" it read, and beneath "La Cienega 20." The post was old and in bad repair. A cross bar beneath the fingerposts read "Camino Monosabio"—wise monkey road. Wise monkeys apparently avoided this highway although it once might have been a major thoroughfare judging from its surface. It ran straight as a ruled line toward a gap in the hills ahead.

I sighed and resumed walking.

The sky lightened and the sun came up pale and rosy in the dawn. A house and few outbuildings came into view. They were set back from the road and were surrounded by a high wire fence. The house was low and massively built with small slit-like windows. A dog barked, then stopped its noise as I went past.

Man's animals went where man went either as mature units or as fertilized ova suspended in stasis solutions. And on some worlds where man was extinct, his animals remained. And the symbionts and commensals came, too. The rats, the mice, the insects, the parasites. Man had conquered and man had pested. I wondered how bad Segovia had been treated, and how much native life was still alive.

Chapter Five:

The sun was well toward noon and I was tired and hungry. I had been following a fence line, a high outer fence supported by ceramic insulators and a lower inner fence separated by a three meter space. Every few meters a skull and bones insignia was wired to the fence with a sign "Pericolo del muerte" which was plain enough for anyone. If the insulators were any indication, the fence carried a charge that would kill large animals and incinerate small ones. I wondered at it until I remembered the gray monster I had shot. Perhaps charged fences kept the things away.

There was a gateway ahead, an open double gate flanked by two squat metal cylinders topped with cupolas. Jutting from each cupola was a metallic tube. I eyed them for a moment and decided they were missile weapons. I looked through the open gate. There was a second gate beyond, which was also open.

A sign on the gate read "No Trespassing" but I ignored it. I walked through the gate close to one of the towers. The cupola of the opposite tower rotated toward me and the tube discharged a drumming explosion and a number of metallic pellets. I rolled behind the cylinder beside me which was attempting to bring its tube to bear on me. I was pinned down.

Two three-wheel vehicles came racing toward me down the road that led from the open gates. They skidded to a stop and two men leaped out of the first car with weapons in their hands.

"Who are you, and what are you doing here?" shouted the man in the second car. "Why do you trespass on Don Gonsalvo's land? How did you open the gates?"

I shouted back, "You ask too many questions at once. Get me out of here and I will answer."

The man reached into the three-wheeler and the gun mount beside me stopped humming. "You can come out now," he said.

I came to my feet and walked over to the car. They searched me but found nothing they recognized as a weapon except my knife. This they kept. "Now answer my questions," the man said. He was obviously the leader for the other two said nothing. They merely kept their weapons pointed at me.

"I am José Torres. I am walking to La Cienega. I came in because the gates were open. I did not open the gates. They were open when I arrived."

"They were open?"

"Yes."

"They are supposed to be closed." The fellow took a transceiver from his vehicle. "Rodrigo to base," he said. "Get me the patron." There was a brief pause and an authoritative voice came over the transceiver. "Go ahead Rodrigo."

"I am at East Gate, señor. There is a stranger here who set off the alarm. He is alive although the guns fired at him. Moreover he is not wounded. And señor, both gates were open."

"So?—Discover why they were open and inform me. Bring the stranger to the Casa Grande. I wish to talk to him."

"Yes, señor."

I said, "I have no wish to cause trouble. I have travelled far without food or water and I thought there might be hospitality in a house with an open gate."

"Trespassing can get you a sore back in this region," Rodrigo said. He gestured at the two men who had come in the other car. "Continue the patrol," he said. "Let me know if you find any more soft places."

"Will do," one of them answered. They went back to their car, started it and drove up the road.

"You—" Rodrigo said, pointing at me, "Get in my car."

I did as he ordered. He didn't know much about handling prisoners. I could have disarmed him easily. He didn't know what to do with me, which argued that he was either unfamiliar with combat—or didn't take prisoners.

Rodrigo went to the outer gate, eyed it briefly and pulled a wire from it. The wire extended to the other gatepost. The outer gates snapped shut.

"Bridged," he said. He pulled a similar wire from the second gate. "It's an inside job. We've a traitor among us. We'd probably be fighting for our lives if the goons had been out last night. God knows why they didn't pay us a visit. Maybe they're tired of getting burned. Anyway, this smells more like the Union." He sighed. "So—again we escape—thanks be to God." He slid behind the wheel and drove back the way he had come.

The approach to the hacienda was well-kept with flagstone paths and mowed lawns, but I noticed that there were no trees or bushes. There was not an inch of cover from the bottom of the hill to the top, and the surface had been carefully smoothed so that nothing would be hidden from the massive structure on the hilltop that was more fortress than house.

Beyond the house on the level ground on the far side of the hill were rows of outbuildings whose purpose was instantly apparent.

"One moment," I said, "I would look at your barns. They remind me of my home." And indeed they did. I knew their purpose as though I had built them. There is a functional order to livestock operations that dictates similarity in structure. This was a ganaderia—a place where cattle were bred. It would not be at all surprising if they were not bred for the same purpose as on my homeworld. Terranueva and Segovia were both classical names and quite possibly they had similar traditions and customs. I had been born on such a ranch as this, parsecs from here; but for a fleeting instant I felt at home. Here, as on Terranueva, the old ways were still in vogue. I grimaced. Probably that was another reason I was selected for this duty.

"The señor will be angry if he is kept waiting."

I nodded. A haciendado was a little king on his own land.

I turned toward the house and as I turned a wild cry of dismay came from the paddocks, followed by a woman's scream!

My reaction was pure reflex, swept up from a past where such sounds demanded instant response. I whirled and even as the startled Rodrigo understood what was happening and also began to run, I was twenty meters down the slope, moving as fast as my legs could propel me.

Chapter Six:

Silence fell on the paddock area after that single outcry, but I had pinpointed the source. I ran down the fence line to a sloping earthen wall where a cluster of youngsters stood, and scrambled to the top. I paused for a moment, tore the cloak from my shoulders and leaped down into the ring below.

The inner wall, faced with adobe bricks, fell vertically three meters to a circular area floored with coarse white sand. It was lined by a six-foot wooden burladeros of heavy planks set about a meter and a half inside the earthen walls. A youngster was lying in the ring close to the wooden wall, one leg bright with blood. Two other boys were trying to drag him toward one of the revetted openings. They had courage, I thought, but their attention was diverted and their actions hampered by a monster of a bull whose head swung indecisively from them to the girl who was standing before him, holding a big red cambric cape.

She shook the cape and stamped her foot. Her face was bright and tense with excitement. I thought I had never seen anything as lovely, as courageous, or as foolish. She posed in the classic stance of the matador, erect and graceful in boots, skin tight breeches and ruffled blouse.

The bull made up his mind. He had spiked one cloth-flapper who had annoyed him. He would now eliminate the other. His tail stiffened, the muscles of his rump bulged, and he charged. I swore mentally as I regained my footing from the leap that had carried me beyond the burladeros.

The girl took the bull on the cape in an acceptable veronica and moved aside. It was neatly done, but the cape was a little too large for her. She lifted it, but not quite high enough. The bull caught the cloth on his horns, hooked it from her grasp and whirled it into the air with a twist of his muscled neck.

The girl gasped in dismay and began to run toward the nearest opening in the wall as the bull looked for an instant at the cloak, then whirled and came rushing after her.

She wasn't going to make it, I thought. The bull would get her before she could possibly reach safety. I whirled my cape in my hands and shouted as I ran toward them. The bull never saw me. His attention was fixed on the running girl. I put every bit of my old skill into the motion that flipped the cape over the bull's horns. Blinded, the bull hooked viciously, skidding to a stop on braced hind legs as he drove his body upward. The girl reached the burladeros and went through the opening to the alley as the bull tossed the cape aside, and at almost the same moment the two boys managed to drag their wounded companion out of the ring.

The bull was angry. He wasted a few seconds worrying the cape and then turned his attention to me. He was between me and the nearest openings in the burladeros. The others were clear across the ring, too far to be reached. It was the bull's game and he knew it. He trotted forward, head up, eyes fixed on me. I reached for the big cape the bull had torn from the girl's hands, picked it up and shook it. It felt like the ones I knew, a stiff heavy capote of tough cambric cloth. It felt good in my hands. I turned to face the bull and the same excitement blazed on my face as had shone on hers.

"Hey!" I called, "Eh!—Eh! Toro! Here! To me!" My voice coaxed and demanded at the same time.

The bull stopped, his ears swung forward. My voice aroused an ancestral memory in him. Thousands of his generations had been bred to respond to such a voice. He shook his head, sniffed the air, and pawed the ground with a cloven forefoot, throwing sand over his shoulders. He lowered his horns and snorted.

"Father of fat!" I shouted. "Here! To me!" My voice was brittle as glass, "Eh! Toro!" I held the cambric up and stamped my extended foot.

The bull charged and I met him with a veronica. The bull came down, whirled, was trapped in a demi-veronica and led helplessly around his target while I finished the pass with an insulting rebolera that left him standing alone and puzzled while I stood to one side.

A fair bull, I thought. Good breeding. Straight on the charge—but slow. I turned away and walked through the burladeros to the safety of the alley. The bull did not move. I didn't hurry, I even swaggered a little. It had been genuine joy to feel the pure flame of danger for a moment. But I wasn't going to push my luck. My footwork was bad, my timing off. I was not in fighting condition but fortunately neither was the bull. He stood alone in the arena. His enemies were gone. He was a little wiser in the ways of men and capes, but he had not been hurt, so the lesson was not driven home, and in time he would forget.

From the earthworks came a spatter of applause. There were a score of people standing there, I noted with surprise. I hadn't even known they were present. Hands reached down to help me aloft. Voices said "Well done, matador!" Hands touched me. In microcosm it was the same as it had been before the Navy recruiter had seen me and recognized what he saw. After that, José Torres had gone to cadet school and specialist school and had become an officer in the fleet; a prestige position that made even a matador poor by comparison. And since then there had been many worlds and some adventures greater than a corrida de toros.

I walked slowly around the earthwork. I wanted to find that brave fool of a girl, and that stupid fool of a boy. I found the boy first. A man was finishing a thick bandage around the injured thigh.

"Will he walk?" I asked.

"He will live and he will walk," the man said, "But he will limp."

"That is good. It will keep him from the bulls and perhaps he will die of old age."

"Perhaps," the man's face was disapproving, "and perhaps it would have been better to have died than to be crippled."

"No man need be crippled in spirit," I said. "Nor is it certain the boy will be crippled in body. That is for time to decide."

"For God to decide, señor," the man said.

Ahead a lean gray man with a heavy authoritarian voice was talking. I heard him plainly since my hearing can be hyperacute because of the amplifiers implanted in my mastoids. His words were unkind. I recognized the voice as the one which had spoken to the guard Rodrigo.

"Inez," the voice said, "You are twice a fool. Once for permitting Ricardo to go into the ring with the bull, and twice for trying to rescue him. Brave you may be, but God does not love fools."

"Was I to let Ricardo die?"

"Better he than you. He will never be more than a servant. You may be the mother of greatness."

"I am not one of your prize heifers!" the girl said. "I am not breeding stock!"

"What else? You are a woman. Accept your destiny and be

content with it. Like Ricardo, you cannot become a matador."

She tossed her head angrily. "To live here is as bad as living in the prison run by the Aliens!"

"Close your mouth," the gray man said, "We do not speak of Aliens."

"Yet you trade with them. You sell the scabs meat. You take their gold. You become rich by dealing with them. You are not much better than a scab yourself, my father!"

"And you, my daughter," the man said. "Do you wish to call yourself the daughter of a scab?"

"It makes me ashamed. Why don't you stop?"

"Enough! You know why. You know our enemies. You know what would happen were we to become weak. The rancho would be overrun. I would be dead. You would be certified or perhaps the bride of Aspromonte."

"I'm sorry, father," the girl said, "I don't mean to offend you, and I do love you, but this life is boring. There are so many days which are the same. I am stifled."

"Why don't you visit your relatives in Santayana? Go—" the haciendado stopped. "Later we will talk of this," he said, "Here is the stranger." I flexed the muscles that turned off the amplifiers. Now that we would be face to face they were not necessary.

"The matador?" She turned quickly, saw me and blushed. The color was becoming, I thought. She was as beautiful at close range as she was in the arena. She would be beautiful under any conditions. There was an aliveness to her that was extraordinary. I could feel it with that peculiar added sense possessed by some Terranuevans. She had piquancy of spirit. Her incongruous blue eyes were bright and her shining black hair a smooth heavy cap on her small proud head. She made a tiny gesture, half curtsy-half nod. "Thank you, matador, for saving me from hurt," she said. "I am in your debt."

"It was nothing," I said with a shrug. "I would be delighted to save you from hurt every day."

"Young man, I am in your debt also," the gray man said. "I am Gonsalvo Corréon."

"It was nothing," I said.

The gray man looked a little piqued. He had given me his name and apparently the name of Corréon should mean something. I'd have to play this by ear.

"Who are you?" the haciendado asked. "What are you doing here? Where did you learn those passes? What—"

"Patience, father!" the girl interrupted. "All in good time. You overwhelm the poor man with questions as you once overwhelmed the bulls with cape and sword. He hasn't had time to answer your first question and you are at him like an inquisition. It is too much."

He is a stranger. The east gate was open. He was there," Corréon said, "but you are right, I go too swiftly and without courtesy. Now—again—señor—first question—who are you?"

"My name, matador, is José Torres," I said carefully. "I am a traveler. I am going to the city on the coast, since I know something of ships. I expect to find work there." The gray man looked a trifle mollified, and I sighed with soundless relief. So Corréon had been a matador—probably a great one if this ganaderia was the product of his earnings in the bullring. At any rate—with the first step established the others should be easier.

"You would find better work in the arena," Corréon said.

"Your pardon, matador, but I am an aficionado," I used the term in the classical sense of "amateur" rather than "fan." "I enjoy the art, but I do not have the skill to perform before a crowd."

"If I think you are good enough—" Corréon began, and then stopped. "But this you should know. You are not so young, and I am not so long retired that my name should mean so little to you."

"Mother of God!" I gasped. "You are not *that* Corréon! Maestro!—forgive me! I didn't realize—in this context—in a ganaderia rather than in the arena. I am stupid!" I laid it on a little. I didn't know Corréon from Adam, but the man was obviously a personage—probably a premier matador and to lay it on a little thick did no harm so long as one sounded sincere. Anyway, a numero uno on any classical world was a great man—and an even greater one if he had sense enough to retire when he was past his prime, and the courage to stay retired in the face of popular demand to return and be killed.

Corréon looked mollified. "Ah—you could make such a mistake," he said, "That is understandable. But you would indeed be a good torero, even though you are a little old."

"Thank you, matador," I said.

"And now, señor, how did you come to the basin?"

"I walked." I gestured toward the East. "Over the hills."

"There's a Ring up there."

"I did not see it."

"Are you not afraid of the goons, those monsters which the Aliens made to kill and eat men during the war?"

"Of course. Who isn't? But I live only once and I can die only once. I have never let fear keep me from doing as I wish."

"You amaze me."

"I am a gambler, señor. A professional. And I carry my profession into my life. It is all a matter of odds. And they are in my favor."

"You would make a great matador. You have the right mentality."

"I am an amateur. The bull was a sire. He was fat and slow."

"Fat, perhaps, but not slow," Corréon said. "Under my tutelage you could—"

"Father," the girl said. "Your manners—"

"My daughter Inez," Corréon said, "She corrects my social errors while behaving gracelessly herself."

"Señorita—I am delighted!" I answered.

"Thank you for saving Ricardo's life," Inez said. "He is dear to me."

"She is a spoiled and willful girl," Corréon muttered.

Inez smiled brilliantly. She was out of place here, I thought. I hadn't seen anyone quite like her since my duty with the Mystic Matriarchate several subjective years ago. God knows how many objective years that might be, I thought. That Imperial scout could have messed up pseudotime to a fare-ye-well. I wouldn't put anything past a computer with a sexy voice and maternal instincts.

"I take after my father, so I have been told," Inez said.

I smiled. The comparison with a Mystic was not appropriate. First of all, they were not human, and she was. She was also more unrestrained, more aggressive, and less polished than a Mystic. She demanded attention, where they accepted it.

"You do not answer me," Inez said, "Have you gone dumb?"

"Your beauty stills my voice," I said.

Her eyes widened. "That is a better compliment than any I have heard this month," she said. "Do you say that to all the girls you meet?"

I shook my head. "No—only to the very beautiful ones."

"You're teasing."

"I'm not. I really mean it. You are very beautiful. You are very young and alive. God has blessed you more than most. You should be grateful—and keep your loveliness from harm."

She turned abruptly from me.

"He speaks truth," Corréon said heavily. "You are beautiful—and you are a woman, and as our guest implies, you are a headstrong fool."

"My apology, señor," I said, "But I did not imply that."

"Nevertheless, that is how it was understood by my father," Inez said, "and as I think about it, I understand it the same way."

"I regret. It was not so intended."

She didn't look at me. Instead she faced Corréon and spoke as though I were not present. "Father—I do not think I trust this one even though he saved my life. I watched him well as he caped

Ferdinand. He was clumsy—yes—but it was a clumsiness that comes from lack of practice, not lack of skill. He is not unskilled. And he taunted the bull—laughed at him—cursed him like a professional. And his passes had traces of an elegance such as I have never seen; not even in your work, my father. They were different; slower, more refined. They stopped time, made it hang, like a suspended instant in eternity. With practice he could be superior to Manolo Ruiz, for he is tall and would be deadly with the sword. Tall ones are always better killers. He is a matador. Yet I do not know him, and I know them all."

"I have eyes," Corréon said abruptly, "and memory."

"I am an amateur," I said. "I am not a professional."

"Your actions call you a liar," retorted Inez.

"Inez! Your manners!" Gonsalvo said. "If he is an amateur without formal training, it would explain why his passes are different. He could have taught himself. I have seen good self-taught amateurs."

"But not such a one as this. Listen to his speech, father. He is an educated man—not a country boy. Such a one wouldn't—"

"Ah—but he would! He is precisely the sort who would be like this—a man of good family who could afford private training. A true aficionado."

I listened and smiled. They were making me a background, and were so engrossed in their argument that for a moment I was ignored. I coughed.

Gonsalvo turned to me, face flushed with embarrassment. "Forgive me, señor," he said, "I was rude."

"It is nothing. But to keep your lovely daughter from worrying, I shall impose upon your hospitality for only a bath and a meal. Then I will take my leave."

"Nonsense. You must stay at least for the night. And I will transport you to Santayana in the morning."

"That is too much," I said.

Inez was smiling, half-hidden behind her father. "I am sorry señor," she said. "But I am suspicious. You are exactly the sort of man who could gain my father's confidence and then destroy him."

Corréon's face darkened. Without looking at his daughter he snapped, "That's enough! I have decided that Señor Torres will be our guest and that we shall treat him as one to whom the family of Corréon is indebted. Is that clear?"

Inez's eyes sparkled but her face was sober. "Yes, father," she said mildly. She looked at me and winked. "I am delighted, señor, that you will be our guest."

I hid my amusement. The girl was devious. Possibly the old

man would not have given me the time of day, but she maneuvered him into a commitment, and had done it so neatly that he probably didn't realize he had been manipulated. And now with the die cast, Corréon had no recourse but to follow through. I would have liked to laugh, but politeness and politics forbade it.

"My house is yours," the old man said.

The formula was ancient, but the spirit behind the formula was even older. It went back beyond the time of space flight, before the Extraterritorial Migrations, back to the time when men ruled only the homeworld of the race. All descendents of Empire knew the formula. My own people on Terranueva had a version of it. Men on several hundred worlds still knew it and used it. Its meaning and implications were the same on every world. The offer of a man's house was unqualified. You became a part of the family so long as you stayed.

Chapter Seven:

Corréon suggested a way to penetrate Segovia that I had not considered. I expect I was too conscious of my chronological age, for bullfighting is a young man's game. Yet many of my years were essentially unreal. The gerontology techniques of the Confederation kept citizens at their physical peak for decades.

If I could become a torero I could move through this world without hindrance. Virtually everything would be open to me. If I wanted to investigate this world there was no better way to do it. The season should not last more than half a year, and the other half would be my own. I would be expected to travel to towns, shrines and ganaderias. I should be able to see everything. Evars must have had this in mind when he selected me.

"I think you could become a matador," Corréon said. "You have talent, but there would be much work."

"How much?"

Corréon shrugged. "Ask an easier question, José. You cannot become a matador by training alone. You need courage and adaptability, for no two bulls are alike. You must learn well, because your life depends on it. I have seen good matadors come from novilleros in their second year. Emilio Herbert-Garcia was never a novillero, and he was one of the best until he died."

"A bull?" I asked.

"No—a car accident. He was drunk. Yet he was a good matador. He drank to forget the pain in his leg where he had been gored."

Corréon sighed, set down his brandy shell, and spread his fingers. "But I have also seen men who have never gone past novilleros, who never took the alternative, but remained with the little bulls for their entire careers because they lacked skill or courage. There are all kinds of men, Señor Torres."

"I am not a boy," I said, "I might find it hard to learn."

"Nonsense! You have had training. Alfredo Gomez started at twenty seven. He was older than you, and not nearly as quick, but he was very good."

"I have heard of him," I lied.

"When he was not afraid, he was great, but his blood was unstable. One never knew whether he would fight or run. He was a man of moods. Yet his corrida at Sanlucar was sheer artistry. I have seldom seen its like."

"I heard of it," I said.

Corréon shrugged. "Not all of us can be where destiny strikes." He looked at me in the fading light. "But why do you want to be a matador? For money? Thrills? Fame? Pretty girls?"

"I don't know," I said, "Money, of course, and fame, I suppose. But I think it might please my father."

"Ah!"

"I have not been a good son," I said, "Yet I might have been better if we were not both such hotheads. But his temper is mine, and now that he is dead I regret things I said to him."

"A horse without spirit is fit only to pull a plow."

I nodded. "Yet I could have been more kind. He wanted me to be a cattleman. I wanted to be a gambler."

"When one's life is involved," Corréon said, "There must be more than gambler's courage to stiffen the spine and keep the feet planted."

"I think I regret my father," I said. I was extemporizing and that was dangerous, but I was sure I had Corréon evaluated. "You see, señor, my father's death was swift. And because of his love for bulls, it might be fitting to send some to accompany his spirit."

"And you think this is enough?"

"For anyone but you, señor. The truth is that I love bulls. And there is the great gamble. I understand the odds, and I use my skill to turn them in my favor. I do not completely trust luck. You should never gamble with me, señor, for you would probably lose. But I truly enjoy hazard, and there is no greater wager than one's life."

"You have not said you were unafraid."

"That would be a lie, señor. I am not one of those who spits in the face of danger to show my lack of fear. My mouth was filled with dust when I faced that bull. A man would be a fool not to fear a toro de lidia, but along with the fear there was joy and a sense of power."

Corréon's nostrils dilated.

I've got him! I thought triumphantly as he rose from his chair and looked down at me. "José Torres," he said, "You speak well. Tomorrow let us see if you behave as well as you speak. You will train under me and when I feel that you are ready, we shall have a faena, and if you acquit yourself well, I shall see that you become a matador. Would that please you, Senor Torres?"

"It would indeed," I said.

Chapter Eight:

We eyed each other across the strip of sand; two masses of different hue and form. I, in one of Corréon's old suits of lights, a gleaming slimness of gold and silver, and the bull, black and massive with a varnished sheen of dried blood across his shoulders and six gaudy banderillas hanging in his hump.

The ordered ritual was drawing to a close. The people of the ganaderia, clustered around the ring had screamed their pleasure and shouted "olé" to the passes of cape and muleta. Ciclón was their bull. I had dedicated him to them, and every man and woman and child around the ring knew that this was their faena to remember and savor.

Breathless and intent, they waited for the kill.

Ciclón was tired. His bright orgasmic rage had dwindled to a slow pulsing hate. His head hung low on his wounded neck and his breath came in long slow sighs. But he was not subdued. His eyes were alert, his ears forward, his attention fixed on the muleta in my hand. For twenty minutes he had spent his strength in repeated efforts to kill me. He had endured the harsh pain of the goad, and the bright stab of the banderillas that I had set in the muscles of his hump. He had bawled with rage then, but now he was silent. For twenty minutes, except for that one glorious charge into the padded flank of Arrucinada's horse that had sent the picador sprawling, he had been frustrated and deceived with swirling capes and last second movements of his enemies. Now he stood still, husbanding

41

his strength, held in a strange compulsion that made us two parts of a single organism, united by the death that lay between us. We savored this moment, Ciclón and I. There was nothing in all the world except us two standing there in the sand awaiting the moment of truth.

I eyed Ciclón, conscious of his mass and power, the blackness of his hide, the smell of his blood and sweat, the sour scent of his gushing breath, the curve of his horns, the hump of tossing muscle in his neck, and the frozen ferocity held in brittle stasis.

Yet even as I watched the bull, I wondered how it was that imminent death frees the mind of the participant even as it focuses the eyes of the watchers. Right now I was closer to death than I had been at any time during the corrida, yet my mind was on wings. It had been a great faena; too good for a ganaderia. It had been technically and artistically satisfying. There had been no mistakes, no wasted motions. Ciclón had been magnificent, and the action had built to this suspended instant between life and death that transcended brutality and became something at once sexual and spiritual.

The peones felt it too; the thrust of life—the pang of death. Ten thousand years of civilization and hundreds of parsecs of space lay between the spectators and their ancestors who watched with the same titillating lust and terror the combat of gladiators, the martyrdom of saints, the public executions and the ritual sacrifices to dark and ancient gods. It was all here, woven into this tableau in the sand.

Yet it seemed a shame that all the bull's courage and nobility should end. It was terribly cruel that one so brave, so strong, so simple and so beautiful as Ciclón should so soon be dead and turned to meat on which the people of the ganaderia would feed. I drew a slightly deeper breath and the armed head before me lifted and the ears pricked forward.

I set my eyes upon the cruz, that little spot between the plates of the shoulderblades where the sword must enter to cut the vessels of the heart and bring swift clean death.

I slid the curved sword from the upper edge of the muleta, moving steadily and smoothly so as not to rouse Ciclón from his trance.

I lifted the hilt to eye level, profiled my body to the bull, rose on my toes and sighted down the polished blade. My life lay along the steel and in the precise timing and disciplined reflexes that would drive it home. I drew a long slow breath and let the adrenalin flow into my muscles. I fluttered the muleta ever so gently to break the spell, stamped my foot and called softly and urgently as I would to a loved one.

"Eh! Eh! Toro!"

The bull stirred. His eyes fixed upon the rippling muleta. Great muscles bunched beneath the thick black hide. The sharp horns swept downward and forward as he lunged.

I brought the cloth to the right. The armed head followed the lure. The horns moved aside as I leaned forward over the right horn, placed the point of the sword in the cruz and stiffened my arm. The thrust of the bull carried the blade into his body.

"Al recibir!" The shout from the rim was clear above the indrawn gasp of breath as we touched for an instant before I stepped back. A tag of braid fluttered from my tight breeches where the horn had touched me.

Ciclón stood alone, his legs planted stiffly, the hilt of the sword protruding from behind his shoulders. Slowly he sank to his knees, coughed, spewed bright blood from his mouth, and died. He twitched once and lay still, a black impersonal blot upon the sand. I stood looking down at him, my hands spread. I didn't really feel good about what I had done, but I had done it well and cleanly. It was my first kill, and there was an ambivalence to it that I feared would always be with me.

And then pandemonium broke loose! The entire mass of spectators leaped into the ring and mobbed me. They screamed and babbled and wept. They patted me, pummeled me, kissed me. Corréon had both arms around my shoulders. Arrucinada, divested of his iron boot, caught my hands in a crushing grip. I was hoisted into the air and borne off on the shoulders of the peones who carried me out of the ring and up the hill to the Great House.

I grinned down at the flushed excited faces. I heard the noise, I smelled the sweat and excitement, but somehow I was not caught in it. My mind was back with Ciclón and the ridiculous ease with which the sword had slipped through his skin and muscle and into his heart It was so fast, so smooth, so quickly ended.

Ciclón should have had a better fate than an anonymous death in a ganaderia. He should have gone to his end before a multitude. And then the irony of my thoughts struck home. For after all, what difference did it make where he died. He had been doomed in any event. What difference did it make if he died in the Plaza Nacional or in the training ring of Rancho El Primero? The fact was death—not where it occurred. For even if I had not killed Ciclón he still would have had to die. For in that half hour in the ring he had almost learned the thing no bull should ever know; that it was the man and not the cape which should be attacked. He would have been infinitely more dangerous and totally unfit for use had he lived.

Even on Terranueva, mnemonic erasure was not tried on adult bulls.

Later, when the peones had returned to their houses and the excitement had died, Corréon invited me to sit with him in the patio. He was still excited and wanted to talk about the faena. His eyes were bright as he looked at me.

"It was beautiful to watch," Corréon said, "especially the kill. You held him in your hands Joselito. It was a culmination and a fulfillment. So much life and passion requires the counterpoint of death. It makes the corrida complete, particularly when the kill is a work of art, executed with beauty and precision. You will be a great killer of bulls, José Torres. With your height, your grace and your finesse, you will be a hero."

I wasn't sure I wanted to be a hero. The two parts of a corrida that had always bothered me were the goading and the killing. The goading, of course, is cruel but necessary if matadors are to live, and the kill can actually be less painful than the methods used by butchers at the abattoir, for the bull is filled with excitement and anger and never feels the sword if the thrust is clean. Still, there is always the poor kill, the bumbling thrust that glances off bone, or the bad day when nothing goes right. Those were the things I dreaded. It is not wrong to kill, I thought, but it is wrong to inflict unnecessary pain. I guessed that if I were to offer a prayer before a faena it would be that I might kill cleanly and quickly and with mercy. I never considered that Ciclón might kill me, yet I knew with cold certainty that somewhere in my future my name would be written on a horn.

"Ciclón was brave," I said.

"He was a good bull," Corréon agreed, "I have fought many worse. He ended well, with nobility and dignity; like a king."

"The king has died," I said. "Let us drink to the passing of his soul."

"We shall have a storm this evening," Corréon said, gesturing at the hills to the East. "It is probably an omen of your future."

I looked at the clouds piled above the hills and then at the clear western sky. The sun was dropping toward the horizon and the air was calm. I shivered a little. I am not superstitious by nature but already the mystique of the bullring was entering my mind and spirit.

"Does a storm always come this way in this region? With such calm to herald it?"

Corréon shook his head. "It comes in many ways; this is but one of them. When the wind is from the East there is likely to be violence." He rose to his feet. "I must leave you now, Joselito, for I have many things to do and I have indulged myself too long this day." He went into the house and I stayed outside, fascinated by the approaching storm. The sky darkened and the sun hung in orange splendor above the patio wall to the west, compressed in a narrow strip of clear sky between the top of the wall and the clouds. The clouds moved steadily westward, bringing with them a crepuscular darkness. The ornamental trees within the patio bent before intermittent gusts of wind. The air was electric and oppressive. I could feel my scalp prickle as a ground charge built beneath my feet.

"This is foolish," I murmured to myself, "the way I feel I should be looking for a place to hide instead of standing here." But I stood erect in the open, facing the sunset, legs spread, feet flat against the flagstones, waiting.

A blue-white flash hit the hillside just below the house. Thunder followed it instantly, the crack of riven air virtually simultaneous with the flash. I flinched. My arm came up to shield my eyes from a brilliance already vanished. My nostrils crinkled to the reek of ozone, my ears rang, and my eyes were dazzled by the afterimage of the bolt.

I didn't run for cover as the rain fell. I held my place like a bull on querencia, bareheaded to the storm, as the first scattered drops became a downpour that hissed earthward. The horizon closed in, obliterated by the rain. Wind crumpled the downpour into wet folds, and tossed the branches of the trees. Leaves fluttered wildly on the thrashing limbs and turned their pale undersides upward to the heavier gusts, as they shivered and rustled to the impact of the rain.

Clouds rushed across the sky, black and formless, their darkness intermittently split by strokes of lightning that threw nearby objects into stark relief and flashed a brief lurid panorama of rainswept air. An instant later the dark was back, blacker than before, and the crack, growl and rumble of thunder tumbled and echoed across the reverberating sky.

I moved under the edge of the eaves until the tumult passed and the thunderheads moved westward. The wind rushed smoothly now and my spirit moved into the flowing air and swept upward toward the clouds. The rain came down steadily and softly in the wake of fury past. Now—*this* was how I should have felt at the end of the faena, I thought, as I watched the quiet rain. I laughed, mocking myself.

"One would think that you would derive more than laughter from such violence, matador," Inez said. Her slim hand touched mine.

I turned surprised. I had known she was there, but I thought she would retire without revealing herself. She had done this before in the past weeks—had come into the range of my perception—lingered awhile—and then departed. This time she had chosen to announce herself. I looked at her and knew why she had decided to let me know of her presence.

"You shouldn't be out in this rain," I said gently as I drew her into the shelter of one of the archways. "You'll look like a wet kitten. Your father will be displeased."

She shook her head. Her hair was plastered limp and heavy against her neck. "He is always displeased. I have displeased him from birth. I should have been a boy. That was my first mistake. And when my mother could have no more children because of what my birth did to her, his displeasure was increased. It was my fault. And my mother died, filled with inadequacy." Inez's voice was soft and remote. "Now he looks to Dolores to bear him sons and treats me more indifferently than before."

"You should not say these things. They are not true. He loves you and is concerned for you. I saw that the first day I was here."

"I must say them to someone. You will be gone and my words will go with you." She moved toward me and fitted the curves of her body against me. She stiffened as my arms went around her shoulders, and then slowly relaxed. We stood there in the darkness quiet and unmoving, listening to the rush of the wind and the patter of the rain. There was no need for words.

The silence endured until finally she spoke. "Señor, I would know what you think of me. Do you think of me—as a person?

"As one to desire?—As a woman?"

"Yes."

I wondered if I should lie. "You are the daughter of my host," I said. "Such a thought would be disgraceful, wouldn't it? Hospitality and the rules of good behavior—"

She smiled. "Thank you José Torres. I understand."

I started to say something, looked down at her face and changed my mind.

"I'm glad," I said.

"For what?"

"That it was I to whom you turned." I tipped her chin and kissed her gently on the mouth.

She returned the kiss with an ardor that surprised me. "I think I love you, Joselito," she murmured. She slipped her hand in mine and squeezed my fingers. "I must go now, but I shall see you later tonight."

"I shall look forward to it," I said.

She turned away from me and went up the outside steps to the second story. She had hardly gone when Gonsalvo came out of the shadows of the cloistered walkway around the patio. I was surprised. I had no idea he was there, until he moved. My attention must have been entirely focused on Inez, and that was disquieting. I hadn't realized that I was so interested in her.

"I was watching," he said. "You behaved as a gentleman should. Under normal circumstances I would welcome a declaration from you. But our lives are not normal. The haciendados must join together to combat the encroachments of this little caudillo Aspromonte. Inez will marry Ernesto Herrera and bring together the two largest ranchos in the basin. Together we can check Aspromonte's ambition."

"Has she agreed?" I asked. I didn't pursue the subject of Aspromonte. I already knew enough about the local Guardia Civil leader to fill a small book. The peones talked and I listened. He was one person, even more than Corréon, who was a constant topic of talk. I had heard so much that I wanted to see the man and discover if he was real. He seemed to be the sort around whom legends are built when they are still alive.

"No—but she will. She is intelligent. She understands the logic of power."

"You have not asked her? Are you sure she will obey?"

"I am."

"Perhaps she has her own life to live."

"We all have our problems," Corréon said, "she will do what must be done."

"I think it is best that I leave," I said, "I do not wish to defy your authority nor make trouble in this house. But if I stay and she wants me, I shall take her. Therefore, the sooner I go the better. I want no anger between us. I do not wish you for my enemy. I think of you as a father."

"I appreciate the honor," Corréon said. "I was right when I said you were a gentleman—no matter that you are also a liar."

"Oh yes—a great liar." Corréon smiled. "I, of course, do not know why you lie, but I know you do. And that is part of my unwillingness to let you have Inez. A false suitor makes a poor husband."

"You have reason for saying this," I said. My voice was cold. "Why should I lie to you—and why do you doubt me?"

"I do not know why you should lie to me. As to why I doubt you, I probably know Segovia as well as any man alive today and beyond the mountains there is nothing but flatland. There are no ganaderias. There never have been. In that region there is nothing but grain and farms where cattle are fed for market."

"I did not say I came from there," I said. "I came through there." I had done a great deal of research in Corréon's library in the past weeks, and now I knew my story. It would need more nailing down, but it could withstand any pressure Corréon could put on it.

"And you say that you are an amateur—and self-taught. Ha! You insult my intelligence! You handle yourself with grace and face bulls with disciplined fortitude that cannot result from anything except experience. You were a matador before you entered my gates. You are a better one now but you were one then. Yet your name is unknown to me and your face is unknown, and I know everyone who deals with bulls; so you lie."

"I am *not* a matador!" I said. "I have no alternative." I spoke the truth. On Terranueva where desire was the teacher, I had swung the cape for the fun of it. I was a natural, a fenomino, one of those rare ones who learn by instinct rather than instruction.

"Who was your teacher?"

"Except for you, no one."

"Again you lie." Corréon shook his head. "I know," he said. "I know my trade."

"If you cannot recognize truth, I am sorry for you," I said. "Goodbye, señor."

"Wait! I have written letters. I shall get them. Liar you may be, but at this moment you are the greatest matador on Segovia except for Manolo Ruiz. You are good enough to fight in any corrida in this world. I have said so and my words have weight." He sighed. "And you cause me no distress except sadness, but I shall press you no further."

"I am telling the truth," I said, "but you will not see it."

"If you fight in Santayana as my pupil, I will underwrite the corrida. If you do well, I have arranged for your immediate alternativo. Such things can be done and Mendez-Lobo at the Plaza de Toros will sponsor you at my request. There is a selfishness here, Joselito. I want you to appear like a shooting star. I want the publicity. There is money in it, and I need money."

"You do not like dealing with the Aliens?"

"I am not a scab in my heart," Corréon said. He sighed. "I shall tell Inez when you have gone. I do not think it wise that you see her, yet my heart weeps a little. Tomorrow when you are far from here, I shall tell her why I did this thing, and what you said to me. It is right that she should know."

"She will not love you for it."

"I know, but that is part of being a father."

I grimaced without humor. "It is heavy work, I think. Perhaps you are wise to spare me such a fate."

"There are compensations," Corréon said. He turned away.

48

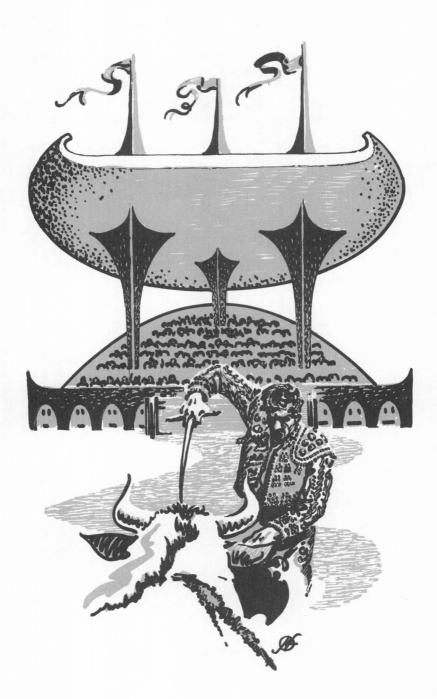

"Wait here," he said. "I will return."

He was back in a moment with a thick envelope. "Arrucinada will drive you to Santayana," he said, "Here are your introductions to Mendez-Lobo. He will see to it that you are given a place in a local corrida. He owes me that much."

"Thank you, señor," I said. "And, señor—as to my origin. Think northward to the Oriente Archipelago. Sandoval Island to be exact—the one the goons destroyed. There was a ganaderia there, if you remember."

"I remember," he said. His voice was soft in the darkness. "But the name was not Torres."

"The name is my mother's," I said, and left him standing there. He did not move and I did not feel good about what I had done.

Chapter Nine:

The brassy blare of the trumpet cuts through the brassy air to herald the last faena. Manolo Ruiz and I are mano á mano again. We have been at each other for the past two months. He is still number one, which is why he has the last fight of the corrida, but I am hot on his heels.

Last year Manolo had been unchallenged best. I had come to the scene too late to get more than a few press notices. The media, however, had been good to me and I started this season with a claque of reporters and sports commentators that had grown with each passing week. Gonsalvo Corréon's sponsorship had done me no harm, and I had an incredibly good string of fights that Mendez-Lobo had arranged for me as a replacement for Carnicerito who had gotten spiked at Pontecorvo and had been out for weeks. This year I had a good enough press to challenge Manolo, and we went through a series of corridas that had people talking of the legendary Manolete and Joscelino. And, indeed, if history could be relied upon, our styles were similar.

Like the great Manolete, I am a torero corto—a limited performer—with a cape repertoire that includes only the classical veronica, demi-veronica and chicuelina. I seldom use more than four or five different passes with the muleta, and I leave the adornos or ornaments to Manolo. But what I do is done with such perfection and temper that I create an illusion of prolonged movement, as though time itself is lengthened. The cape and muleta are living things in my hands. They mesmerize the bull, control his explosive ferocity and turn this violence into the ordered measures of a dance. Yet never for an instant does the performance lose the suspense and terror of mortal combat of a man against one of the most keenly honed, precisely developed agents of destruction on the six hundred and thirty-two habitable planets that compose the Confederation. Manolo is my exact opposite. He is the Joscelino type; small, incredibly agile, a wizard with the cape and muleta, but too small to kill a large bull with grace and artistry.

All talk of artistry notwithstanding, all panegyrics about cape work aside, all the babble of the aficionados apart, the main thrust of a corrida is the thrust of horn and sword. Death is the heart of a corrida de toros. For in every bullfight the bull always dies, and there is always the chance that a man may also die.

I have sometimes wondered why men, women and children return week after week to watch this repetitive formal tragedy of furious and explosive action that drains away bit by bit in an iron ritual and ends with a quiescent mass of meat upon the sand.

Death plays a part in the attraction, but is not the entire story. For these people in the stands are ordinary folk, who in the course of their lives would probably be incapable of drowning a cat or pressing life out of the chest of an unwanted puppy. Yet they pay good prices to come to the Plaza de Toros for their look at death, and week after week they come to watch the tragedies on the sand.

One of the factors that produce this action is probably the matador's suicidal exposure to a singularly messy death. A torero makes the bull dodge him. I once took an extraordinary bull through fifteen naturales with the muleta without ever moving my feet or changing my position except to shift from the right to the lefthanded pass, and the rhythm of the "olés" was a slow even chant from the hypnotized stands. I was a hero that day, and Ruiz was green with envy as he congratulated me for drawing so good a bull. We know each other better now and we are friends, but then our rivalry was hotter, even though no fiercer than it is now.

But the greatest factor is the bull himself and the taurine mysteries that run back thousands of years into our past. Bulls have a religious aura; at times it has been divine. Their enormous strength, masculinity, ferocity and nobility are male symbols carried to the ultimate. And in a colonial or a frontier world the male symbols are dominant. The bull is notable among animals for his regal grandeur. He comes innocent to his fate, in the pride of his power and strength. He knows his might and glories in it. Seldom is he a coward, and to the moment of his death he tries to kill the man who faces him. And until the end he thinks he will succeed.

It is an unfair contest. The bull is skillfully weakened, manipulated and tricked into a position where he can be killed with relative safety, and the tragedy is completed within half an hour. The speed is necessary, because under the stress and pain of the arena the bull quickly loses his innocence and can become a terrible agent of destruction if he learns to charge the man and not the lure. Yet with the steel deep within his body he retains his nobility. He sinks to the sand and dies at the feet of his enemy without protest and without humility; and most wonderful of all, he dies in silence. He is not the only animal that is quiet in his dying. Sheep and camels die uncomplainingly, but they have neither the grandeur nor the charisma of the bull. With them it is submission, with the bull it is majesty.

And there is something about the death of a god or a king that is removed from reality, and in the ordered death upon the sands of the arena there are elements of royalty and godhead. The bull, not the matador, is the hero—and his ordered death translates the act of slaughter to a spectacle. The bull becomes a symbol; remote, removed from comprehension, identification, terror or compassion. And men watch eagerly and come to watch again because the silent death of the taurine king evokes no emotion except excitement and satisfaction; stimulation unaccompanied by guilt.

More—or less—sensitive people have inveighed against bullfights for thousands of years. Hundreds of thousands of pages have been written against corridas, yet the spectacle continues. Somehow it strikes a responsive chord in the human soul which cannot be struck by any lesser stimulation. It fills a need—more present in times of despair than in times of success. Bullfights rise to their greatest heights in lands or on worlds where life is harsh, where there is little beauty and less hope. A desperate people sublimate their despair in the majestic tragedy of the bull, which is enacted on such simple and forceful terms that even the most hardened and stupid can feel it. And one of its inevitable outcomes is a translation of the supreme masculinity of the bulls to the libidos of the spectators.

Many times in the past year and a half people have asked me if I am afraid, and always I say "yes," but that answer is only half the truth. There is always fear before the corrida begins, but once it is under way fear becomes absorbed in action and I am filled with exaltation that leaves no room for anything else. It is no small thing to be the executioner of a god....

I go to one of the openings in the burladero and look at the toril through which the bull will come. The crowd in the stands is silent as it waits, its attention focused on the door. It opens and the bull bursts into the arena—a black mass of pulsing energy, innocence and destructive fury.

"God!" I breathe, as I watch the beast run with marvellous lightness across the yellow sand and hook his horns into the revetment of the burladeros around which one of Manolo's cuadrilla is peering. The bull is fiercer than he had looked in the corrals— huge, quick, and a hooker to the right. He is going to be troublesome for Manolo. Ruiz doesn't have the height to kill such a monster with grace, although he will undoubtedly do the job with skill. Today, I think with smug satisfaction, Ruiz is doomed to second place unless he performs a miracle. For in the last analysis it is death that the crowd comes to see, and my kills had been exemplary—almost surgically precise.

I tense a little as Manolo Ruiz goes out to face his bull. My thoughts are not properly disciplined or ordered, and certainly not appropriate while a corrida is in progress. I still have a part to play in the action during the quites, and I had better keep my attention on the bull or I can suffer from its lack.

Manolo moves forward confidently behind the big cape. He is an artist with it and can make it do things I cannot possibly imitate. It is something I do not really understand, but the tricky passes and the flashy adornos with the cape are the unchallenged property of mighty midgets like Manolo Ruiz. A big man only manages to make a fool of himself if he tries such things.

I like Ruiz, and in the arena I respect him; but I never really understand him. For Ruiz is obsessed by bulls. They are his life, and he goes to every corrida as though it was the wonder of the world, like a hungry novillero eager for fortune and fame. Yet Ruiz is a millionaire twice over. He has been on top for nearly ten years and eight of those he has been the number one. Only this year is his supremacy in doubt, and that is only because of me. In our hand-to-hand struggles across the breadth of Segovia's single continent our positions on the corrida alternate from week to week so close is the rivalry.

My simple austere style, and cool precise movement is a perfect foil for Ruiz' fiery brilliance. Between us we have made a hundred average bulls look great. We draw fabulous prices and acquire mutually antipathetic hordes of followers who quarrel bitterly even though we do not....

Manolo rests behind the burladeros as the banderilleros do their work. Probably he should plant the darts himself this day, but even perfect placement would not overshadow my brilliant kills, and since I had not planted darts, neither would he. A black pride holds him back. If he cannot overshadow my performance according to the rules I have laid down he will not win. And, anyway, he has little opportunity to beat me, for I have been very good indeed, and have collected trophies on every faena. He has matched me once, but in this fight he must collect two ears and the tail to beat me....

When the traditional passes are finished and we complete the quites where our contrasting styles are most apparent, we take a breather, where Manolo waits for the signal for the last act. He grins humorlessly. "I think you've got this one in the bag," he says. "I'm lousy. My timing's off."

"Not so," I reply. "It's touch and go, and you know it. I drew a good bull last time and he made me look better than I was."

"Ha! The bull was lucky to draw you. You made him immortal. Five munits will get you a hundred if there isn't a statue of you in the Plaza next year. You gave them something to remember, my friend." Ruiz scrowled briefly with honest envy and then smiled brilliantly, his heavy-boned face lighting. "Ah well," he says, "if I am to be beaten by anyone, Joselito, I would rather it be you than any man I know." He shrugs and gestures at his mozo del estoque. "I'll have the muleta now. It's time to get this ended." And as he takes the sword and cloth the trumpet sounds.

Ruiz goes out into the arena, makes the traditional request to kill, and then, holding cap in hand pivots in a circle to include the entire audience before tossing his cap into the stands. I grin in fierce admiration. There is no one quite like Manolo Ruiz. He would challenge God if God fought bulls. He shakes out the muleta, spreading it with the sword.

The bull is on querencia, his special piece of ground, and is doubly dangerous since in this spot he will fight a short-charging counter-punching action that will force Manolo to come to him and thus put the matador at a disadvantage. But Ruiz, with consummate skill, routs him off his station to another part of the ring where he charges freely. It is a thoroughly competent job, but it looks abrupt and awkward. The bull is making the matador look bad.

Manolo takes him through a series of de castigo passes that are necessary but so functional that he is unable to draw more than a murmur of approval. Yet not once has Ruiz made a bad move. They are simply not good in comparison, and the bull is far from the equal of mine.

The knowledge seems to make the little man desperate, for his actions take on suicidal overtones. He starts classically with a series of right handed naturales that leave the crowd gasping with excitement and terror before he switches to the even more dangerous left hand. He does the pase de la muerte, a kneeling pase por alto, and finishes with an estribo that has the crowd screaming

"No! No!" But he is not getting either the rhythm or the rapport. It is thrilling and deadly play, but it has no touch of exaltation.

He does the dangerous manoletina and finishes with a wrenching por alto that fixes the bull as solidly as though its feet were cemented to the sand. I had killed *al recibir*, with the bull furnishing the power for its death, but Manolo can't do that. He isn't tall enough. He has to go *volapie*—on flying feet—leaping off the ground in and over the horns and away. And he has to do it with grace.

Ruiz sights down the blade, rises to his toes, leaps and thrusts. The blade strikes the cruz and sinks through skin and muscle. The horns come up and past his body when suddenly the bull hooks sharply to the right. The point of the horn catches Manolo deep in the right leg and lifts him aloft.

Ruiz gets a hand on the bull's crown and pushes his body away from the horn as the power of the enormous neck hurls him a dozen feet in the air. The bull looks up, sights Manolo's helpless body as it falls, poised to spike the man to death as he hits the ground, takes a slow step forward and crumples dead beside the man he has gored.

"I am first at Ruiz' side. Ruiz opens his eyes; his face is distorted with pain. "Did I kill him clean?" he asks as I wind a tourniquet around the wounded leg to stop the bleeding.

"You did, maestro."

"And did I cut an ear against you?"

A banderillero comes toward us from the bull. He thrusts black, hairy, blood-dripping ears toward the fallen matador.

"Both ears, maestro," I say.

"That's more than I expected," Ruiz says. He closes his eyes and his bronze face turns faintly green.

"Shock," says a voice from the ring of men around us, "Get him to the surgery at once!"

"Will he live?" I ask.

"It is in the hands of God, but I think he will. You did well with that tourniquet, matador. The bleeding is minor."

Manolo is lifted and carried away. The crowd follows, and I am left alone. I walk slowly over to the burladeros where my cuadrilla is clustered awaiting my return.

Chapter Ten:

At the hospital I waited beside Ruiz' bed until he came out of the anesthetic. He returned to consciousness quickly and smoothly, which spoke volumes about the quality of medical care in Santayana. Men had lost many things on this world but not their skill in medicine.

"How am I doing?" Ruiz asked.

"At a guess, you will be running in a month," I said.

Manolo sighed. "That'll be too late to catch you. I guess you'll be number one this year."

I grinned. "I haven't won that honor yet. I hardly think I should after the faena you gave them."

"It wasn't the equal of yours," Manolo was silent for a moment. "I don't think I have ever seen anything quite like what you do." He said. "You have a peculiar variation of the classic passes, and it is beautiful."

"I experiment," I said.

Manolo nodded. "I extemporize often," he agreed, "but such acts are not your nature. You represent schooled perfection. Those passes are schooled."

I said nothing as I watched Manolo Ruiz with placid eyes.

"When we began to meet mano á mano," Ruiz said, "I checked your past. I could find nothing about you before that scab Gonsalvo Correon introduced you in Santayana. Yet you obviously, even then, were a first-rate matador—and despite the fact that your alternativo was bought, your skill was so great that you had no difficulty at all in getting good reviews in this most difficult and demanding profession."

"I am naturally good," I said with my wry grin.

"Tell that to the Guardia Civil. No man—ever—is naturally as good as that. Yet there is no record of you anywhere."

"I came from the North, from the Archipelago." I said. "My people owned property on Sandoval Island. All were killed, except me, and I escaped because I was not there."

"I checked that story," Manolo said. "It holds. It might even hold under detailed checking. But there is no one alive who remembers your family and their dossiers are not in the police files."

"Why should they be? We in the Islands cared nothing for such records. And nine out of ten other Archipelagans were just like us," I said stiffly. "That was why we lived there. We liked our freedom."

"Don't get angry, dear friend," Manolo said. "It is my nature to talk this way. I am incapacitated. I need someone I can trust to take my place, and I know no one I trust more than you. You have never taken an unfair advantage, nor have you ever said an unkind or ungenerous thing about your colleagues. And, in this profession, that is so strange that it is almost frightening. But I worry that I can find nothing about your origins other than what you tell. You are a mystery. Yet despite this I trust you."

Ruiz eyed me narrowly. "I who am conditioned to trust no Segovian—trust you. It is incredible unless I accept the conclusion that you are not Segovian."

"You're joking."

"No, Joselito. I am serious. There are many things about you which are strange. Little things. Small acts of courtesy which are not our acts, like standing aside for a woman, like bowing with the head up rather than down. Like saying "Goodbye," rather than "Go with God." These are little things, each one alone meaning nothing but in the aggregate meaning everything. You were raised in a society like ours, but not ours. I cannot prove this but I know it as certainly as I know that I am in this bed with my leg torn open."

"It's closed now," I said, "the doctor sutured it."

"Ah!—See! This is what I mean. You say sutured. I would say sewed."

"They're the same."

"Yes, but your word is obsolete," Manolo raised himself on one elbow. "You are not of this world," he said. His voice was flat with certainty. "I know—as do all of us—that there are other worlds peopled by men, and that in time they will find us, and help us against the Aliens. I believe you are from those worlds."

"And if I were," I said. "What makes you so sure that I would help you?"

"Because you are a man and they are not."

"Could it be that outsiders have passed the point where being human makes the difference between friend and enemy?" I asked softly, "Assuming, of course, that I am from another world."

"No," Manolo said. "That would be impossible. Man is man and blood ties are stronger than any other. By blood alone men would fight on our side."

"No matter if they had known the Aliens longer than they had known you?"

"No matter. We are men. We stand together against outsiders although we may fight each other to the death."

"That is not rational."

"That is the Brotherhood of Man," Manolo said. "We are all mad, perhaps, but we are all men and will aid each other in the face of an outside danger."

I shook my head.

Manolo chuckled. "That will gain you nothing, my friend. You cannot escape the logic of your race or the ties of your blood. You and I, Joselito, stand as one man against the Aliens."

"And what about scabs? Do they stand against the Aliens?"

"Bah! They are not men!" Manolo's lips twisted. "They are animals!"

"Yet they are of your blood and mine."

"If I thought for a moment that there was a drop of that coward blood in my body I would open my veins and drain it out."

"You hate too well."

"And you, Joselito, do you not hate at all?"

"Very little."

Manolo smiled bleakly, "Then you cannot be Segovian," he said.

I sighed. "You are incurably romantic, Manolo. But believe as you will. I cannot stop you."

"You can help me."

"How?"

"By carrying out my mission. You are my brother in arms against the bulls. You work for the state. You belong to Action, even as I do."

I shrugged. Ruiz undoubtedly had friends in Cuidad Segovia. Although all matadors and their cuadrillas are registered by the state, they are not all Action agents. Agents aren't supposed to know each other. Theoretically, it would be twice as bad if a knowledge-able but talkative soul fell into the wrong hands.

"I had to know," Manolo said apologetically. "Your mystery

demanded it." He paused for a moment, his face twisting with pain. The nerve block was wearing off. "Our months of mano á mano have taught me that I can trust you with my honor."

"I want no such trust from anyone, Manolo."

Ruiz ignored me. "I want you to accept my mission."

I shrugged. "I don't suppose I can refuse."

Manolo shook his head. "You can, but you won't."

I smiled. "Under the circumstances, how can I fail to do as you wish?"

Manolo frowned. "Don't joke. There's a difference between doing a thing because you must, and doing a thing because you want to. If you want to do something—" he sighed. "Why should I lecture you?"

"Thank you," Manolo said. "You will take your cuadrilla to the town of La Cienega."

"I know the place—Gonsalvo Corréon lives near there."

"That scab!" Ruiz snorted. "But he is not your concern. You are to meet with Bernardo Aspromonte, the local Union leader. He will tell you what to do." Ruiz' voice weakened. "It is important. It may help destroy the Aliens."

"Destroy!" I said. "Why must we always destroy? Why can't we live in harmony?"

"They invaded our world."

"We invaded it, too."

"But we did it first." Ruiz shrugged. "Anyway—that is the way of men. We cannot be inferior. We must conquer or die."

"The scabs wouldn't agree with you."

"Pah! Scabs! Animals! Slaves! Spineless worms! Not men— never men!" Manolo's face flushed. "Talk no more to me of scabs, Joselito. They anger me and I cannot afford that luxury. I am in pain."

I said, "One final question. Do you know anything more about this mission or this man, Aspromonte?"

"My manager has his dossier, but the mission is secret, as usual."

I nodded. "I'll check with him," I said. "Now rest and get well. I'll take your mission if I can handle it."

Ruiz smiled. "I was sure you would. You cannot resist an appeal to friendship." He winked and rubbed his nose.

I made an obscene gesture.

We both grinned.

"You're a bastard," Ruiz said, "Now get out of here. I will inform our Headquarters that you are taking over." He sighed. "You know, I hope that my dream is right and that you are an Outsider."

"Sorry," I said, "I'm just a citizen whose parents were old-fashioned." I lied well enough, I thought. Not that there wasn't some truth in my words. I was a citizen and my parents were old-fashioned.

Chapter Eleven:

We came into the La Cienega Basin in two cars, a Pegaso convertible and a Centaur carryall. Jorge Gonzales, my picador, drove the Centaur and Jaime Villareal, my number one banderillero, drove the Pegaso. He and his two partners, Paco Sandoval and Enrico Guiterrez and I rode together. I liked the bandilleros, since they were gay light-hearted young men who talked a lot about inconsequential things and were unabashed by my long silences. The ones with Jorge were a gloomier and more serious lot; Ernesto Robles, my manager; Alfredo Lamas, the number two pic; Luis Palermo my valet, and Miguel Cardenas, the grim little mozo del estoque—the sword bearer. Counting myself there were nine of us. We were an action group, a combat team, and although we had never been called into action, we had drilled and rehearsed our roles until we were, we thought, letter perfect.

I was the only one who knew that we had a long way to go before we were half as good as we thought we were, but I didn't give voice to my opinions. I merely tried to set up problems that would train without giving the idea that training was necessary. Right now I was drilling Jaime, Paco and Enrico on terrain analysis as we rolled down Camino Monosabio toward La Cienega.

I remembered the first time I came down this road and felt an odd stir of anticipation as we came to the goon fence that marked the edge of Corréon's land. Soon we would be passing the main entrance. In half an hour we would be in La Cienega. In minutes thereafter I would be talking to Inez on the phone, and if God and Gonsalvo Corréon were willing, I would be seeing her tonight. It was four months since I'd seen her. She had been with an aunt, a ferocious bulldog of a female who kept us from saying what was in our eyes.

Since I had left Rancho El Primero nearly a year ago, I had not been alone with Inez. Instead, we wrote letters; mine cool and careful, requiring much reading between the lines; hers warm and passionate, full of life and love. I had not heard from her for nearly a month, which was mildly distressing but not alarming, since her last letter had indicated that things in the Basin were not too stable. There had been considerable bickering between the Union and the haciendados, and Bernardo Aspromonte, the local caudillo, had been organizing raids against the Herreras, and the Herrera vaqueros had retaliated. Until her last letter, no one had been killed, but it was only a matter of time.

There was one good side to the trouble. Corréon had stopped pressuring Inez to marry into the Herrera family, and had started thinking of his protege who was well on his way to becoming the number one matador in all Segovia.

"Absence, my dearest Joselito," she had written in her latest letter, "makes you larger in Father's eyes, even as it does in mine. He reads of your exploits with pride and watches you on video whenever you appear in a corrida. When you have had a bad day he is unbearable, and when you are good he beams with pride and says that since he trained you it is no wonder you are perfect. He amuses me, but I think I may have done too well about changing his mind. Perhaps he will someday feel that I am not good enough for you— which is, of course, the truth. He tries so hard to deny you, my darling, but he cannot. You are kindred souls—" It was the last letter I had received and that one had come to me at Sanlucar three weeks ago. I had hoped she would be in Santayana, but she was not. I had tried to phone her but could not get a call through, which was not too unusual, since phone service outside the cities was a chancy thing at best, and with the Basin in an uproar it was more than likely that phone lines might be cut. But that didn't bother me, since I knew the defenses of Rancho El Primero. It would take an army to breach them.

The car was coming up to the main gates of the Rancho and I looked outside, straining for a glimpse of the hacienda, which was barely visible from the road.

And then I saw the gate. It was ripped away. The gateposts and their automatic weapons were gone. Craters pocked the soil and the shattered hulk of an armored personnel carrier lay in the ditch beside the gaping hole in the fence where the gates had been.

"Go airborne," I ordered and Jamie took the convertible off the road and presently was circling the Great House and the corrals and pens. It was a shambles. The house looked as though a giant boot had stamped it into the ground. The roof had caved in, the interior was gutted and blackened. The barns were burned. The livestock was gone. Nothing living was visible. El Primero was dead.

My voice and my heart froze. I thought of Inez; her beauty, her love of life. And now she was dead. Nothing could have survived that holocaust. Now I knew why she hadn't written. It dawned on me with a sense of shock that I had loved her more than I realized. That was why, I thought with sudden anguish, there was no spice in women. That was why I had changed from a middling womanizer into a man who observed the amenities but didn't try for extras. That was why Paco called me San José and the others nodded agreement. Somewhere down in that ruin was my love, and there was a hollow ache in my gut and a fire in my mind.

"All right—go back to the road," I said and lapsed into silence, and for once the banderilleros didn't say anything. Paco and Enrico looked at me quickly and then looked away. Jaime kept his eyes on the road and presently we were again rolling toward La Cienega at 90 k.p.h.

We passed a guard station and slowed to go through the opening in the goon fence surrounding the town.

"Grim little place," Paco said.

"It's better in the center of town," I said, "There's a Ring nearby—"

"And towns don't do too well near Rings," Jaime said, "The young men grow up and move away. The girls get married and leave. The old folks stay around and get older and slowly the town withers and dies."

"La Cienega's not that bad," I said.

"I've been looking at the houses," Enrico said. "The place is a fort. And that goon fence is in working order."

"There's a Ring nearby," Naime repeated.

"I don't like the feel of this place," Paco said. "There's something wrong with it."

"There are no women on the streets," Jamie said.

"There seldom are in these country towns," I said. "A few shoppers, maybe, a scattering of indentures, and that's about it."

"Here there are none," Jaime said, "this town is scared."

"Of what?" Paco asked.

"Of us, maybe."

"Not us," I said. "The Basin is boiling with trouble. Hey! Hold it!

Turn left here."

"Why?"

"Because the hotel's down that street," I said, pointing. "You can see it down at the end of the block."

"That dump?" Jaime asked.

I had to agree with him. The hotel was appreciably older than it was a year ago. It had a starved look.

"Hmm, living in this place should be a real treat," Jaime said.

"Or a treatment," Paco replied.

Enrico said nothing, but the expression on his face was eloquent.

"We have no choice," I said. "That's all there is. Well, let's park the car and see what's in store for us."

"How about Jorge and the others?"

"They'll have to come here."

"Five'll get you ten the joint's so old that it has central air conditioning," Paco said.

"No bet," Jaime said. "We're about to begin living dangerously."

The hotel was old fashioned—hardly more than a flophouse on Santayana's water front. It still used porters. There was a cashier's desk with a man behind it. There was an antique elevator in the lobby that carried us creakingly aloft and disgorged us on the third floor.

"Now where do we go?" Ernesto asked.

"Down this hall, señor," the porter said, gesturing to his right. "You can get confused. The numbers on the rooms aren't sequential."

"Why not?"

The man shrugged. "I wouldn't know, señor. This place was built before I was born." He picked up our bags and set them out in the hall. "I'll show you your rooms and then bring the rest of your bags." He picked up four pieces of luggage and moved down the hall, turned into a lateral corridor, set the bags down and began to unlock a row of doors. "Rooms 314 through 320, sirs; 314 is on a corner."

"That's yours, maestro," Ernesto said, "the air will be better there."

The porter moved with practiced speed, setting out baggage, turning on lights, opening windows, collecting tips. And then he vanished.

I looked about my room. It wasn't bad, nor was it good. The bed was old, the rugs threadbare, the furniture scarred, but the room was clean and smelled fresh. Even with the heat there was no dusty odor in the air. I had stayed in worse places.

I looked out of the window. There was no one in sight below. The street looked hot and empty, baking in the sun, dotted with a scattering of parked vehicles along the arcade that surrounded the square. I stared at the empty vista and shrugged. I had intended next month to return to La Cienega as a premier matador, to a fiesta that would be the talk of the year. Instead, I had come now; without fanfare, almost stealthily, on a job that was not of my choosing. I was being used, and I didn't like it, but I was soldier enough to do what must be done. This time I had no voice in my actions. Next time would be different.

With both Gonsalvo and Inez gone, La Cienega was a different place than the town I had known. Aspromonte was now in control, and from what I could see the town was suffering. I knew too little about him. The peones had talked, but they didn't say much and the Corréons had seldom mentioned him. Jorge's knowledge of the man was superficial. But from relative obscurity he had emerged in less than four years to become leader of the La Cienega Basin.

Chapter Twelve:

I spent the better part of two hours checking records at the Town Hall, trying to find out what had happened to Corréon. The clerk who showed me the records was full of helpful information. He told me that Aspromonte had placed a formal charge with the alcalde, that accused Corréon of consorting with the local Aliens. When Corréon refused to answer the charge, Aspromonte had attacked El Primero and destroyed it. That was the record. The only trouble with it was that the record lied. The clerk was easy to read, and after a few key questions I had the true story. Aspromonte had placed no charges until the attack was over. The alcalde was told about what had happened after Corréon was dead. The whole thing was a violation of the code which prohibited the Guardia Civil from punitive acts without proven cause or a bill of attainder from a jury of Corréon's peers. Aspromonte had used his power to put the alcalde in his pocket and force the mayor to support his policies after they had been carried out. It was thoroughly illegal, but it had gotten rid of Gonsalvo Corréon.

I also discovered that Corréon had some idea of what was coming, since no women nor children were reported in the body count after the attack. There had apparently been enough time to get them away from the hacienda. I had no idea of where they had gone, but apparently neither had Aspromonte for there was a wanted notice out for Inez, Dolores, and her two boys. This, of course, was natural enough, because the proscription of Gonsalvo could also include his dependents under Segovian law. But the law didn't say that a man could be killed and then proscribed.

I wasn't happy about what I had learned, but there was nothing I could do about it now. The records were superficially correct, and no one on Segovia had knowledge of Sorovkin muscle reading technique. I had no hard evidence, and it was true that Corréon had consorted with the Aliens. But the way Aspromonte had acted did nothing to make me like or admire him.

I went back to the hotel and tried to quiet my desire to strangle Aspromonte. The telephone inturrepted me. I picked up the receiver and looked at the screen. It stayed blank. Whoever was on the other end was using a hushphone. "Are you ready, señor?" a voice asked.

"Yes," I said.

"Be in the parking lot at 1840. A car will be waiting." The line went dead.

I listened for a moment and replaced the receiver. I looked at my watch. It read 1705, which left me plenty of time for a cleanup and a quick meal. I needed both.

I spent more than the usual time in selecting armament after I got out of the refresher and slipped an elastoplast over the pink skin inside my left thigh where El Sobrante—a big alipio—had grazed me at Los Altos a month ago. The wound hadn't been serious, but for some reason it was slow to heal, and still gave me an occasional twinge. The elastoplast kept it from hurting and I wanted nothing to impair either my concentration or coordination.

The radiotransparent derringer in a power holster strapped to my left forearm and the equally transparent knife in my right boot didn't trigger ordinary alarms. The flat 9-millimeter magnum autoloader in my shoulder holster and the razor sharp knife in a right forearm throwing holster were steel and perfectly visible as they were meant to be, but the plastic explosive disguised as ornamental buttons, the knockout capsules, the garrote and the various bits of detection gear incorporated into my clothing were even better hidden than the transparent knife and gun. I looked at myself in the mirror, clapped my flat varnished hat on my head at a rakish angle and went downstairs.

The dining room was reasonably clean and sparsely populated at this early hour. The service was good and the food was excellent. I didn't try the local wine, but the local beer was as good as I remembered. I signed the chit, and walked out.

It was 1840 hours when I entered the hotel parking area. A dark Pegaso convertible was standing in the driveway with its turbine purring. The driver looked at me from the half open window.

"Union," he said.

"Forever," I replied.

"Get in," the driver said as he leaned across the seat and opened the rear door.

Three alarm mechanisms in my clothing registered simultaneously. I swung the door wide and looked inside. I could see nothing.

"Your pardon," I said. I walked around the car, opened the door to the front seat on the side opposite the driver and slid in. The alarms were quiet. I took my 9 millimeter from its holster and placed the muzzle against the driver's ribs. "For your information, señor, this gun has a hair trigger. It can blow a hole clear through you. And I have quick reflexes."

"Don't worry, friend," the driver said, "I'm not looking for any trouble."

"Neither am I."

"I'm just here to give you a ride," he went on. He flinched his narrow chest away from the gun.

"I'll hold the gun while you drive. I'm the suspicious type."

"Just don't hold it too close. I get nervous around those things." He engaged the drive and the Pegaso moved sedately out of the lot. Outside, he turned toward the lake north of town, angled into the flight strip and pushed the throttle forward. The convertible leaped forward with a surge that made me blink, the rotors cut in with a howl and we were airborne. This job had *really* been worked over! Seconds later, we were over the lake skimming along at two hundred k.p.h. a meter or two above the glassy surface that broke into foam and wavelets as our turbulence struck the water.

"Well, that's that," the driver said, "Why not put the gun away? It won't do you any good now. Shoot me at this altitude and you're dead in the crash."

I smiled. "Maybe and maybe not," I said. "But you'll sure as hell be dead. Besides, I keep thinking of those things in the back seat, and somehow I don't like their implications."

"Hey! You're good!" the driver said. "How'd you spot them?" There was honest admiration in his voice.

"It's my business," I said, "and to make sure nothing goes off up here I have you on the end of Betsy." I poked the gun gently into his ribs.

"It figures; you're probably the vindictive type. I just don't get the breaks."

"How come you tried to boobytrap me?"

"Orders. Aspromonte wanted to know how you'd react. The stuff backside is not lethal. But it can make you feel real bad."

I grinned.

A red light bloomed on the dashboard. "You're being challenged. Use your IFF," I said.

The driver flipped the IFF switch. "See that big pile that looks like a pyramid with a flat top?"

I nodded.

"That's where we're going. That's State Hall—It used to be a resort hotel before the Aliens came. The goons wrecked it trying to get the guys who holed up on the top floors. That was in '84, I think."

"They make it?"

"Yep—ate every one of them. The place was a wreck when Aspromonte took it over four years ago. He peeled off the six top floors and rebuilt the rest. It'd be a damn good goon that could get in now. It's almost as strong as a Ring."

"This fellow Aspromonte sounds like a real pusher," I said.

"Yeah—a real avanti-type. Can't figure why he wants you."

"It is strange, isn't it?"

"Take your finger off that trigger, friend," the driver said. "We're going down now." The car skimmed along the surface, skittering like a flung stone, sending clouds of spray into the air. The speed slackened, the wheels came down, caught the edge of a hard surfaced ramp and dragged the dripping car out of the water and onto a metalled road that wound around piles of scrap toward the immense loom of the building. Brakes squished briefly as the car swung around a large jagged mound of debris and into a black orifice that led downward.

"Motor pool," the driver said as he brought the car to a stop. "We're here, and believe me I'm glad to get rid of you. You take the stairs to the right and check with the guard at the main desk upstairs. You can't miss it."

I looked around. We were in a huge underground room supported by massive concrete pillars and beams, and dimly lighted with glow tubes. It was always what it was now, an underground parking facility. There were vestiges of numbers on the pillars and in the dim light I could see row after row of military transport. Trucks, cars, and armor all stood shining in polished paint with serial numbers and the clasped hands of the Guardia Civil symbol stencilled on their sides. There was enough transport for a regimental combat team! I whistled softly. If the upstairs was any reflection of the motor pool, this place was crawling with troops.

The vehicles were not new. None had air-float capability although many were rolligons, and had good cross-country mobility. Most were probably salvaged from the Agua Fria disaster of '84 when the goons proved once and for all that no conventional military force had a chance against them. However, no matter how much tactics had changed, transport was still needed to move men from one place to another, and these vehicles, old as they were, were still useful. Apparently the Guardia had levee capability in the Basin, but it was hard to figure the necessity for such a force unless Aspromonte had larger ideas than a local dictatorship. I shrugged. If the man had delusions of grandeur that was none of my concern.

"Well, I'll not be seeing you again, I hope," the driver said as he started his engine. "Here comes your escort."

Two armed men approached the car, and frisked me as I got out. They found the 9 millimeter, the derringer and the steel knife. They missed the rest.

We went upstairs through a lobby almost as big as the motor pool. It was now used as a drill floor and several squads were going through a by-the-numbers drill under the bored eyes of a gaggle of non-coms. The big room was virtually empty. Beside the main staircase was a guard post, a message center and a row of self-service mechs that dispensed soft drinks, stim pills and other goodies. No one paid a great deal of attention to us as we went up the stairs past a guard kiosk on the mezzanine and another on the second floor.

The second floor guard halted us, asked for our destination and phoned our arrival. We went down the hall to an office, were welcomed by a cold-eyed security non-com and my escorts were relieved.

The non-com eyed me closely and nodded. "You're Torres," he said at last. "Come with me. The chief is waiting." We went through the office, through a door into an anteroom, through a second door that opened with an interlock, and into a room that literally reeked of masculinity. It was furnished with a working fireplace and a picture wall on which scanners were imprinting a view of the lake with a small boat in the foreground skimming over the rippling surface of the water. Good paintings and a Second Century pastoral tapestry hung on the other walls. The jetwood furniture was upholstered in sheared lambskin and the thick handmade rug was a masterpiece of weaving. The air, although fresh, had that curious dead quality that goes with first class air conditioning and soundproofing. It muted the repetitive tinkling of a tiny bell. The security man closed the door and the sound stopped.

Standing in front of the fireplace facing us was a man almost as impressive as Admiral Evars. Force radiated from him and filled the space between us. He was big and square with a heavy, hard-featured face, slab-cheeked with a hawk's beak nose, cold hazel eyes, high forehead and crisp brown hair that was almost wiry. His jaw was heavy, but his mouth was incongruously beautiful. His lips were as soft and sweetly formed as those of a painted angel.

I recognized the raw ruthlessness of the man, the odd quality we call leadership, the anger, the impatience, the burning desire to win, and the ambition that drove him. I liked him no better than I did when I saw the wreckage of Corréon's hacienda, but I would obey his orders. Such was the measure of the man. He was oddly like Evars in some ways, and I responded automatically to the air of command. Discipline, I thought wryly as I recovered control of myself, makes one do the strangest things.

He waved at the room. "My house is yours," he said, but he didn't mean it and I knew it. "Welcome," he added, and he didn't mean that either. He eyed me with the appraising eye of a butcher looking at a side of beef.

"You'll do," he said. "That'll be all, Eduardo." The security man saluted, executed a smart about face and left the room. "Sit down," he said gesturing at a chair.

"Just for the record," I said, "How do you know who I am?"

He smiled. "You've been scanned twice and the records compared with Cuidad Segovia's. You're José Torres, premier matador de toros, head of Action Group 23."

I nodded. "What else do you know?"

"That you probably could kill me right now and I wouldn't be able to prevent you," he said. "Surely two guns and a knife aren't all of your armament."

I laughed. "I feel better," I said. "I don't like to work for incompetents. They make life hazardous."

Aspromonte nodded.

"Why do you need my group?" I asked.

"I don't. I need you.'

"All right. Why do you need me?"

He smiled. "You're better than Ruiz," he said. "All he can do is talk about bulls and liberty. You get down to basics. I like that. I'm not at all unhappy that he was spiked." He touched a button. One of the men from the other office appeared with a gear sack. He opened it and took out something I recognized instantly. It was my space suit.

"What's that?" I asked even as I wondered how it had gotten into Aspromonte's hands.

"Damned if I know. It looks like a diver's suit except that it isn't. I'd say it was a space suit. Anyway, it seals out the environment. My engineering staff thinks it will fool a goon."

"Why?"

"They're supposed to be attracted by scent. A man in this gives off no odor."

"Are you sure?"

He shrugged. "It's been lab-tested,—and that's why you're here. You're going to field-test it."

"Why don't you use your own people?"

"Two reasons: survival chances and National's orders. They want it tested by an action group. They think you have a better chance for survival in case it doesn't work at goonfooling."

I wondered briefly why I'd never thought of the space suit as a protective device against goons. Possibly it was because I never considered it as part of a weapon system.

"Put it on," Aspromonte ordered, "I want to see how it fits."

"How does it work?"

"Here—I'll show you."

I let them help me into the suit. They were incredibly clumsy. I could have gotten into it alone in half the time.

I discovered somewhat to my surprise that the suit still functioned. There was still about eight hours life in the systems. The holster pocket still contained my service Kelly. I'd have to get Aspromonte to explain it to me. It wouldn't do to be too familiar with the equipment. But that would all come in due time and order. Meanwhile there were other comments to be made.

"This isn't our technology," I said. "Where did you get this? From the Aliens?"

"We found it up at Laquna Estrella—near the Ring. And it's not Alien. It's made by and designed for a human being. Note how it fits you."

"That means that someone like us, from somewhere else, is on Segovia."

"That's right."

"Is that good?"

He shrugged. "Who knows. Possibly they're as bad as the Aliens. But they make good protection suits. This one is far beyond our technology."

"You want me to test this against goons?" I asked.

He nodded.

"Where are the goons?"

"There's a whole Ring full of them about forty kilometers from here."

"And if the suit doesn't work."

"The gun that goes with the suit will stop a goon."

"Have you tested it?"

He shook his head. "Not against goons," he said.

"Then I'll believe that story when I see a dead goon."

"Believe it anyway. It makes our best weapons look like toys.

73

But just to make it a little safer for you, I'll hire some of Ramirez' boys to protect you."

"Who's Ramirez?"

"A local nomad chief. His people used to herd sheep in the hills before the goons came. Now they run cattle. They're a tough lot, and they don't worry about goons. They've got a technique for killing them that works. They've also got the riflemen to make it work."

I nodded. I had heard about these people, or ones like them. They were an independent lot, and perhaps the best fighters on a man-for-man basis on the planet.

"I have the whole plan worked out," Aspromonte said. "If the goons can't detect you, there's no reason why we can't destroy the Ring. I've been working on this ever since I came here, assembling the material and praying for a break. I think we've got the break, and with luck and skill one man could take them."

"You want me to try?"

"That's why I requested an Action group."

"Have you cleared this with National?"

He nodded. "Let's go down to the operations room and look at my plan. I have a sand table and model layout. I can show you better there. Also, there's a book of photos and all the equipment that'll be needed. I've always intended to knock the Ring off. I despise the lot of them." His voice was cold and filled with hate.

Chapter Thirteen:

We had walked nearly five kilometers over mountain trails in the dark. Neither Jorge, Jaime, nor I were accustomed to this kind of travel, and considering our deficiencies, we held up rather well. For the last kilometer we hadn't said a word, not because there was nothing to be said, but because Juanito, our guide, had insisted that we remain silent. There was always the possibility of making a noise at the wrong time in an operation like this, and it was best that we stop making any. We passed orders by finger code, a thing which I had never used since I learned it in Cuidad Segovia. I had never thought I would have to use it, which went to show how wrong I could be.

The Ramirez brothers, Juanito and Vittorio were apparently used to this sort of travel, for they moved swiftly and silently through the woods and acted as though they could see as well as though it was broad daylight. Possibly they could. It was certain I couldn't. They were an odd pair, Vittorio—broad, massive and heavily muscled—looked deformed under the enormous pack he carried on his shoulders. Back at Headquarters we had agonized over every milligram of material that had gone into that pack, since I would have to carry it for a part of the journey, and I was nowhere near as muscular as Vittorio.

Juanito, the other half of the Ramirez team was long and lean. He carried no pack, but instead carried two heavy scope mounted rifles and a bandolier of ammunition. I had never seen projectile weapons quite like them. They fired a much longer and heavier cartridge than any I had seen before. Goon guns was what Juanito called them. Jorge and Jaime carried the more conventional high velocity weapons that were used by the armed forces and were designed to kill by hydrostatic shock.

Finally we came to a fold in the ground with a low hill cresting in front of us. Juanito stopped and we all followed suit. We gathered together in a tight little group and conversed in the code. We had come to the end of our journey. Over the hill ahead of us lay the La Cienega Ring. Juanito gave instructions to my two men and they slipped off into the darkness to take up positions covering my route of advance. Vittorio slipped the pack off his massive shoulders and took off the first layer of the contents—my space suit.

I let Vittorio and Juanito help me into the suit, sealed the seam tabs and put on the helmet. The pack, I noted with mild satisfaction, was considerably smaller.

"Think you can make it?" Juanito asked in a subliminal whisper that my amplifiers picked up and transferred to my ears.

I nodded, and watched while Vittorio sprayed me with a chelating agent that removed odors. The two men helped me shoulder the pack and then gave me the universal thumb and forefinger salute for good luck.

I looked at my timepiece as I moved out down the faint trail that led over the hill ahead. I had almost half an hour to reach the outer defenses of the Ring. The suit was functioning perfectly. Whatever those people at State Headquarters had done, they hadn't damaged the suit's mechanisms. The pack was heavy but bearable. The weight of the Kelly in the holster pocket was comforting. I didn't feel too badly about making this foray into Alien territory. In fact, I was rather excited about it.

I crossed the hill and went down the other side. Somewhere ahead, in good position I hoped, were Jaime and Jorge. Juanito and Vittorio were following behind. As I went down the sloping path to the valley below, I visualized the model on the sand table in Aspromonte's operations room. It had been constructed in meticulous detail, and so accurately that I knew exactly where I was. The Ring lay in the center of the valley, beyond the dense screen of trees that hid it from my sight at the moment. It was a circular central area of paved or plasticized soil utterly devoid of vegetation. In the center of this bare area was a square windowless block of a building fully a hundred meters on a side and about twenty meters high. Supporting buttresses set about twenty meters apart supported the walls against the thrust of an arching roof. Beside the building stood the ovoid shape of an Alien spaceship, a wingless craft of unfamiliar design about the size of our Canopus-Class cruisers. At Headquarters, they couldn't tell me whether it was a warcraft or not. I hardly thought it was. It was too potbellied. Warships tend to be lean and mean.

Surrounding the bare area was a raised embankment which supported two ill-defined rings of what looked like pipe or conduit that coalesced into a single pipe that ran to the central building. These were probably the defensive shield and screen generators.

Surrounding the embankment was an egg shaped area filled with regularly spaced trees and surrounded by a roadway some four meters wide, which was in turn surrounded by a two meter woven wire fence with a "Y" of barbed wire on top and fitted with glowtubes every ten meters along its length.

In the smaller end of the egg shaped bulge at the lower end of the valley lay Ringtown, the scab settlement. A ruined road led from Ringtown through a gate in the peripheral fence and through a gap in the hills to the Agua Fria Valley. Once, long ago, it had been a highway. Now it was hardly more than a track through the thick second growth of trees.

Ringtown itself was a hollow square of dormitories and communal buildings that housed a population of about fifteen hundred. These formed the labor force for the Ring. Yet their isolation said that they were not completely accepted by their Alien masters, for their quarters were outside the maximum defense zone.

Outside the fence there was a cleared area that supported a scattered growth of low brush. This, according to reports, was heavily sown with mines and spotted with detection apparatus.

And now as I came out of the screen of trees I saw it in reality. The peripheral fence was a few hundred meters away, outlined by its lights, and stretching off into the distance up and down the valley. Even from here I could see that it was appreciably curved. The fence lights faintly illuminated the thing for which I was searching, the thing that made this caper feasible. I moved along the border of the woods and the cleared area scanning the terrain in front of me and moving only when I was certain that the way was clear. I needn't have worried. This outer area had no mantraps. It was simply a cleared area, possibly to give the defenders a field of fire. However, I didn't relax my caution, and it was well that I didn't for there were scattered pieces of detection apparatus along my route, and these had to be avoided.

There had been a violent storm in the area a couple of weeks ago and a tree had blown down across the cleared peripheral strip I was skirting. It was huge, one of the ancient forest giants that once had covered this area. The giant trunk had cut a swath across the strip and its top had impacted against the ground a bare ten meters from the peripheral fence. The upper part of the trunk and branches had been ripped and torn by the mines, but it made a pathway across the cleared area, and this danger spot had not yet been repaired and restored to its prior effectiveness. The defense was sloppy, I thought, but perhaps the Aliens had a reason, and the reason might be the spaceship with its obviously freighter conformation.

The tree was the one thing that had made me consent to try this caper, and was the reason Aspromonte had called for an Action group. I found the base of the trunk, climbed to the top and began to make my way down the natural bridge across the minefield. This was a piece of cake, I thought as I came to the first of the thick limbs of the upper branches. I looked at my timepiece and decided to wait. It wouldn't be too long before a goon was due to pass along the fenceline, and I didn't want to be too close when it did. I had a great deal of respect for those deadly androids. There was at least ten meters of minefield to cross after I left the tree, and I didn't want to be caught out in the open with that much ordnance around me and a goon in front of me. I stopped in the thickest group of still leafy branches, burrowed between a few small branches near the trunk, and lay still.

I watched the fence. It was electrified—probably with a charge strong enough to contain a goon and keep it walking on its prescribed rounds, but not strong enough to keep it in if it were stimulated by human presence. The lights on top of the fence didn't worry me. Although they seemed bright, they didn't penetrate the folds in the ground or the branches of the fallen tree, and I was effectively hidden. I didn't think anything could see me, but thinking of that one encounter I had with a goon made me take the Kelly out of its holster. There was no percentage in being too confident.

As I waited, I thought of the briefing room where Aspromonte, the Ramirez brothers, Jaime and Jorge and I reviewed what I was about to do. So far everything had gone precisely as planned. It worried me a little. Things shouldn't go so well. The periphery shouldn't be this poorly maintained. The tree should have been removed. There should have been alarms. I couldn't help wondering why there weren't—and some of the ramifications of that wondering were unpleasant. Of course, the laxity could be due to over-confidence but it could be because the Aliens considered the defenses obsolete and had constructed better and more sophisticated systems inside this fragile outer shell. That was an unpleasant thought indeed.

Now there was no concealment. On the hard level surface of the central ring I was nakedly apparent to any eye turned my way, and the pack on my shoulders would focus eyes even though it was smaller and lighter now. My only recourse was direct and bold movement, that would—I hoped—be taken for the purposeful and proper actions of one who was authorized to be in the area and had a job to do. Since no one should suspect I was not authorized, the advantage was all on my side.

I walked openly across the intervening space toward the central building. Despite my apparent confidence, the walk was a five minute exercise in fear of discovery that left me quivering with reaction in the shadow of the gigantic central building.

It loomed above me, an immense structure of alien material. The hum from its interior drowned my world in noise and effectively smothered any sounds I might make. I slipped the shrunken pack from my shoulders, took out a drill and bored a spaced row of holes in the buttress against which I crouched. The corundum drillpoint cut readily into the material, which was oddly light and soft. I hadn't expected this, and it made me pause a moment and lean against the buttress while I fingered the resilient curlings from the drill. I felt the faint vibration of the building as it resonated to the forces at work within it. I nodded to myself. The material had a vibration period.

I gathered a small pile of drill shavings and thrust one of the probes of the resonator into them. This was the final test. Everything I had done so far was to bring the last item in the pack— the resonator—into contact with this building. The resonator wasn't a new device. The principle had been discovered millennia ago, long before the Empire had appeared. It worked on the principle of augmenting molecular vibration to the point where the substance composed of those molecules would dissociate and break down. Singers and stage magicians still used the trick to shatter crystals. The machine I had brought this far with such effort was the mechanical equivalent of the performers' voice. I turned the resonator on and began the simple process of tuning it to the pile of shavings. The drill curlings quivered, wavered and dissolved into a thin watery goo. I grinned in the darkness. The device was going to work.

I finished boring the holes, inserted the probes, sealed them with adhesive, pushed the resonator into the corner made by the buttress and the wall, covered it with the neutral non-reflective material of the pack which promptly took on the infra-color of its surroundings as its thermoceptors adjusted to the wall temperature. I set the timer knob on the surface of the resonator for six minutes and without a backward glance began to walk across the cleared area toward the spot from which I had come. Now that I was free of my burden I made better time. I checked my watch—0115. By 0121 the building should come tumbling down. I should be outside the force screen, and perhaps halfway to the peripheral fence before anything happened. After that no one would see me because everyone's attention would be riveted on the center of the Ring.

I made it to the repeller field barrier without incident, passed slowly across the surface of the generating band and stepped across the detector screen generator, trusting in the previous setting of the distorter field to get me through.

It was a mistake. The screen was variable polyphase! The setting was almost right, good enough to let me through, but off enough to cause a belated triggering of the defense. With a crackle of disrupted air, the repeller field hardened into impenetrability. The detector screen glowed, and an automatic weapon coughed and chattered, spewing a lethal stream of solid destruction down the face of the screen. Lights winked on, throwing the area into daylight brightness.

They revealed nothing, for I had sprinted for the shelter of the trees in the parklike grove that separated the central ring from the periphery. As soon as I hit the ground I rolled, and behind me a tree burst into flame as the fire control computers analyzed my movements and trained a laser on my predicted path.

I rose to my feet and ran, hit the dirt, rolled, rose and ran again, varying my speed and direction each time. Fire crackled around me until I got out of range of the sensors that directed it. I grinned. Computers simply couldn't compete with a trained and elusive target.

But I was far from safe. Goons were undoubtedly closing on the area, and there was literally no place to hide. I was out in the open and easy prey. My flesh crawled at the thought of the obscene things goons could do to me before I gave up my hold on life. Discipline fought with terror, and terror won. I ran, swiftly and openly, directly toward the hidden opening I had made in the fence. I ran until my lungs were searing flame, and the suit regenerators choked from overload. I ran until my muscles could drive me no longer, until my system collapsed inside the viciously overtaxed suit.

No protective suit was designed for such violent activity, but the technicians who had built it, had constructed it with loving care and meticulous attention to detail and finishing. Therefore the suit survived. Its mechanisms did not collapse, and—because of my panic—I was nearly a half kilometer from the spot upon which the goons converged.

I drew the Kelly as soon as my nerves subsided to controllable quivering. The goons would certainly search outward from the area, and one might yet stumble across me, or one could follow along my panicky flight line. My trail should be plain even at night. It would be logical, I thought, to watch my backtrail. I looked at my watch—0120—less than a minute to go!

The second hand dragged across the luminous dial as I searched my backtrail through the infra glasses. The goons *had* come from the center. I refused to accept the thought that they might come from the periphery. If they did, my suit should conceal me from detection. It was only along my back trail that I had left any trace of movement.

I was right. There was a shimmer of brightness against the fainter pattern of the trees. It was a goon. There was no mistaking the outline of the beast. I raised the Kelly and the goon stopped, its body slowly rotating on its hips as it searched the area.

I sweated inside my suit. I dared not move to bring the gun to bear. The slightest sound would turn that questing body into onrushing destruction, that might well kill me even as I killed it. Desperately I forced my eyes past the menace. The resonator should be going into action now—attuning itself to the frequency of the molecules of the building and augmenting their movement until the giant brace collapsed. My eyes strained through the barrier. Was there a change in the shape of the central building?

There was!!

With horrid deliberation the central section of the vast windowless mass folded inward upon itself. The roof sagged and collapsed. The walls crumbled. There was no sound. The repeller field stopped that. It was like looking at a shadow play. The toppling walls and roof disappeared into a gaping hole that belched glare and steam. The repeller shield flickered, then hardened as secondary power sources took over automatically. There was a bright orange flash of an explosion—and the entire central area was lighted by a glow of supernal brilliance.

I automatically closed my eyes, but the goon spun around, and stood frozen as the brilliant glow enveloped it. The ravening hell of heat and light lanced at the barrier and recoiled. The heat, sound, and shock were trapped inside that insubstantial screen. But the light came through.

I opened my eyes. The goon was still facing the ravening hell of the center, pawing at its eyes with its clawed hands as though it would beat vision through its seared retinas. I set the Kelly on full intensity and medium aperture and drove a two microsecond bolt through the goon's body. There was a puff of oily smoke, a heavy detonation, and the goon, shocked into iron rigidity by the violence of the explosion of its tissues toppled face forward into the dirt.

I grinned. A service Kelly did the trick. Not even a goon could withstand the force of that blaster. I triggered another blast at the goon's head, just to make sure, but the Kelly hummed feebly and died. Out of charge! Probably the damn fools at headquarters had run it dry testing it!

I looked back at the screen. A hellish red luminescense now filled the interior and rebounded inward from the screen, turning the area into a lurid furnace straight out of hell. I hesitated a second and then hurled the Kelly toward the force field. I felt a little sick at the thought of what had happened inside that shell. The La Cienega Ring was dead, melted into a seething puddle of slag. It was victory!

I ran toward the peripheral fence. The repeller shield wasn't going to hold that cauldron of melt much longer. The auxiliary power source would collapse and that lake of lava would come rushing down on me. What I needed was distance. Goons might be dangerous but the stuff inside that shield was certain death.

I checked my watch. If Aspromonte's observations were correct, a goon was due any moment. Overhead, clouds obliterated the stars and veiled the slow low-hanging moon. The night was dim and quiet. A hush had fallen on the night noises as it always did when a goon was near.

A faint drizzle of rain sifted downward from the clouds and through the heavy air. A rising wind blew the misty rain into thin streamers that fled through the fence and toward the buildings in the center of the Ring. I wished for a moment that I could move like that.

The rain increased and beat a rustling tattoo on the leaves around me and I felt the familiar crawling of my guts that came upon me whenever I entered a bullring. But here the positions were reversed; I was the quarry, not the maestro.

A pulse hammered softly in my temples. With a bull I knew what to do; with a goon I did not. I remembered the gray monster I had killed with the Alpharzian Kelly. I clutched the checkered butt of the service weapon.

I wasn't supposed to have nerves, I thought wryly. Toreros, according to popular belief, were inhumanly calm, incredibly efficient pieces of biological machinery with a sublime contempt for danger and death. Like most popular beliefs it was wrong. I was afraid. The adrenal responses, the sweat, the quickened pulse, the icy quiverings of anticipation, the desire to run with a blind passionate terror were all present. I didn't want to die in the merciless grip of a goon, and be picked apart and eaten. I had seen films of goonwork and the memory sickened me.

God! Where was the beast? My ears, straining into the helmet amplifiers, caught a whisper of sound. My eyes caught a flicker of movement. And the goon appeared, a darker mass in the misty

darkness. It moved as silently and softly as a puff of smoke, a huge rounded mass of sloping shoulders, muscular arms and barrel chest set above a wide belly and thick heavy legs. Nearly two meters tall, its head was almost level with the top of the fence. I couldn't see its features, nor did I wish to. All I could do was breathe a silent prayer that whoever built my spacesuit had done a good job.

The goon hesitated momentarily, its huge head swinging outward toward the tree. I held my breath as my fingers tensed on the Kelly. Then the hesitation vanished and the goon moved forward. In a moment it was gone. I sighed. The suit worked. Unless it saw me, a goon couldn't detect me.

I crawled to the fence, avoiding the mines, shrugged out of my pack, and opened it. The package I wanted was ready to my hand. I took it out, opened it and removed the bridge wires with their metal clips and bridged the alarm circuit of a meter wide section of fence.

"Now for the cutter," I murmured under my breath as I took one of the aerosol cans from the packet, fastened a nozzle to the delivery hole and set its tip against the fence wire. Gingerly I pressed the stud on the can. Moving quickly, but without haste, I spread a semicircular line of the sticky stuff on the wires and tossed the canister back toward the tree. Five seconds passed and with a faint hiss, canister, nozzle and sprayed section of the fence disappeared.

I pushed the cut section of fence down, pushed my pack through the hole, and crawled after it. Turning, I lifted the section back into place and took a squeeze tube and another nozzle from my pack. With careful hands, I set drops of sticky material on the cut ends of the wire mesh, and with infinite care pushed the cut section of the fence back into place. The weld flowed together, coalesced and hardened, leaving the fence apparently intact. A sharp blow would shatter the union, but unless one knew where the mended section was, the defect would not be noticed.

I dismantled the bridge and let it fall to the ground outside the fence, tossed the can of welding compound over the fence and into the branches of the fallen tree, smoothed out my tracks and moved across the peripheral path into the parklike glade that lay between the outer fence and the inner glassy circular area of the original Ring. I was meticulously careful about erasing any evidence of my passage. It was slow work, but it could be life-saving. The time element bothered me, since patrolling goons, while methodical, were not clockwork automatons that could be absolutely predicted. If the next patrol came early I could be caught in the open, which would mean either my death or an aborted mission, and one would be as bad as the other. But if I was careless and someone noticed my tracks, it could be just as bad.

I sighed with relief as I reached the glade of well-spaced trees and dropped down behind the largest one I could find. Now to wait until the next goon passed before I moved any farther. The fact that I was the first man in Segovia's history to have directly penetrated a Ring didn't thrill me. Others had done by guile what I had done with technology. It might be a notable accomplishment, but it was no victory. It is an axiom in my business that it is always easier to enter the jaws of a dragon than to leave them—except by way of the stomach.

Once across the screen and barrier I could move with relative freedom since anyone seeing me would imagine I was a scab. Scabs were common inside a Ring, and some of them were always about.

I grimaced. I felt no genuine hatred toward scabs. I despised them for their slave mentalities and their loyalty to the Aliens, but I realized that generations raised in slavery had no concept of freedom. Still, I had never felt grateful to them until tonight. Now they were the protective cover that made my task easier.

I waited, watching the fenceline through infra red glasses until the ruddy figure of a goon drifted wraithlike across my field of vision. Infra red didn't make them look any better. The monstrous figure made me twitch uncomfortably, but I was far enough away for the movement to remain unseen. The goon moved steadily along the fenceline and disappeared around the gentle curve of the periphery. I watched until it vanished, then rose to my feet and walked quickly toward the center of the Ring.

Through the glasses, the trees and grass appeared an eerie reddish color against the darker background of the sky. Off in the distance loomed the fiery mass of the central building, as the giant cube glowed with the heat emissions from its interior. My suit compensators, I noted with satisfaction, blended me into the background and made me virtually invisible in this weird heat-world.

I climbed the embankment and stopped outside the screen and shield rings. They lay black and quiet against the ground, two conduit-type ring generators curving off into the darkness. I reached into my pack and took out the next item of the combat load. It was a neat, handmade rig that National's labs had sent out to the field headquarters some years ago. They called it a disruptor, but what it really was was a frequency analyzer and a heterodyning circuit that could literally bore an undetectable hole in a detector screen. I analyzed the pattern of the screen with meticulous care. The screen was on standby, which merely meant that it wasn't operating at maximum capacity. However, it could still detect. Like other Alien devices I had seen, it depended on triggering, on breaking of its pattern by a solid object of definitive minimal size. Since the Aliens realized that small animals were always present, the screen was set so that these small creatures would not trigger it. Objects as big as a man, however, would augment the screen, raise the barrier, alert the goons, turn on lights, alarms and automatic weapons.

The screen, however, had been observed for years, and its composition was fairly well known. The disruptor I carried in the pack should be able to dilate a section of it enough for me to slip through undetected. I checked the disruptor and adjusted it to the shifting frequencies of the lattice that formed the screen. I pressed the activator button and moved slowly across the generator ring and through the screen. Nothing happened, and the air sighed out of my lungs. I hadn't realized that I had been holding my breath.

I walked across the ten meter gap between the detector screen and the defensive shield. Like the screen, the shield was on standby. It wasn't the push-pull barrier we used in the Navy. It was an older principle and worked on inertia rejection. The faster an object impacted against the shield, the more forcefully it was rejected. Missiles travelling hundreds or thousands of meters per second bounced off the shield like it was so much armor plate, but when it was on standby a slow moving object could ooze across the barrier with relative ease. Moving with snail-like slowness I slipped across the generator tube. My body tingled as the shield's energies impacted against my cells. It was an eerie and unpleasant sensation and I was glad when it was over.

A kilometer away, reflected in the glassy black refractory surface of the inner ring, stood the great central building. At one end the pale oval of a spacecraft stood in its revetment and pointed its blunt nose at the sky. Beyond, the black hills of the Sierra Chicas rose to rounded summits.

I ran along the fence, found the tree, kicked out the weak spot, wriggled through, came to my feet and went first along the tree, then on the fallen trunk until I cleared the strip. I was lucky and I had a good memory. I got out alive. I labored up the slope with my lungs afire, and flashes of light flickering before my eyes. The roaring of my pulse dinned in my ears and my mouth was a mask of gasping agony. I stared half-blind at the figure that rose from the trail beside me.

"José! Stop!" Jaime's voice cut through the fog. Hands tore off my helmet. Other hands pulled me out of the suit. Quick strong arms supported me as our group ran for the ridge line and plunged over it into the shadow of the slope beyond.

"You made it!" Jaime's voice was relieved. "Now let's see what's happened to you."

"Nothing," I said. "That suit's proof against anything I ran into down there." I let my head droop between my knees and drew long sobbing breaths. From behind the hill came a sudden whoosh of superheated air and a flash of light as the trees outside the collapsed screen caught fire and burned. I wondered how many lives had been snuffed out in that coruscating hell I had made. The thought made me ill. Something else was making me ill, too. I couldn't get enough air, my muscles twitched uncontrollably, my eyes rolled in their sockets. Damn! I thought—damn these almost right worlds that have almost everything an outworlder needs. This one had almost enough air a thousand meters above sea level. It was almost enough to support my violent exertions, but not quite.

Chapter Fourteen:

I didn't see what happened to Ringtown, but I heard about it, and what I heard made me sick. The melt destroyed the center of the Ring and whatever had been inside the inner shield, but when the shield collapsed little more happened. The superheated gas fired the belt of trees, but the puddle of lava was already cooling and didn't go anywhere. It never touched Ringtown.

Aspromonte had started his men moving at the first flare of light from the hills. They arrived at the Ring within an hour. Most of the goons had been trapped in the melt. The rest were blinded and disorganized. The few that survived were quickly disassembled by Aspromonte's combat teams. Ringtown had been spared until Aspromonte's men arrived. They went through the place like scythes. Goons could hardly have done better. There had been over a thousand scabs in the town and of these less than two hundred survived; girls and women all—no children—no oldsters—no men. They were the sort of prisoners a Segovian would consider worth keeping, or worth using. The others were killed.

Prisoners kept coming into the Headquarters building all morning in coffles of five or ten, stripped to their skins and linked neck to neck with lengths of rope. They were a bedraggled lot, dusty, sweaty, and showing numerous signs of ill-usage. There was no fight left in them if there had been any in the beginning. They were dazed with the disaster that had overtaken them.

I stood at the bottom of the staircase watching them pass, wondering why I had ever gotten mixed up in this affair, and how I could get away from it. This was something I hadn't expected, and it bothered me. The Confederation wars were far less personal, and even though the destruction was more severe, it was more remote.

"It's a nice haul," Aspromonte said, "Your cut's about ten percent. They'll bring a good price at the Fall Assizes."

I turned. I hadn't heard him come down the stairs. "Forget it," I said. "I don't need that sort of money."

He shook his head. "I don't understand you, matador."

"Maybe it is because I am a matador. I fight bulls, not cows."

He laughed. "You have them right," he said. "They're cattle. The Aliens bred the spirit out of them long ago. We helped by killing off the brave ones who used to raid us. If you kill enough of the brave the timid will eventually dominate. Now only the true cowards remain. These will do as they're told. They won't be a bit of trouble, and since they are already slaves, it won't make too much difference if they are owned by the Aliens or by us. They'll get along."

"Without consideration and without mercy. It makes us no better than the goons."

Aspromonte shrugged. He wasn't interested in what I said. There was no sense talking to the man. He was obsessed. The death of the Ring was not catharsis enough to shake him out of his hate.

"Let's close this out," I said. "I want to get out of here. I have a corrida in Pontecorvo."

"I'll lend you a car," he said.

"I'll go with my cuadrilla."

"They've left."

"Without me?"

He nodded. "You were exhausted after your run. You needed rest and your man Ernesto figured you could come later. Most of the preliminary work doesn't need you to make decisions. So they went on to Pontecorvo and let you sleep."

"That's a kindness I could have done without," I said. I shrugged. It was like Ernesto. He was always protective. It was logical, I suppose. After all, I was the meal ticket and I should be coddled a bit.

"I'll go to the motor pool and arrange for a car," Aspromonte said. "Then I'm off to Cuidad Segovia. National's been burning wire over what we've done."

"Make it a convertible," I said. "I want to look at the Ring."

He nodded and left me on the stairs. I watched more captives pass and managed to achieve a kind of impersonality toward them. They were merely bodies, I kept telling myself—and presently that was all they were. I was surprised how easy it was to fall into the attitude of mind that turns human beings into faceless entities or into discrete bits of dehumanized flesh called units. The procession of captives was neither interesting nor exciting, but it was unpleasant. I have an active mind and some experience with the brutalities of primitive cultures. I didn't like the aftermath of what I had done. Nevertheless I had a compulsion to see my handiwork. I suppose the ego that lies in all of us demanded a look at the Ring, and I had told Aspromonte no more than the truth.

I went down to the confusion of the motor pool where the last truckloads of loot were being unloaded, found the duty officer and located the car Aspromonte had set aside for my use. It was a four-year-old Pegaso in good condition, much like the one which had brought me here. I checked the rotor mounts and the power takeoff, the two weak spots in convertibles—and found that they were in good shape. This buggy had better than average capability. Aspromonte had picked me a good one. Well—he should. I'd made him a hero.

I drove north along the west side of the lake until I came to the fork that went toward La Cienega Ring and east to El Camino Monosabio. I turned west and went air-borne. A few minutes later I was circling the Ring. The area was deserted. The center of the Ring was a circle of black smoking slag. There wasn't a sign of trees or buildings or spaceships or anything else. The outer fence was intact, except where Aspromonte's men had breached it, and Ringtown smoked from the fires the troops had set. I hovered over the concentric circles of the dormitories and common buildings of Ringtown, and looked down at the ruins. Smoke poured slowly from them. Holes had been blown in their ferroconcrete walls. Bodies littered the annular streets and the central plaza, and already the gray furry rats and sheftas were beginning to feed. In a week, the bodies would be bones. There were no vultures, and for some reason I missed them. Indeed, except for insects and some flying marsupials that preyed upon them, there was nothing remotely resembling a bird in Segovia's skies. It was one of those things that made this world different, but the insects and the rats and native marsupials were excellent scavengers. There was no need for vultures.

I sighed as I looked at the desolation, and overcome by impulse I set the convertible down by the revetments that guarded the entrance to Ringtown. There was a narrow road leading from the entrance into the surrounding woods. Its surface was broken and scarred with the ruts and tracks of Aspromonte's vehicles. The air was still and deathly quiet as I got out of the car and looked at the pockmarked exterior walls of the dormitories which formed a wall around the town. I went through the torn entrance gates and into the central plaza. I stopped, looked and fled. Never again, I swore, would I help Segovians operate against each other. I have a strong stomach, but the remnants of insensate brutality scattered in the streets and the paved surface of the plaza were more than I could take.

I went back to the car and took off. I headed across the shallow northern end of La Cienega Lake toward Monosabio road. I wanted no more of this place. The more kilometers I put between myself and Aspromonte the happier I would be. I was about a quarter of the way across the marshland before I was aware that the port rotor was not performing properly and was halfway across before I realized I was in trouble. The blades were vibrating and the vibration was being transmitted into the frame. I crossed my fingers and looked at the opposite edge of the marsh. It seemed far away. I wondered if it wasn't too far as I began gingerly to drop into the thicker atmosphere cursing Segovian mechanics and mechanicals in a low fervent monotone.

The Aliens had put a ban on fixed wing and jet propelled aircraft by shooting them down, and Segovian aircraft—such as they were—were either helicopters or rotor-lift convertibles that doubled as ground vehicles. The helicopters were fairly safe and the convertiplanes fairly dangerous, but the convenience of being able to go airborne for short distances made up for the danger. Air capability cut down long detours to get from one major highway to another. So there were the Pegasos—light, bulky vehicles that served a dual purpose and carried up to five passengers.

Right now, the one I was in was less than reassuring. It screamed and vibrated, but somehow managed to stay airborne until I saw a relatively level meadow near the Camino Monosabio. I dropped the Pegaso into it and shut off the engine. I sat there, letting the fear and the adrenalin run out of my system. The rotors drooped like wilted leaves as the engine shuddered into silence and the metallic screech of the power takeoff died. I could smell hot metal and fuel and I suddenly got the idea that I would live a lot longer if I got out of the driver's seat and ran like hell.

Which I did.

There was a stream at the bottom of the meadow a hundred meters away, with a cutbank facing away from the car. I reached the edge, slid over it—and the Pegaso blew. I've seen things like that on video, but never before in real life. There was a flash, a ball of flame, and a fireball that roared skyward on a pillar of smoke! Rocks, dirt, debris, and torn bits of metal sprayed the area. A rock struck my left shoulder. It hurt and I yelled. A drive wheel whizzed past, leaped the stream and vanished crashing into the brush on the other side. And then there was an aching silence punctuated by the crackle of flames as the less volatile parts of the vehicle were consumed.

The highway was less than a kilometer away, and I had no desire to wait by the wreckage on the off chance that I might be rescued. Somehow I didn't think anyone at Union Headquarters would be looking for me. And for a moment I toyed with the idea that someone could have sabotaged the convertible—but I shrugged it off. That would be a stupid thing to do. I was no danger to anyone at State Hall, and certainly no one wanted my scalp—but perhaps someone wanted Aspromonte's. I grinned wryly. That was possible.

I shrugged and started walking towards the highway.

Chapter Fifteen:

I tried to flag the vehicles heading northwest toward Pontecorvo, but had no luck. Segovians were wary of hitch hikers, and distrusted strangers. It was surprising to me that the enclave philosophy extended so far as to refuse help to someone obviously in trouble, since there were still a few goons roaming the open country. The military, of course, would pick people up, but the highways were not policed and troop movements in the late months of the year were relatively rare. It amused me that I continued to think of seasons on this seasonless world, but it made me realize that I was as much a creature of my environment as Segovians were of theirs. I adapted, but basic changes in ideas were harder to make.

I didn't worry too much, despite a subliminal uneasiness and a feeling that I should get out of the La Cienega basin as fast as possible. A bus would be along in the next few hours and it would stop for me. So I composed my soul in patience, found a comfortable spot under a tree by the roadside, and rose to my feet and waved futilely whenever a vehicle went past.

Finally a rattletrap truck creaked to a stop. It was so decrepit that I wondered why I had bothered to wave at it. The driver opened the door of the high cab and beckoned as the highway howled electronic anguish that a vehicle should have the temerity to stop on one of its control strips.

"Hey! Matador! You want a ride?" the driver yelled.

I looked inside the cab. "Juanito!" I said, "What are you doing here? I thought you were back with the rest of your tribe."

"I stopped overnight in La Cienega and saw some friends. Spent Aspromonte's money this morning for supplies. But how about you? How come you're afoot?"

I climbed into the cab and as he got the truck rolling again, I told him what had happened. His only comment was to shake his head and mutter something about damn fools and puddle jumpers. It didn't make me feel too good, because I had already decided I was a fool to trust my neck to someone else's convertible.

"I can't take you to Pontecorvo," he said. "My old man would kill me if he knew I had you aboard and didn't bring you in for a visit. Judging from the phone call I had with him last night, you're his number two hero—a millimeter or two back of Aspromonte."

"That's a rotten comparison," I said.

Juanito nodded. "I agree, but my father Carlos has a different idea of Aspromonte than we do. Anyway, the Old Man owes you something since you revenged his father's death. Grandpa was killed by La Cienega goons at Agua Fria, and Dad has never forgiven the Aliens."

"You people hate long and hard."

"Is it any different anywhere else?"

I shrugged. "It's better hidden," I said, "but I suppose the suppressed majority always hates the dominant minority."

"Especially when the minority is a different breed of bull that doesn't give a good goddam about what we are, how we think, or what we do. Sure—I'd probably hate the Aliens anyway, but I hate them double for their indifference. The damn supercilious beasts gripe my soul!" Juanito closed his mouth into a thin line and drove for a couple of kilometers without saying another word. I was unhelpful and let him stew until he boiled some of the bile out of his spirit.

"You think they will figure we're responsible for killing the Ring?" he asked abruptly.

"If you mean you and me, the answer's no, but if you mean the State, the answer is probably yes," I said. "If I were an Alien I'd be suspicious as hell. That caper was too well organized. The troops were too handy. You remember I told Aspromonte not to put troops in the area, but he was so damned eager to kill scabs that he wouldn't listen."

"He gets that way at times. He has a one-track mind about Aliens and scabs. He hates them and anyone who has anything to do with them. Carlos thinks this is an admirable trait."

"I don't," I said. "He's going to get in deep trouble some day. What he doesn't recognize is that Alien technology is far more advanced than ours. They have space ships—we don't. They have atomic power—we don't. I could go on but why bother? Sure—we have nuclear fission, but they probably have not only fusion but a lot of other gadgets we may have had when we were part of the Empire, but that was a long time ago."

"What we've lost we can rebuild."

"Sure we could—if they gave us time, but they don't give us time. We come up with a new development and if it has war potential they smash it. They know everything we're doing."

"Not quite," Juanito said. "We got them at La Cienega. We'll get them everywhere."

"Maybe," I said. "We don't know what they're going to do about this caper." I sighed. "Somehow, I wish we hadn't done it. It gives me a sick feeling in my gut when I think about it. Aspromonte stampeded us. We should have investigated and then pulled back and built enough gadgetry to smash them all at once."

"That would have been smart," Juanito said, "but it wouldn't have been natural."

"That's our trouble. We don't work together. We don't have any coordination. Every corner of the world does pretty much as it pleases."

"We've got Cuidad Segovia. They're a central government."

"And how much real power do they have? Aspromonte's a good example of how well they can control their local leaders."

. Juanito shrugged. "Argue with Carlos, matador. I can't compete with you. You've been all over. I'm just a local boy."

I laughed. "Don't play games with me, Juanito. You know what's going on."

"Maybe I should worry," he said, "but I leave that to Carlos. Which reminds me—I'd better let him know you're coming. He doesn't like unexpected guests." He took the transceiver mike off the dash and started calling. A minute passed until an answer came.

"Okay Juanito. I read you. What's up?"

"I'm bringing that matador—José Torres—home with me. He blew his car and I picked him up. Told him you wanted to see him."

"I do. Thanks for letting me know."

Juanito closed the circuit and put the mike back on the dash. He fed more fuel to the turbine and we moved faster to the accompaniment of increased squeaks and rattles. "She sounds like rolling death," Juanito said, "but she's better than she sounds. We'll make it."

He turned off the main road onto a dirt track just beyond the edge of the La Cienega Basin, and a few kilometers later we came to a place he called the Camp. It was a walled electrified perimeter backed against a rocky cliff. A small stone dam furnished water to operate a turbine surrounded by a goon fence. There were mounted quick firers on the wall. The gate was massive and striped with electrodes.

Inside was a single street fronted with stone and log buildings built against the perimeter wall. At the far end of the street a massive stone house nestled against the overhanging cliff. Everything was squat, heavy and incredibly strong—as goon-proof as could be made with stone and iron.

"There's a shaft behind Cliff House," Juanito said. "It goes to the top of the mesa. The ladders inside won't support a goon, and unless they learn how to fly, we're safe enough."

"Not bad," I said as we drove up the street. Dogs came from the houses and barked at us. People were present in fair numbers, watching curiously as we passed. A few men sat on benches in the shade of the overhanging porches, determinedly doing nothing. Older girls and women in calf-length dresses and short boots waved at us. Small children played around the houses. Large boys, however, were notable by their absence.

"The boys are in school," Juanito said, answering my unspoken question. "Carlos believes in education."

"How about the girls?"

Juanito shrugged. "How about them?"

"Don't they get education, too?"

"Sure. The old women teach them all they need to know."

I sighed. Segovia had a long way to go.

We parked the truck beside Cliff House and entered. A gray, lean, and oddly youthful man came towards us. "My father, Carlos Ramirez," Juanito said. "This is Señor José Torres, the matador. I have told you of him."

Carlos smiled. "I am delighted. Welcome to my house. It is yours."

This man meant what he said, I decided. He was not like Aspromonte.

"Aren't you going to introduce me?" a high voice said from behind me. I didn't have to look. I knew. It was Inez Corréon. So this was where she had gone. I doubted if I could have thought of a better place.

I turned, and she was in my arms.

Carlos laughed. "You should marry this woman, Señor Torres. She is too beautiful to be hidden, and her soul is too free to be indentured. And she loves you. She talks of you constantly."

"I have been searching for her," I said.

"So has Aspromonte," Juanito added.

I eyed Inez. "Would you marry me?" I asked.

She blushed. "This is no place for such a question. Such things should be asked in private."

"Why?"

"It is the custom. It is less painful for the suitor to be rejected privately."

"Do you plan that for me?"

She shook her head. "I would rather have you than anyone I know." She managed to put enough invitation into that one sentence to make me feel uncomfortable, for I was flying false colors. Any marriage I might contract would be subject to Navy approval, and the Navy was not noted for sanctioning marriages between Special Service officers and natives of Class III planets. But my doubts were smothered by her nearness, and the shock of finding her alive.

"We can be married in Pontecorvo," I said.

"Why not here?" Carlos asked. "I am the village chief. I am authorized to perform marriages."

"Why not?" I echoed.

It was Inez's turn to hesitate. "I have no dress. There have been no banns. There is nothing special about such a marriage."

"But it is legal," Carlos said, "and that is what you need. As long as you do not have a legal guardian, you are subject to indenture. You have already been stubborn enough to refuse my best men because you love this madman who teases bulls. Now don't compound your stupidity with shyness."

"You sound like my father," she said.

"I always admired his courage," Carlos replied, "even though I hated his activities as a scab-lover. Gonsalvo was basically a good haciendado. He treated his people fairly. His only fault was too great a love for gold."

Inez bowed her head.

"In any event," Carlos went on, "this would be only a civil ceremony. You could have your show later at the cathedral."

"I doubt if the priest would allow me to wear white," she murmured, and looked at me with half-veiled eyes. I had seen such looks before, but somehow this was different. My thoughts must have reflected on my face because a light of mischievous understanding illuminated her smile.

Carlos laughed. "Here is a woman for you. She will not be a disappointment."

Inez blushed again—more crimson than before, and I—who had seldom seen this phenomenon—felt almost as uncomfortable as she looked.

"A marriage would honor my house," Carlos said. "No

Sanmarco has ever been married here." He turned to Juanito. "Go, my son, and get your brother. Bring your wives. There is a dress in the great chest in my bedroom. Your mother wore it when she wed me. We will do this properly for the Señorita Corréon y'Sanmarco, and it will reflect honor upon us."

I looked questioningly at Inez. She nodded and that was all I wanted. I was fond of Inez and I didn't think this act would be a blot upon my record.

Carlos brought a bottle of Sanlucar brandy. Juanito and Vittorio appeared with their women who hustled Inez off into the back of the house, while the four of us found glasses and Carlos poured brandy into them.

I sipped appreciatively, so did Carlos. Juanito and Vittorio gulped. Carlos looked at them disapprovingly. "My boys," he said, "have not yet realized that there are some things more important than simple practicality. They think a fine brandy is good only for getting drunk and a fine woman good only for getting pregnant. They have much to learn about living, and perhaps they will in time. I have, I expect, been a bad father. I should have married again after their mother died, but for some reason I could not."

"There wasn't anyone pretty enough to attract him," Juanito said.

"Beautiful enough," Carlos corrected. "There is a difference."

I nodded.

Juanito and Vittorio looked at me owlishly as Carlos filled their glasses. "Try the liquor slowly this time," Carlos said. "Savor the taste, enjoy the bouquet, let the glow permeate your nose, your brain, your stomach. Enjoy, my sons, don't merely utilize."

I laughed. "You sound like Aspromonte," I said, "although the advice you give is different. Bernardo would say you have it backwards."

Carlos nodded. "Yes, he is a pragmatist. He looks at the end rather than the means. He uses people and he doesn't care how he uses them. He had three malcontents who needed hanging, a feud with Corréon, and a town that was appalled at what he had done to the Herreras. He had the men killed rather horribly—did most of the bloody work himself, so I am told. Then he took the bodies into La Cienega and left them in front of the alcade's office as a "warning" from Corréon. The townsfolk were furious since the three were local citizens. They went over to Aspromonte en masse and helped destroy El Primero. Now the town is committed to the State. There is no balance of forces in the basin. The Guardia is paramount. The Aliens and the haciendados are destroyed, the town is in Aspromonte's pocket, and for the first time since the Alien invasion, the basin is under the control of one man." Carlos grinned ferociously. "It takes a man like Aspromonte to bring us together. We need him. And now he will move upward."

"Which should make him infinitely more dangerous."

"Or more useful. For as surely as night follows day he will eventually control Cuidad Segovia, and once in power it will be La Cienega all over again, a time of building, a time of battle, a time of victory."

"Do you believe this?" I asked.

"I do. He loves power, and power gravitates to him. He has the mentality of a conqueror. He can inspire fanatic loyalty. He can plan intelligently. He can execute. He is absolutely ruthless when ruthlessness is required. He is the sort of leader we need to destroy the Aliens. If he succeeds he will restore our world."

"Do you think so? If your evaluation is correct, he is a megalomaniac. Every success will lead to new desires. There will be no end to them and if he succeeds he will inevitably end by controlling everything. The man's mad."

"Of course he is. All great men are mad. But his potential for good outweighs the evils of his character."

"How do you figure that?"

"Look what he has done. He's cleared this region of both Aliens and scabs. It's ours again. And if he gets the power, he will clear the world."

"'And assuming the Aliens are willing to be destroyed—and won't destroy us first—Aspromonte will end up becoming so firmly entrenched that he cannot be removed."

"He is human. He will eventually die."

"And do you think that will solve things? Do you think the system he creates will die with him?"

"Of course. He cannot endure opposition any more than he can share power. There will be no one capable of taking his place and the old institutions will have to be restored."

"So you would not oppose him?"

"Lord, no! I'd help him any way I could. He's the hope of the world."

"And you think I should help him? I did—and he turned butcher. It was his orders, or lack of them, that murdered Ringtown. I saw those bodies. Not even goons do worse."

"Even so. For you cannot do what he can. You are a hunter; a man of great cleverness and skill, but you do not work with large numbers of men toward great ends. He is an organizer, a planner, a mover of men, and he knows the power of the pack. I think he can save Segovia. To me Bernardo is the hope of mankind, the leader of a resurgent people."

"And yet you hid Inez from him, knowing that he wanted her."

Carlos looked at me with frigid dignity. "She was put in my charge by her father. Would you have me break faith?"

I didn't smile.

"There is a difference between matters of honor and matters of policy. In policy I follow Aspromonte. In honor I follow my conscience."

"Yet you would promote tyranny."

"If it is necessary. For there is no freedom without the power to defend it. And as for the freedom of my people, that can come only after we have freed our world from the Aliens. In the long run tyranny will die, but Segovia will live only if we rid ourselves of these invaders. I want to feel like a man. I do not want to feel inferior to something inhuman."

Well, I thought bitterly, here it was—the racism, the chauvinism of mankind. It was the Brotherhood of Man all over again —the thing that had destroyed the Empire and had almost scuttled the Confederation in its constant effort to establish superior and inferior rankings between men and others, and between men and other men. The Confederation kept this under strict control, but here on this tortured world it throve. I swore silently with repressed frustration.

Outside the house the warm red glow of evening disappeared in a bloom of actinic light. Brighter than the noonday sun, it swelled in the South and then abruptly flickered out, leaving the evening darker by contrast.

"For the love of God!" Ramirez gasped, "What was *that*?"

Then the shock wave hit. Slates flew from the roofs of the house. Men and women were picked up like dolls and hurled through the air. A whole section of wall collapsed with an earsplitting crack of ruptured timbers and broken stone. Dust rose in a choking cloud!

"Sound the alarm!" Ramirez shouted to Juanito. "To the mine! Everyone! On the double."

A siren howled and the earth rocked and trembled as the earthquake struck.

"Inez!" I shouted.

"Here!" she came out of the confusion and stood beside me. People came running into the Cliff House, through the central hall and into the rock beyond. Inez and I stood with Carlos and his sons and watched the exodus from the Camp. "And this is what you want for Segovia?" I asked.

He looked at me with cold eyes as the flow of people ceased

abruptly. A man stopped beside Carlos. "Twelve men are outside, Chief," he said, "and there are six left in the camp. The storage barn collapsed. They were inside."

"Dead?"

"We did not stop to find out."

"Good. We will look for them presently."

The man went on into the cliff and we followed when it was apparent that there were no more to come. Some distance inside the rock we came into a large well-lighted chamber at the end of a corridor filled with barriers and guard posts. It was crowded with people watching a battery of video screens that lined one wall. I looked at them with mild astonishment.

Ramirez smiled without humor. "We're not so primitive as we seem," he said. He raised his voice to be heard above the background noise. "What's happening?" he asked a man at one of the control panels.

"La Cienega's gone," the man said. "A fireball hit right on the town. We're getting no broadcasts out of the basin now, and our wire coverage is poor. There's a lot of snow and static."

"Any radiation?"

"Minimal. The readings are mostly heat, but you wouldn't believe the readings," another operator said. "Fireball went up to ten thousand meters and flattened out," another voice said. "It isn't moving. It's just hanging there."

"There's a pretty fair wind blowing south," the first operator said. "It's moving about 10 k.p.h."

"How about electronics?" Ramirez asked.

"Nothing but static, and there's a steady stream of that. It's directional—all from the basin."

"Chief!" an urgent voice came from the control consoles. "Look at the big screen! I'm working the direct wire scanner just north of the Palo Verde grade."

"God! Would you look at that!" Ramirez breathed. "That's hell itself!"

"Don't look at the fire—look at the ground," I said.

"Why—wha—" Ramirez' voice stopped. Below the scan axis in the bottom of the screen the level floor of the valley stretched southward, and in a long curving line across the valley floor the fire raged, pouring billows of gray and black smoke into the sky. But the fire went no farther than the line. It stopped abruptly, and overhead in a hemispheric mass roiled and glowed the raging fires of the fireball. Already, even as I watched, the flames began to flicker and die. Yet the smoke continued to pour from the scorched earth beyond the razor sharp line that divided the green of the surrounding trees and grass from the scorched incinerated ruin of the Basin.

So the Aliens had something like our tactical barrier, I thought grimly. That meant a Class IV or maybe V, technology. The barrier was one of the accomplishments of Confederation science—and look as I would, I could see nothing that was generating it. Yet it confined the damage to a circle twenty kilometers in diameter, which was big for a barrier screen.

"Can you traverse that camera?" I asked.

"Sure—I'll scan the area for you," the technician said. The scene shifted as the camera pivoted.

"It had to come down with the warhead, or right after it," I murmured. "Since we felt the shockwave, I'd say right after—but what kind of generator do they have that can withstand that heat?"

"What are you mumbling about?" Ramirez asked sharply.

"I was wondering," I said. "What do you do to the fields when you have harvested your crops?"

"We burn them," Carlos said.

"Why?"

"To kill the pests and parasites that would destroy the next year's crops."

"But you don't burn indiscriminately do you?"

"No—we make a fire break around—" Carlos died away. Finally, in a low shocked tone he said, "Do you mean that they're burning out the basin because they think it's infested with vermin—they think we're *vermin*?" His voice rose on the last word.

"You haven't really thought about the Aliens, have you?" I asked softly. "You should. It's a chastening experience. You see, they don't think of us at all unless we become a nuisance. Occasionally we are an annoying sort of disease which needs controlling. They don't care if we live or die, just so long as we don't bother them."

"And so we're vermin!"

"That's higher on the scale than bacteria. I hope they have the idea that we are intelligent enough pests to learn from experience."

"But—"

"Don't object!—Pray!" I said. "Just pray that they don't treat our cities like we do our garbage dumps. Pray they don't wish to go to the trouble and expense of exterminating us. And in the meantime, you might as well call off this underground huddle. There is no radiation. There will be no firestorm. Some of the Basin folk may still be alive. The perimeter didn't cover it all. Get your people out of this hole and start saving lives."

"I am going to Pontecorvo after you marry me to Inez. I'm no good here, but with my cuadrilla I may be able to do something."

"What?"

"Frustrate Aspromonte. For if that maniac tries to kill another Ring the Aliens will surely do more than cauterize an infected area."

Chapter Sixteen:

"I wonder about you," Inez said as she watched me dress. "You are different from other men."

I laughed. "What do you know about other men?" I asked. "You were a virgin."

She blushed. "I don't mean that way," she said, "I'm thinking of those lines on your body, as though you had been cut many times with sharp knives."

I shrugged. Every line was a chronicle of battle. I've taken my share of lumps and while Fleet surgeons are expert at putting people together there are the inevitable traces that neither grafting nor tissue clones can completely erase. The hairline scars—so unlike primitive surgical healing, were outside Inez' experience, yet she felt a subliminal unease even though they were not difiguring, or even noticeable unless the light was right and one looked closely.

"There have been men and goons, and bulls," I said, "and none have been kind. Fortunately I heal quickly and do not scar."

"But—so many?" She sighed, half vexed at my answer. Her attitude said "All right, you won't tell me yet—but I can wait and you will tell me in the end. Someday I will know everything about you, but will I be happy when I know?"

She wasn't hard to read. Her body was a lovely expressive extension of her mind. It was a mirror of her thoughts. But she had no idea of the extent of my understanding. She didn't know what I really was and I didn't enlighten her. To her I was a Segovian who had led a peculiar life before becoming a matador, and now the peculiarities were enhanced. But she knew matadors and their strangeness on the day of a corrida and the queer things they did before they faced the bulls. And knowing this, she didn't ask questions. We were happy with each other and the weeks that had passed since we left La Cienega had been pleasant. Today was the last corrida of the season. Tomorrow we would celebrate our second month of marriage. I had thought I was in love before, but I really didn't know the meaning of the word. There was an affinity between us that was beyond logic and reason.

She flipped aside the sheet that covered her and stood beside me. Her fingers traced a tingling path down my back. "Torres agonistes," she murmured. "How can I sleep when you are wakeful? How can I be calm when you face the bulls? You leave my side and I feel lost. I love you."

I said nothing; just stood there and enjoyed. Were this not a faena day my actions would be different, for I never tired of her. There was a pleasure in her that I had never known before. It was not the driving urge a Mystic could inspire, nor yet the more subtle lust a Dibrugarhian could stimulate. It was something else, something softer, something deeper, something more elemental and more real.

"It is a good thing those lovely ladies in the boxes behind the barrera cannot see you now," she said with gentle malice. "They wouldn't have such inflated ideas about your heroism and imperturbability. You shine, my love, in the brilliance of your faenas, not in your preparation for them. You shudder like a hermit on his wedding day."

I grinned. "Eagerly but with trepidation, eh? There is poetry in you, my darling; unkind poetry."

"I am jealous of your bulls. They demand too much."

"They die, and you do not. And they demand me only one day in every two weeks."

"That is too much."

I laughed at her.

"I mean it," she said. She shook her head. "I say I love you, but those are words that have been said uncounted millions of times by uncounted millions of people. I cannot tell you how I really feel, yet when I am with you I am close to heaven. I fear every day that this will end and rejoice every day that it does not."

I looked at her with love. Her body and her spirit were a flawless blend of interlocking curves. There was poetry in her—and music—and abiding joy. A woman like Inez didn't merely happen. She was specially created. And for the lucky man she favored, she was the ultimate masterpiece; a delight to the senses and to the soul. I sighed and reached for her. She came to me like thistledown on the wind. I sighed and held her close. "Stop tempting me," I said. "This is no time for love. There is a corrida this afternoon."

"And when it is over you will be too tired, too harrassed, too busy with your friends and foolish females even to think of me."

"Dreamer." I said.

"And that is why I hate the bulls. They take you from me." She left my arms, went to the closet, chose a dress and put it on. Already it was too warm for underwear, and it promised to be hotter, a brassy strength-sucking day that marked the towns close to the equator. I wondered why I was such a fool as to have chosen Sanlucar for my last appearance of the season. Even the feast of San Jaime and the crowds that came for the ceremonies and the food weren't enough to make the town palatable. Inez settled the dress with a wriggle of rounded hips. "There—my lord and master—is the package less attractive now that it is wrapped?" She grinned a gamin grin and pivoted before me.

"Hardly," I said, "for I know what is inside." I sighed with exaggerated regret and reached for my trousers.

"You want me to make breakfast?"

"No—let's eat downstairs."

"In that coffee shop? I'd choke." She shook her head. "You should eat here. I do not trust this hotel's cook. He might poison you. I hear he follows Manolo Ruiz."

"Then we should educate him." I watched her as she moved, the dress curling and folding along the lines of her body.

"You watch me as you watch a bull," she said.

"But not for the same reason." I thought fleetingly that the cuadrilla watched her too—looking for the first telltale swelling of her slender waist. I knew the wagers on her pregnancy although I didn't speak of them. But their eyes asked questions. There was machismo involved, and getting one's woman with child was a social positive that had evolved into a status symbol during. Segovia's slow recovery from the Alien War.

"I know why you won't eat, but it's silly," she said abruptly.

"It won't be silly if I get a horn in my belly," I said. "Both you and the surgeon might be unhappy."

She put her hands over my mouth. "Hush!" she said. "You're tempting fate."

Her phobias weren't mine, I thought, but my braggadoccio had holes in it. I had my own superstitions. I had a certain order of dressing before a faena. My cravat must be tied in a double overhand knot, my zapatillas had to have white soles, my undergarments must be Matamoros wool. I dressed precisely as I did for my first faena with Ciclón at Corréon's ganaderia. Superstition? Probably. All matadors had their peculiarities and I was no exception. This stated contempt of the bull's horns was another part of the mystique of magic that ensured my remaining alive. I didn't really believe in it, neither did I disbelieve.

She shrugged. "I wish you could relax," she said. "Of all the faenas I have been with you, this one promises to be the worst. I die a little already."

"It's the last," I said, "and the last is always the worst—until the bull comes through the toril. Then there's no more time to worry. It's the waiting that's hard, not the fighting."

"Not for me," Inez said, "Those first moments when you go into the ring drain my strength. I watch. I ask myself if you have noted how the beast moves, how he hooks with his horns, how he stands, whether he will charge the cape or you." Her eyes were wide. "I ask too many questions and I fear for you."

"Don't tell me. I do not want to be conscious of your fears."

"I understand," she said. "I will be happier when I have your children. Then nothing can take you completely from me." She sighed. "I am twenty years old and childless. It is a disgrace to womanhood."

"Ah—machismo in reverse," I said. "But right now I'm not interested in babies. I want a lover—not a pregnant wife. I want you for myself, not as a nursemaid to some squalling brat."

"Squalling? Ha! Who would care? He'd be your son." She laughed at me. "Just what do I have to do to prove I'm capable of taking care of you and your child at the same time?"

"Get pregnant." I said.

She stamped her foot. "You know I won't until you permit it."

"Disconcerting, isn't it?"

She glared at me and I shrugged. Meeting Days were never the best days of the week. They started wrong. There was always the corrida. But after today there would be no more of this until next year. It would be better when this day was over and the excitement had died. There would be five whole months of no bulls, no rings, no hurried arrivals and departures. I sat on the bed, then stretched out on it and let some of the tension flow out. Inez was no help to me now. I had to build to an emotional peak for a good performance and she was a distraction. She stimulated the wrong emotions, but it wasn't easy to separate her from my life or to suppress my desire for her. It was never easy. How does one stay cool beside a fire? I grimaced. A good way might be to do something other than play with the flames.

"It's odd about attitudes," I said. "I often wonder why you do not hate me. After all, I work for the agency responsible for your father's death."

She eyed me doubtfully. "Perhaps I should, but I don't. You didn't kill Padre—Aspromonte did. Nor was it your fault that Ringtown was savaged when you melted the Ring." She shivered. "I never liked Ringtown although I was there for a year after my mother died. Scabs aren't really human. They're something the Koalber have made. They look like people, but they neither think nor act like people. They think the Koalber are gods."

"Koalber?"

"The Aliens. I used to talk with Nasuvon and I didn't think they was a god."

"They—was?" My voice was curious. Inez used words like a machinist uses tools. She seldom made errors, and she was not making one now. I was sure of that.

"They're amphisexual—functioning male and female in the same body. They work in pairs. The Pair that ran the La Cienega Ring were Nasuvon. I had rapport with their female principle, and I was something of a curiosity—like a talking dog. They can't believe that individual units are intelligent. They think our works are instinct. They would talk to me for long periods of time, and even did it occasionally after I left them and returned to the ranch. Once they talked to me in Cuidad Segovia. They wanted my father to do something for them. I forget what it was."

"They talked to me when the Ring was destroyed. It was not really to me, it was to everyone; so I heard what they said. Nasuvon knew they were going to die and they sent a warning about a structural weakness in the dome. But they were puzzled. There should be no weakness. They thought it might be possible that humans were involved, that it was a forty percent probability."

"It was a hundred percent," I muttered as my mind kept screaming "*jackpot—telepath!—gold mine!*" at me. My hands were shaking and I could taste a faint flavor of bile. It was pure elation that cramped my gut. I wasn't philosophical. I didn't ruminate about the fact that people can live together for months and share love and dreams—and still know nothing of each others' lives. We are islands with transient bridges to other islands. I knew that and it wasn't strange. Nor was I surprised about Inez' knowledge. Things like this happen to me. I accept them and do not worry why they seldom happen to others. Coincidence is the handmaiden of Special Service agents. Without her, we don't stay alive.

Aspromonte, I thought briefly, *would give his soul to possess what had been given to me.* With Inez, I had a pipeline to the Aliens. I had suspected they were telepaths after the La Cienega burnout, but now I knew.

"They discussed Nasuvon's estimate and decided to destroy La Cienega," Inez said. "I didn't know what they meant, or I would have warned Carlos. One doesn't talk about cauterizing an ulcer and mean incinerating thousands of people."

"That's what they meant," I said. "They don't think of us as people."

"I wish I couldn't hear them when they talk between Rings."

"Be glad you do. Perhaps you will save the world."

"Don't be dramatic."

"I'm not. I'm stating a fact—" a fact that would be logged in the scoutship's tapes if I ever got back to that sexy mechanism. I grinned. It would be fun to give the computer a bad time. I hoped Inez would be with me when I did it.

The probabilities of that were remote. Bur Pol would probably dragoon her for Koalber contact work and I'd never see her again. The Services were hell on romance. I had an idea what her future and mine would be and I didn't like it, but it was probably inevitable. I wondered if there were other wives and sweethearts in my past—and how far my past really extended back in time. Inez was right. There were too many hairlines on my body; too many I didn't remember. I wondered briefly about my own reality and the childhood I could envision so clearly. Was I really from Terranueva? Did I really do what my memory told me? Was I really Senior Lieutenant José Torres, or was I someone else entirely? I shrugged. I didn't know and I wouldn't know. All I really could hold certain was that I was someone valuable enough to be restored and reused a number of times, and that I had better get as much as I could out of Inez and this cycle of existence before it disappeared. Selfish? Sure, it was selfish, but if my total life belonged to the Navy, the discrete parts of it belonged to me and I would get as much from them as I could.

"My love," I said, "I want you to do something for me."

"Name it."

"I want you to tell me everything you know about these Koalber, everything you can remember, everything you have heard, everything you have guessed or reasoned about them."

She didn't ask why. She was with me when La Cienega was cauterized and she knew I worked for the State. She didn't approve, but she understood. She slipped her hand in mine and led me back to our bed. She held my hand as she talked, and the sun rose until it was directly overhead before she was done.

I went to the window and looked out into the city square. The

109

bells in the cathedral were ringing. The sun was a ball of brass in a sky yellow with heat. I felt a familiar tingle along my spine as I stood there. I looked at my hands. They quivered a little. I felt myself sliding into the familiar introspection. The corrida was coming into the forefront of my mind.

Chapter Seventeen:

I went to the corrals for the little ceremony where the alcalde holds the lots and the matadors draw for the bulls. I picked a pair called Diabolo and Furioso, inappropriate names for a religious festival honoring a man of kindness and mercy—but then the entire idea of a corrida on the Saint's day was strange.

The other two matadors were dressed in funeral black. They looked uncomfortable. One was Carnicero. He had gone through last year with me, but had been left far behind in the race for the top. He was a good man but erratic. I extended my hand—"Good luck," I said.

Carnicero shook it and smiled to cover his embarassment. "It is good to see you maestro," he said. "It has been a long time. I am happy you are here."

"It should be a good faena," I said. The third matador came up, hand extended. "I am Pepe Gomez," he said. "Grandson of Alfredo Gomez."

"Your grandfather was great," I said, "as you will be with his blood in your veins."

Pepe grinned. "My blood is rosewater," he replied. "I could use some of my grandfather's right now."

I chuckled.

"A good faena—God willing," Carnicero said.

I was neither attracted nor repelled by the good wishes. I felt that it was foolish to call upon anything except my own resources.

But many did. I shrugged. Possibly that was why there were so many second-rate matadors. They looked for outside help, and God—so the ancient proverb went—helps those who help themselves. I depended upon myself and my cuadrilla. I knew what they could do. Possibly it was this dependence on Divine favor that made Carnicero a second-rater. The man had all the moves, but he wasn't daring when he should be and too daring when he shouldn't be. I remembered one time when he tried six times to put a sword into a bony bull who could not or would not spread the cruz. And in the end the bull had gotten him and laid him up for a month, while one of his fellow matadors had to pith the animal with the descaballo. Now if I had been in Carnicero's zapatillas, I'd have tried twice with the sword and then would have gone for the descaballo, and pithed the bull. Sure, I would have been booed, but there are worse things than the anger of a fickle crowd. Getting gored is one of them. There is no reason to take stupid chances when the odds are against success.

As befitted my rank, I led the way through the ruedo and walked across the sand of the arena. It hadn't been raked yet and was lumpy underfoot. Moreover it wasn't the good golden sand from Oro del Mar, and it probably would give poorer footing than I liked.

"Not too good," Carnicero said.

"A lousy ring," Gomez agreed. "I've been booked in them all year. They're murder."

I nodded. The bad rings were murder. Eighty percent of the deaths occurred in these ill-equipped places. Most of the major bullrings were relatively safe. At least a man had a medical team ready for him if he goofed. But this one was new and not well staffed or equipped. They'd be lucky to have a country doctor. And the facilities—I eyed the burladeros with disgust—too low. It needed at least another boardwidth of height. Any halfway agile bull could clear that wall and get into the alleyway or the stands. And no matador liked to cape a bull out of a mob of fleeing people.

Everything was cut to a minimum to ensure a maximum of profit for San Jaime. Ordinarily I wouldn't let my agent schedule a place like this, but the festival was important. There would be a big crowd and publicity San Jaime received among the faithful made it one of the better end-of-the-season spots. It did my image no harm by giving the impression that I was not too proud to work here, or that I was not so greedy as to deny the saint his due.

Jorge came across the ring to where I leaned against the burladeros. "Not too good, eh maestro?"

"It could be worse."

"How?" Jorge shook his head. "Personally, I'm gonna be damn glad when this is over. I don't like working these half-finished rings.

You'd think men would learn something in four thousand years. We took the stars, but we still don't build decent bullrings. It grabs me."

"You're not alone," I murmured. "But think of San Jaime. We do a great work for him this day."

"And for what? The guys who need it don't get it; the cathedral does. And what good does a few more ornaments on San Jaime's statue do anyone?"

"We get expenses—don't forget that."

"I'd rather have the gold."

"And lose out as numero uno in the vote. There are going to be a hundred thousand aficionados here today."

"How can we lose?"

"Ruiz is doing Cuidad Segovia today."

"He healed quick. He had a big hole in him."

"He's dedicated—you know what that means, and he's going to be after our throats."

"Pah! He can't touch us this year."

"Don't run him down. Manolo's a genuine hero around Districto Nacional."

I shook my head. I was loaded with introspection and I could no more maintain a mood for bulls than I could fly like a bird. What was wrong with me? Was I tired? Was it too much Inez? Was I ill? Was I looking for something else? What was the odd uneasiness which obsessed me?

Why had I become a matador? Was it only because the cover was good and because I could travel unmolested? Or was it because I was a compulsive gambler and the gambling of my life was the highest stake?

I hadn't wanted—and indeed I knew it was foolish—to exacerbate Alien-human relations, yet I had entered almost eagerly into the plan to destroy the La Cienega Ring. What was this fire inside that made me look for danger? Why had I gone out among the stars? In the six hundred worlds of the Confederation intelligent beings lived and died upon their home worlds and never once wanted to leave them. Most of the billions of intelligent entities that composed the dominant races of the Confederation knew little and cared less about other worlds. They knew the Confederation only as something that bridged the stars and the Brotherhood of Intellect as a foggy ideal without flesh or bones or blood. What did I owe to such as these—or they to me? What did killing two bulls in a town on the Southeast border of the continent mean in the march of unity across this quadrant of the galaxy? What was the reason for such a man as Aspromonte or such creatures as the Aliens? Where did I fit into the scheme of things, and what was the scheme? Where were we going?—and why? Was it all a cosmic grab bag, a lottery, a random game of chance, or was there a reason for these moves and maneuverings?

Actually, the Aliens were probably more my business than the Segovians. There wasn't much hope that the humans on this world would be of sufficient culture or technological stature to be admitted as full members of the Confederation, but there was every indication that the Aliens were. So why had I fought them? I was not obliged to hate them, nor was I obliged to love Segovia. Was Ruiz right when he insisted that in the last analysis species affinity was the dominant reason for behavior and that man supported man merely because of similarities in anatomy and physiology? If this were true, then the whole Confederation was built upon a base of sand.

I sighed. I really didn't know. A year was not enough to learn the basics of this culture, let alone of the Aliens. It was too big a job for one man. Evars should have sent a team.

I shrugged. There was no profit in this thinking. I had a corrida in less than four hours and I had better get ready for it mentally or I was going to make a mess of the performance. Possibly the best thing I could do would be to go to my quarters underneath the stands and try to get some rest. I wasn't about to get into the proper mental attitude with all this fruitless speculation.

I looked for Inez, but she wasn't in sight. I beckoned to Jorge and the picador came toward me.

"I am going to try to get some rest," I said. "I feel edgy. If you see Inez, send her down to guard the door."

"I'll get Jaime now," Jorge said. "I know where he is. And I'll look for your woman. Go below—I'll see that you are insulated for as long as you like."

I opened the door to my rooms beneath the stands, and came to an abrupt halt. Seated in my dressing chair was Bernardo Aspromonte.

"Where the devil did you come from?" I asked.

"I've been waiting for you," he said. "I hear you've acquired Inez Corréon. I want her." His angel's lips curved into a smile, but his eyes were flat and his face was hard.

"I didn't think you had that much gall. She's my wife."

Aspromonte chuckled. "You don't really know me."

I shrugged. "I don't really want to. What I do know is enough for a lifetime. You're responsible for what happened to La Cienega Basin."

"No more than you, matador. You destroyed the Ring. All I did was kill scabs."

"Six thousand dead Segovians aren't my fault. You knew the

Aliens would react."

"I didn't kill those people. The Aliens did. They reacted like a bunch of paranoiacs. It was entirely out of character."

"You can be singularly stupid," I said. "You know as well as I that the Aliens think of us as we think of pestilence."

"So they wipe out the Basin. They couldn't possibly have known that we had a hand in the Ring's destruction. Sure, we took advantage of the melt to wipe out Ringtown, but that's natural and they don't care about scabs. Any Segovians would do what we did."

"Where were you when La Cienega was burned?" I asked.

"In Cuidad Segovia."

"You deserved to burn with them."

"Don't get so damn pure. You set off the melt."

"I know it, and I don't feel happy about it."

"Conscience?"

I nodded.

"I'm lucky. I don't have one. Now let's get back to Inez Corréon. When can I have her?"

"Never."

He looked aggrieved. "Just what have you got against me?" he asked. "I ought to be the one who's complaining. You stole her , but I'm not angry. I have half a dozen women who are better looking and better behaved. I don't want her body."

"Or her property?"

"Hell—it's yours now—or didn't you know? As her husband you exercise all legal rights." Aspromonte stood up and walked over to me. "I don't want that stuff. It's not worth much with La Cienega gone. She's got something far more valuable. One of the scabs I brought to Cuidad Segovia told me about it. She can talk to the Aliens; so I want her."

"Over my dead body."

He looked at me appraisingly. "It's an idea," he said.

"Try it."

He shrugged. "Not here. Not now. Later maybe. Right now I want to know about Aliens. I intend to smash them."

"If you're smart, you'll leave them alone. The destruction of the Basin was not a warning. It was not revenge. It was simply a precaution, like sterilizing an abscess to prevent further contamination."

He made a slashing gesture with his right hand. "Don't try to put me off, matador. Oppose me and it would be better for you if your stupid bulls killed you."

My face paled. Accidentally or deliberately Aspromonte had broken one of the oldest taboos in the superstition-ridden art of bull fighting. No one ever speaks of dying in the arena on the day of a corrida.

Aspromonte's voice was heavy and it carried. The door was thin, and Jaime was outside listening. Aspromonte had hardly uttered the forbidden words before Jaime came through the door, his face red with fury. "Dog—and son of a dog!" he shouted, "Get out!"

Aspromonte looked at the slim young man with astonishment that changed instantly to anger. He swung his arm and backhanded Jaime across the mouth. The boy spun around and fell against the wall.

"You'd better leave," I said, "Jaime'll put a knife in you."

"I will if anything happens to the maestro," Jaime muttered as he scrambled to his feet. "Damned fat mouth. If you trample our luck with your big flat feet—"

"You're crazy," Aspromonte said, but he backed away.

"He's right. You have no business here. Get out while you still can." I turned to Jaime. "Take it easy," I said. "Consider the source. What can you expect from some stupid civilian. It is not his fault that he knows nothing. It is his mother's for not bearing him with a brain. What is done can't be undone. Let's talk no more about it."

"He gets out—now," Jaime said, "Or I go for the others."

"You'd better leave," I said. "You've broken about all the taboos there are to break."

"Okay—but I'll see you after the fight," Aspromonte said. "And I'll bring help."

I shrugged after he left. It wasn't his nature to drop something that might further his ends, nor did I think he would yield to threats. La Cienega might have taught him caution, but it hadn't taught him humility. He still thought he could destroy the Aliens.

I went to the bed in the corner, lay down and closed my eyes. This was a bad day. My mood was black and I didn't try to shake it off. Logic insisted that I was simply tired, that the season had been long, that this ring was not the best. There was nothing to the superstitions of the bullring, but I was a matador—a member of that strange breed whose oddness increases logarithmically as the hour of the corrida approaches.

Chapter Eighteen:

I had the final faena with the bull called Diabolo. And he was a
devil indeed. Big, black and quick with all the faults of the Alipio
line and few of the virtues except courage, he would have been a
challenge at any time, but he was doubly so this day. The first faena
had gone badly. Jorge had piced the bull too hard, and although there
were a few boos and catcalls, I made a clean kill and recovered some
honor. It wasn't much of a fight since Jorge had taken most of the
fury out of Furioso, and the kill was so easy that I wished I was
capable of a few Ruiz-type adornos to make it look more difficult
and exciting.

But Diabolo made up for what Furioso lacked. The beast
reminded me of the one that had spiked Ruiz at Santayana. This one
could have been that one's brother; mean, stubborn, querencia-
hunting, and a vicious hooker to the right. He simply wouldn't
cooperate. He charged in short quick jabs that never lengthened
until the banderilleros and I managed to chivvy him off his
querencia and into another part of the ring. Then the animal was
passable. I placed the banderillas despite Jaime's protests, hoping to
make the bull realize that I was the enemy—and to come to me rather
than stay on his station and make me come to him. And for awhile it
worked, but after the quites when I went to the muleta, Diabolo was
back on querencia making life hell again.

"You'd better take him quickly, maestro," Carnicera called to
me. He was right. It had gone far enough. I would probably have to

goad the bull into moving and I never enjoy punishing an animal I am about to kill.

The whole corrida had been tense and sloppy, marred by anxiety and overreaction. It was a poor end to the season. I felt unhappy about my performance, worried about Inez, and uneasy about Aspromonte. It was no mental attitude to carry onto the sand.

The big Alipio watched me come, but made no move to charge. He had decided to hold his ground and beat off his attackers, and his small stubborn mind would accept no other idea. He was perfectly willing to fight but it would be on his terms.

I tried to entice him with the muleta but he didn't move. I came closer, made a decastigo pass and the bull flinched to the prick of the sword, but held his ground. I tried again and had to leap for my life as the bull lunged without warning. Damn! I thought, he's getting the idea that he ought to charge me. I worked closer—using the sword point through the cape to goad the bull to fury. At the third pass I succeeded and drew the bull off his station and through two naturales. The crowd cheered.

But the bull refused a por alto and wouldn't fix. I went back to the decastigo for the fifth time, swearing with frustration. But after a fashion I was fortunate for the beast had moved enough to spread the cruz. There was nothing to do but kill this uncooperative monster as quickly as possible and get the agony over. Nothing was going to be served by waiting. I draped the muleta over the stick, pulled the sword free, and posed until the trumpet notes for the final phase quivered in the still air. Then I leaped—and the bull moved. The sword struck bone, bent, and was torn from my hand as the bull lunged. The horn passed so close that it took braid from my breeches. I pivoted away, recovered the bent blade, caught the bull on his return to querencia, forced him through a por alto, fixed him— and tried again.

This time the blade sunk in, but the bull's head did not follow the cape. He came straight on with a mighty agonal surge and I was enclosed between his horns, picked off my feet and hurled backwards. My head snapped on my neck as the bull hooked. I didn't have time to react. Already half senseless from that paralyzing shock, I was slammed into the burladeros with bonecrushing force.

I heard the gasp of dismay, Inez' shriek, and the concerted howl of pain and fury from the cuadrilla, and that was all. The world went black before my eyes....

I was cold. It was dark. A chill breeze blew across the pain in my head and neck. The hard floor beneath me heaved and bumped.

There was a constant creaking and swaying and a steady rhythmic clickety-clack of metal against metal that seemed to come from somewhere beneath me. The ache split my head into two throbbing parts.

I was weak.

There was something urgent which I must do. I tried to call for help, but my voice wouldn't work. My stomach drew into a knot and I retched. I felt a little better.

I opened my eyes. It wasn't dark after all. I was in a steel box with a wooden floor. The box was about three by three by fifteen meters. There were two doorways in the middle of each long wall. One was closed. The other was half open and sky and trees moved past. It made me dizzy.

I was on a train. A freight car.

It made me feel better to know where I was, but I didn't know where I was going.

I didn't know who I was. I was just me—nameless and lost with a feeling that I must do something.

I could remember pieces of things; falling from the sky in a machine that talked about vectors and trajectory, and sorry about that, boss; a woman whose body was a flame and whose face was the glory of the world; an enormous glowing explosion; the roar of a wildly cheering crowd; a big hateful man with a beautiful mouth, a slab-cheeked face and cold eyes. But I couldn't put the pieces together.

My head hurt. There was a fire behind my eyes and acid in my mouth. I retched again. There was nothing left to come.

I closed my eyes and endured my hurt until it died to a dull pain that lingered endlessly. And at last the car slowed and stopped with a creak of metal against metal and a clang of iron.

I opened my eyes.

A man looked in the door, cursed, reached in and dragged me out. I fell onto the embankment.

"On your feet, bum. Get going," the man said.

I understood the words, but I didn't know where to go. I stood and the sharp stones hurt my feet. My shoes were gone.

The man pushed me over the edge of the embankment, with his booted foot, and I rolled and slid to the bottom. Stones cut and bruised my flesh and cut my tender feet.

I lay at the bottom of the embankment, breathing shallowly.

Then with infinite pain I rose and stood unsteadily, head hanging, too hurt to care. I took a step and then another.

The train guard watched me for a moment, "Drunk," he said, and then continued his walk down the line of cars.

There was a tiny pond. Green things grew in it. I was thirsty. I drank the water and retched again. The water softened the matted blood and hair on my head. I felt the pain subside to a dull ache. I buried my face in the water, more blood came out of my hair. I rose to my knees and pressed my hands to my throbbing temples. I rose and moved on.

I found another pond and drank again. This time it stayed down.

There was a dirt road beside the embankment. I walked down it, leaving blood spots from my feet to stain the sharped-edged crushed rock surface.

And presently I came to Cantown. The sight of the place made a neural connection and from somewhere in my brain I remembered an axiom. *"To penetrate a culture, start at the bottom. There is plenty of room, and there is anonymity. Those who count won't notice you, and those who don't count, don't care.'*

I looked at Cantown, at the miserable collection of squalid shacks aggregated beside an enormous smoking refuse dump. I doubted if anything could be lower than this.

I went from shack to shack until I found one that was empty, I went inside.

I would start here and work up.

I had no idea why I should start or where I would go, but I was certain that it was what I must do.

Chapter Nineteen:

Manuel Espinosa was drunk. For him, it was an ideal state of being, a nirvana that could be achieved for greater or lesser periods depending upon the amount of money available. Could it be proved that death was the gateway to perpetual intoxication, Manuel would have been an eager suicide, but fear that some other fate lay behind life's boundary kept him alive.

On those rare occasions when he looked upon himself and his world with sober eyes, he wanted nothing so much as the means to drown the vision. Drunk, he had the happy faculty of ignoring both himself and his surroundings.

He had no outstanding quality except an apparently limitless capacity for ethanol. He accepted and metabolized the hydrocarbon in any form that could be swallowed. He was a pariah among pariahs, an outcast among the untouchables of Cantown. His shack, symbolically, was farther down the hill and closer to the dump than any of the others, and when the wind blew from the North the whole choking effluvium of Santayana's offal made the place intolerable. Fortunately the wind seldom blew from the North.

Otherwise, the location was moderately favorable since it gave Manuel first choice at fresh dumpings, but lately Manuel hadn't been working the refuse pile with his customary diligence. The Dummy had been doing the job for him. I was the Dummy.

No one knew much about me except that I showed up one day a few months ago. I had been badly beaten; my nose was broken, my eyes black with blood, and there was a great bruise on my head. I wasn't able to speak although otherwise I seemed no better or worse than other men. I took the shack where Santos had died and didn't worry about Santos' ghost even though the old man had not been buried in holy ground. I stayed there for a week and then moved in with Manuel, leaving the shack to its ghost until the city burned it down.

No one could figure why I would live with Manuel unless Espinosa knew something which gave him a hold on me. Nothing could stand Manuel. Men avoided him. Dogs slunk from him. Even the big brown rats were unhappy in his presence. They avoided his shanty, although they invaded every other shack in Cantown. Only I endured him, which proved that I was well named. There was something wrong with my head.

However, no one really cared. We were left alone—me to my stupidity; Manuel to his bottle. And, in fact, we lived that way in our own personal sphere. Manuel wanted only alcohol—I only wished that Manuel would die. I despised Espinosa more than any creature I had ever known. I loathed him and hated him, yet I shared life with the unspeakable lump of filth and selfishness and did his bidding. For uncounted days I had endured the sour stench of wine and sweat, the reek of urine and encrusted filth, and the nameless other smells that clung to him. For months my will was suppressed and my decisions were not my own.

But it wasn't this menial state that made me writhe in an agony of frustration and despair; it was the fact that this undead corpse continued to live despite habits that would have killed an ordinary man. My mind demanded that I break from Espinosa, but as long as Manuel lived, I could not. I had tried, but had come back. As long as Manuel lived I was tied to Cantown. Yet I had to get away. Something in me, unrecognized and formless, below the threshold of my memory, kept struggling to leave, to discover myself, to do what I must do. And the final frustration was that I didn't really know what I was to do. All I knew was that it couldn't be satisfied here. For I was the Dummy no longer. I could talk. The partial aphasia had disappeared some time ago and with its passing had come a horde of memories. I was gradually turning from a human vegetable to a person. I knew now that my name was José Torres. I knew also that I was not of this world—although I distrusted that memory as wishful escapism. I could remember clearly back to the time I awoke in the freight car. Before that it was like groping through a fog illuminated by stray flashes of light. But there was hope.

I remembered coming to Cantown. The others tolerated me and had even helped with food and a certain rough care for my wounds.

Espinosa had done nothing except look at me with his black button eyes, until finally he was certain that I would live. Then he moved in.

"Dummy," he said, as he squatted on his heels and watched me labor on my shack.

I looked at him dully.

"Don't play games with me," Espinosa said, "You can talk as well as I can."

I shook my head and made gargling noises.

"All right, have it your way. Maybe you can't talk, but you still don't belong here. Want me to tell you why?"

I nodded.

"First, there's your clothes. Sure—I know they're dirty and they're torn, but they're quality material and don't have that look of worn-in dirt. Fact is, they don't look as though they've been worn much at all." Manuel belched and scratched his hairy chest. "They look like you've got money."

"When you came here," Espinosa went on, "you were bloody, but you didn't stink except with puke. You didn't shamble. You staggered all right, but that was because you were beat up. There were no lice and fleas on you. Your hands were soft and smooth. Your nails were manicured. You didn't have any of that crapped out look. You see, Dummy, this is as low as you can get. When a man comes here he's got nothing left. You had plenty left. Yet you stayed. You didn't have all the pizzazz kicked outa you. So you stayed by choice. Now why would you do something like that?"

I turned away. The man was annoying and he asked questions to which I had no answers.

"Don't turn your goddam back on me, Dummy," Espinosa snarled. "I'm talking to you."

And then, for the first time, I felt the compuslion that had since become a major part of my life. Despite my raging internal protest I turned back to Espinosa.

"That's better. Now listen Dummy, and listen good. I got you figured. You're on the run. There's a reward out for you somewhere and unless you're a good boy I'm gonna turn you in and collect it." Espinosa chuckled. "You got me thinking. I was a cop once in Cuidad Segovia before I got booted out on a framed rap; so I know about crooks and scabs and fugitives—and for my money you're one."

Was I? I didn't know. I didn't even know my own name. All I knew was that I must listen to Espinosa.

"You got any money hid out?"

I shook my head, reached into my pocket and took out a thin folder of currency.

Manuel looked greedy. "Give," he said.

I handed him the money. Manuel riffled through it, "Huh—two hundred twenty—," he said. "It ain't much, but it makes you a capitalist compared to the rest of us." He put the money in his pocket. "Anyway, you don't need it as bad as I do. Besides, you probably got more."

I shook my head.

"Now that's too bad," Manuel said. He grinned, scratched and belched a sour stink of wine in my direction. "Two hundred ain't enough to buy me off. But you can work it off. With a big strong fellow like you working the dump it won't be hardly no time before you can give me what I want." He chuckled. "I didn't think I had anything on you, Dummy, but it looks like I hit pay dirt."

I felt as blank as I must have looked. What was the man talking about?—Oh well—it't didn't matter. The idea was clear enough. Manuel wanted me to work on the dump—and that was what I must do. I didn't like it, but I couldn't resist. And it had been that way ever since. What Manuel wanted he got, despite the fact that whole sections of my memory had returned, and I was now perfectly certain I had nothing to fear from the police. There was, of course, someone I should fear. I had an enemy—the man with the beautiful mouth and the ugly face, the one who had caused my injury. But this enemy was not of the police. I knew that much. But the old enemy was hidden in the shadow of the new. Manuel Espinosa was the true enemy, for he could dominate me.

I cursed my weakness. How could I be controlled by something like Espinosa? I was younger, stronger and smarter. All the rules favored the sober man over the drunk, the healthy over the diseased, the dedicated over the waster, but somehow it didn't work out according to the rules.

There was only one answer. Espinosa was an untrained esper, and his talent meshed with the traumatized receptivity of my damaged perceptions. The results were devastating. It was inconceivably bad chance that had brought us two together, while I was weakened and able to be influenced, but as long as Manuel lived, I could not escape. I was as much a slave as if I were certified.

There was only one solution to my predicament. I must kill Espinosa. Yet I must do it in a way that would bring no suspicion upon myself. I had no desire to become enmeshed in the tentacles of justice. My present experience was bad enough.

I had one thing in my favor. Manuel, with a little encouragement, could conceivably drink himself to death. He was already a confirmed alcoholic, and his physical condition was poor. The reek of his breath and the yellowness of his skin and eyeballs indicated a badly damaged liver and kidneys. He couldn't last too long—and with help he might be parted from life a little more quickly. The thought sustained me, and as Manuel systematically destroyed my will, I destroyed his liver. It was a macabre contest. Would Manuel die? Would I become a lump of human putty?

Manuel recognized the elements as well as I did. "Do I die from drink, or do you die from labor?" he asked. "I think perhaps I die first. But it will do you no good. I have placed a paper in the public registry, and when I die the police will learn you killed me."

"That is a lie about the paper," I said. "You know nothing about me, and you do your own drinking. I do not force you."

"You give me money."

"Because you ask for it," I said. "You get it all." I wasn't telling quite the truth. I supplied Manuel with money, but I didn't give him everything. I kept something back. Manuel didn't know about it and therefore didn't ask. I would have been unable to refuse had he asked, but as long as he didn't I could keep my own.

"You will not kill me soon," Manuel said, punctuating his words with a hiccup. "I am still strong."

He wasn't, but I saw no need to tell him that. Every day he grew weaker. One day soon he would die and it would be finished. Then I could leave and do what I must do.

But now there was one more thing to do. It was an imperative. If there were documents I must get them from the public record before Espinosa died. At worst they would be worthless, at best they might reveal more of my identity than my name. And I needed my identity. It wouldn't be too hard to get the papers, but Espinosa had to be made to cooperate. The problem of cooperation could be solved by adding ethanol to the drunkard's wine. This I did and was rewarded when Espinosa passed out. The remainder was easy. I had already made molds of thermoplastic. I greased Espinosa's lax fingers, heated the molds and fitted them over his fingers. I passed them firmly into place and waited until they cooled. Then I marked the molds and removed them. Espinosa didn't stir.

I took the molds to my corner and checked them. Espinosa's fingers were larger than mine, which was fortunate. I could make casts directly over my fingers. I carefully fitted one set of molds to my fingers and poured latex into the space between the molds and fingers. After the latex set I removed the molds and repeated the process with the other hand. I was meticulously careful and by the time Espinosa showed signs of consciousness I had a set of finger caps that looked like skin, fitted like skin, and would last several days before becoming loose. That should be enough.

The next day I went to the city, used some of my hidden hoard to buy some serviceable secondhand clothing to exchange for my rags and took a transit bus to city center. In my pocket was Espinosa's ID which I had taken from its hiding place under Manuel's bed. I went straight to the Public Repository in the Administration Building, found an empty booth, dropped twenty minims in the coin slot, placed Manuel's ID in another, and inserted my latex-covered fingertips in the appropriate scanner cups, and waited.

The machine beeped and clicked. "Your wishes, señor," it said.

"Return my deposit," I said as I took back the ID from the slot. In a moment a plastic cylinder extruded from the face of the machine. Inside was a thin sheaf of papers and some money. I unfolded the papers and began to read. It had been almost too easy. I had operated like a professional thief. Maybe Manuel was right and I was a criminal. However, the papers didn't prove it. They proved nothing. They were all personal documents; a birth certificate, a commendation, a pension warrant, a lapsed insurance policy. Manuel had lied. He knew nothing about me—had no hold on me except the one I could not break.

I put the papers and money back in the cylinder and returned it to the machine, and hitched a ride on a garbage wagon back to Cantown. I took off my new clothes and hid them and resumed my rags and was back in character as the Dummy barely in time to watch Manuel pick his way down the sloping face of the dump. I had no time to return his ID to its hiding place, but I could do that later.

He was appreciably weaker and more unsteady than yesterday. An unbidden feeling of elation swept through me, and on the the the slope above, Manuel stopped and peered suspiciously about. I swore. There must be some feedback in the rapport that linked us, and the old devil's defense mechanisms were still operative. I turned my back on Espinosa and went into the shack. I couldn't afford to let Manuel know I had finally decided to kill him.

From outside came a clatter of falling trash. Manuel had arrived. I took my time going outside. My mind was oddly clear and free from compulsion. Espinosa was lying a few meters up the slope. His upturned face was blue. His breathing was stertorous and shallow. Beads of sweat dotted his forehead. His nostrils were pinched, his eyes open and glassy. His right hand still grasped the neck of a broken wine jug.

I picked him up and carried him into the shack. Elation swept through me. I wouldn't have to kill him. The waiting had paid off. This was *it!* Manuel weighed over a hundred kilos, but I handled him easily. I laid him on his bed and sat down to watch. I was sweating. My hands trembled. I had dreamed of Manuel's death so long that the reality was almost unbearble. I watched—and then I felt the compulsion. It was weak. I could resist it. Manuel was silently screaming for help. "Let him scream," a corner of my mind snarled. "Sit still. Wait. As soon as his respiration turns Cheyne-Stokes *then* go for help. Not before.

I stood up. I couldn't do it. I was going to botch it. I ran up the hill to the other shacks. In the third one I found a man who agreed to call an ambulance. In the fourth I found another who would help with Manuel. Both were surprised that I could talk.

With my unwilling helpers I reached the shack just in time to see Espinosa stagger to his feet and blunder into the stove. The stove crashed over on its side. The pipe broke. Fire, smoke and burning fuel cascaded out. Flames spread across the greasy floor of the shack. Smoke poured from Manuel's jacket as he staggered back. A curtain of flame leaped leaped from the floor.

I screamed in fury and frustration as I plunged into the shack. That damned-damned sot! Why couldn't the drunken slob lie still! Why couldn't he have died? Now with fear pouring adrenalin into him he was awake again and I had to help him.

I reached for Manuel. Blind with fear he jerked back. I felt my foot break through a rotten floorboard, stumbled and plunged wrist deep into the layer of burning coals that had spewed from the stove. I screamed with agony as the latex on my fingers melted and burned. I scrabbled to my feet and lunged for Manuel.

Espinosa shrank back, howling. I picked up his bed and hurled it through the back wall of the shack, grasped Manuel by the jacket and, dove for the hole. Manuel jerked back. The jacket tore as I fell to the gound outside the shack. My clothes were on fire. Pain tore at me. My lungs were seared. I rolled, trying to smother the flames. The man who had come with me tore off his coat and wrapped it around my blazing rags.

Behind us the shack collapsed in flaming ruin upon its owner.

Chapter Twenty:

I awoke in a cool green room that smelled of antiseptic. Faint yellow sunlight outside the window gave a barren view of a wedge of cold sky and the facade of an airwell dotted with windows like my own. I felt unusually clean, and remarkably cheerful. I was obviously in a hospital and the euphoria was probably drug-induced, but at the moment it didn't matter.

I was floating on a cushion of air in a burn bed. My injuries must be fairly extensive, but they couldn't be too severe since there was no evidence of intensive care apparatus. I was conscious of my body and was capable of moving, but I didn't feel like it. Probably it was just as well.

My arms, hands, and face were lightly bandaged. That wasn't good. Bandaging usually indicated replacement and that wasn't a cheerful thought. I had gone through replacement before and if Segovia's medical techniques weren't a lot better than its engineering, I wasn't going to be very attractive.

I was alive, of course, which was the primary thing. And Manuel Espinosa was dead, which was almost as important. I might not look like much when I got out, but sooner or later I would get to Dibrugarh and the finest medical service in the Confederation. Dibrugarh! How easily the thought of the Capital World came to me. Another bit of memory clicked into place. I smiled at the clarity of recall and the limpidity of mental processes. There was no cloying incubus of Espinosa to distort my thinking. Whatever price I had to pay for this, it was worth it. I was alive, aware, and free. That was enough.

There was a discreet noise behind my head. I turned to find a medic regarding me. "Ah—you are awake," the doctor said. "How do you feel?"

"Numb," I said.

"That is good," the medic said. "I must warn you that you will not be the same as you were, but on the whole I would say your appearance is considerably better than it was. Frankly, you were a mess." He pursed his lips and made clucking noises. "You shouldn't treat your body that way. An old depressed cranial fracture, a broken nose, malnutrition, second and third degree burns on face and arms, scars and adhesions involving your internal organs. You were a surgical challenge, and an education to our students. We gave you a new nose, two new ears out of the tissuebank, and a lot of muscle, tendon and skin. There won't be any contractions because we got you promptly and were able to remove the worst of the damaged tissue before secondary infection and lymph stasis had time to set in. You'll work as well as you ever did. Maybe even better. Nothing vital was damaged, but you charred your fingers down to the bone. What were you trying to do? Beat out the fire with your bare hands?"

"Something like that," I said.

"Well, don't try it again. Next time you might not be so lucky."

"I have no intention of ever doing anything like that again," I said.

"You are still going to have trouble. You'll need a whole new I.D. since hardly anything except your overall measurements are the same as they were prior to your injuries. Fortunately your I.D. pix was still intact; so we had some idea of how to rebuild you."

"My I.D.?"

"Yes, Señor Espinosa. We had your photograph and your description. Fortunately it was taken in happier times."

"Oh Lord!"

"Yes?"

"I'm not Espinosa. My name is Torres, José Torres."

"So that is what that friend of yours was trying to tell us. He kept calling you something that sounded like Tonto."

"That's what they called me," I said. "And I guess that they were right. I was stupid. But it was Espinosa who died in that fire, not me."

"Then how is it you had his I.D.?"

"I do not know. Perhaps he exchanged cards with me."

"Why would he do this?"

"Who knows why Espinosa did anything. Ask the others."

"We have. Their opinion of you—er—Espinosa—was very low. I will need your vital statistics."

"I'm sorry. Much of this I do not remember. I was injured. I do not remember anything of importance prior to coming to Cantown. My head—"

The medic nodded. "We found the fracture," he said, "There was considerable compression and some underlying damage." He gave me a look of mild frustration. "You don't mind submitting to narcosynthesis and the polygraph? I don't mind telling you that you have been a trial to us. I have never before encountered amnesia such as yours. It is interesting but frustrating. If there was such a technique as partial mental erasure, I would swear you had been subjected to it."

"Go ahead," I said. I felt no qualms about giving permission. Something deep inside me gave comforting assurance that if I had anything to hide, it would stay hidden. I squirmed uncomfortably. Another bit of memory hung suspended at the edge of consciousness and then sank back into grayness. It was close. Maybe next time it would come.

Technicians brought machines which they fastened to my body. Others injected drugs. Someone asked innumerable questions which I answered or didn't answer. I had nothing to do with the entire business. I was a spectator, aloof and to one side, watching the technicians do things and not particularly approving of what they did.

"Well," the polygraph operator said, "Whatever he is, he isn't a scab. He doesn't relate too well to the government, but he reacts negatively to the Aliens. Not hate, mind you, but indifference. He seems to be a neutral, if such a thing is possible."

"His amnesia, perhaps?" someone asked.

"Perhaps."

"Did you do any better with narcosynthesis this time?" a new arrival asked. This one was in uniform and I eyed him with interest. He was probably police.

"No."

"Then what shall we do?"

"We can try cataloging his remaining scars and feeding the data into the Central Computation System."

"That's a shot in the dark. How about retinal patterns? Or his ears?"

"They're not his ears, and we've never done anything with retinal I.D. There might be a Federal record, but it's not probable. Certainly there is no evidence that he is anything other than what he claims to be, a citizen who awoke brutally beaten in a freight car just outside the city. If he has any memories other than those, they're his secret and we cannot extract them. We'll try everything, but I think it's pretty hopeless. As far as a positive identification is concerned, we'll simply have to take his word for what and who he is."

I smiled. My feelings had been right. If I had any secrets they'd learn nothing about them, or the crazy spaceship that talked to me with a woman's voice. That was apparently forbidden ground, as were those memory fragments of Dibrugarh and places not of this world.

Sometime later, the medic came in with a dark-faced man. He looked hopefully from the man to me.

The dark man shook his head. "There is a resemblance in size and name, but it is not he. I would know him anywhere. He is not our maestro."

"He has been greatly changed."

"If he is changed then he is certainly not our maestro."

"Do you know this man, señor?" the medic asked me.

I shook my head.

"Thank you, Señor Gonzales," the medic said. As the man left, the medic turned to me.

"You know what the Central Computer reported about you?" he asked.

"No."

"It said you might be José Torres, the torero who disappeared last fall."

"Who's he?"

"The best matador on Segovia. He came from nowhere, out of the Archipelago, I think, blazed across last season like a comet and ended as premier; the numero uno."

"Yes?"

"He was tossed by a bull—not spiked but thrown into the burladeros. While his cuadrilla was searching for a medic he vanished. One of his caudrilla was found unconscious in his room. He had obviously been kidnapped. It was at the end of the San Jaime de Compostella festival. People saw him, so they said, but no one has ever produced him, or brought him back from where he disappeared. There have been no demands for a reward. José Torres vanished as a strangely as he arrived. It is a thing of wonder."

"Romantic."

"It's going to be a bad season unless he returns. His presence was sheer drama. I was at the Plaza last year when he killed Campeador. He did it *al recibir*. It was magnificent!" The medic's eyes gleamed. "The computer said there was a forty percent probability that you were he. Retinal patterns were not on file, but you have some of his scars and bone damage. Trouble is, we don't have enough data and you had too much damage. We had to replace too much of you; if you are José Torres, no one can ever say for sure. I rather hoped you were. I am a fan of his."

"I don't think I am. I have no eagerness to fight bulls," I said. "I imagine that I'd run if one charged me. I'd be a fool to say I am a matador. Someone might get me into a bullring if I did. Frankly, doctor, I could have faced a bull when I was young, but not now. The animal would terrify me. I am too old and too slow."

"I think you are right, señor," the doctor said.

I didn't know if I liked that or not.

"How long shall I have to stay here?" I asked.

"Not long. Another week, perhaps. Maybe two. We shall get your identity established and then you can leave. You have been under sedation and intensive treatment for several weeks. You are in good shape, but no one should treat their body as you did. You will have an enormous bill to satisfy, even though much of it can be written off against teaching."

"That's not entirely my fault," I said.

The medic shook his head. "Nevertheless the account will be due. Until the hospital is satisfied there will be a mortgage on you."

"That's a cheerful thought," I said, "Out of one form of slavery and into another."

"You should be grateful you are still alive."

"About the inquest?" I asked.

The medic shrugged. "That is no problem. You go to the coroner's court and give your testimony, and that's it. The hospital's testimony and that of the other peones—er—the people at Cantown, has already been taken. Your statement will close the case. Do you want me to call the court and have them send a bailiff?"

"I have no love for courts," I said.

"Hmm. I suppose you wouldn't. Your kind seldom do," the doctor grinned. "But who does?" he added.

"I am no different from other men," I said. "Except that I don't like the face you gave me."

"Those who rebuilt you wouldn't like to hear you say that," the doctor said. "We are as much artists as those who work with brushes and paint, and we hate to see our work defamed. You have a good face and a good body."

I had to admit that it was good. Except that I looked like Espinosa there was nothing wrong with my appearance. My hands and feet were normal. My new skin was no different from the old. There were no scars. Not even Dibrugarh with all its medical magic could have done any better.

A week later I was ready to leave.

The hospital furnished me a clean suit that almost fitted, and I looked moderately presentable when I came down to the lobby. A slim young man with an eager, bookish appearance was waiting for me.

"Señor Torres?" he asked.

"Yes?"

"I represent the Santayana Coroner's Board of Inquiry into the death of Manuel Espinosa," the young man said, capitalizing the titles verbally. "Your presence and testimony are required to complete the record." He handed me a paper. "You are to appear in court at 1100 hours today to tell the coroner what you know of this affair."

I took the paper. "Very well, I shall be there. Now if you'll excuse me, I would like to go outside."

"Of course," the young man said. "At 1100 hours," he repeated. You have three hours, señor."

I nodded and left the hospital. They had been nice to me, but if I never saw the place again I would not be too unhappy.

I took the transit to the end of the line in the northern district. A kilometer beyond was the smoking pile of the dump.

I walked slowly toward it. Cantown was unchanged except that Espinosa's shack was gone. I shrugged. That was a loss I could stand. But there was something else I could not lose, and I had come back for it. I had gone through hell to save it. There were a hundred munits down in that dump and a billfold with papers, and I wasn't about to leave them there.

A small knot of Cantown residents watched me as I approached.

I waved. "Hello," I said.

They were silent. One or two made horns at me to ward off the evil eye.

"You guys forget easily," I said.

"We don't forget, señor," one of them said, "You look like one who is dead. You look like Manuel Espinosa, but he is burned to death and you are not his ghost."

"I'm Dummy," I said. "The hospital fixed me up."

"They made you look too much like that bastard," one of them said, "but I guess they didn't know any better. When I saw you last you looked like burned steak."

"They didn't know what I really looked like. They did the best they could."

"If I were you, I'd sue them. They didn't do you no favor, but at least you don't smell like him. Are you gonna come back?"

I shook my head.

"Then why're you here?"

"I have some things to pick up."

"Hell, Dummy, the shack burned down."

"I didn't keep anything of mine there. Do you think I'd leave anything I wanted where Manuel could find it?"

"Guess not—say—why'd you stay with him?"

"I couldn't help it. I was weak and he had the evil eye."

The men nodded. This they understood.

They smiled at me, shook my hands and wished me well. The man who had done the talking patted me on the back. "You're out of here now," he said. "Be smart and stay out. Don't come back. This is no place for you."

"I think you are right," I said.

"Get what you came for and go quickly—and may God go with you..."

The coroner looked down from his pulpit. He was a wizened man but the height of the pulpit and the power of his office gave him dignity. "Señor Torres," he said, "we have examined the death of Manuel Espinosa. It has been tentatively found that the deceased perished accidentally by fire, complicated by alcoholism. Have you anything to add to this finding?"

"No sir," I said.

"There is no evidence of foul play," the coroner said, "and since the deceased had no known relatives and no visible means of support, his remains have been held pending your recovery. As his closest associate you are legally his heir and can express your wishes concerning disposal of his body. There is also a small estate of about fifty munits in the public despoitory to which you are entitled.

"I want nothing to do with him, your excellency," I said. "Anyway wasn't he cremated?"

"Almost," the coroner said, "but some portions remain."

"Then why don't you burn them along with the rest?" I suggested.

The coroner was shocked. "Have you no feelings? It is not good to be burned and buried in unconsecrated ground. If you do not accept responsibility for his interment, he must be totally cremated. And this could add further punishment to his immortal soul."

"That may well be," I said, "but his soul deserves no better. I have no love for Espinosa or his memory. In truth, I dislike him almost as much now that he is dead as I did when he was alive."

"Yet you shared his house, gave him money, and in the end tried to save him from the fire."

"I was weak-willed and he was not. Our joint occupancy of his shack was a relationship, not a partnership—and I am ashamed of the relationship. He degraded me. He deserved the fire, your excellency, but I am human. I could not see a fellow man die that way. I was compelled to try to rescue him. Yet I am not sorry he is dead."

"And feeling as you did, you did not leave?"

"As I said, excellency, he dominated my will. I could not leave."

"Is that why the others called you the Dummy?"

"No sir. I was called the Dummy because I am by nature silent—not because I am stupid."

"Could you not find it intelligent to accept responsibility for this dead man?" the coroner asked. "It is an unholy thing to be cremated when one is in sin. The fire for such a soul may be everlasting."

"I am not rich," I said. "I have little money and small possibility of earning more, and I owe a large bill to the hospital."

"That can be adjusted. A job can be found in return for the consecrated burial, Espinosa's estate can form the down payment for his funeral, and you can work off the remainder together with the hospital charges."

I almost laughed. Did this man think I was going into debt for Espinosa—and then work off the debt? What sort of a fool did he think I was? Manuel could burn forever.

"I know a dock contractor who would employ you if I suggested it," the coroner said. "It would be hard work but better than being jailed for vagrancy."

Ah—the hook! I thought. The coroner was determined to have Manuel decently buried, and it might not be wise to oppose him. But there was the job offer, and I could use a job. "I suppose I might bury him if it is not too expensive," I conceded. "Very well, your excellency, I will provide for minimum burial with appropriate rites if you will get me a job. However I do not want too large a bill."

The coroner beamed. "The funeral will cost a hundred fifty munits and the terms will be generous. I commend you on your attitude, Señor Torres. Does it not salve some of your bitterness to know that Manuel will have a chance for Heaven?"

I shrugged. "I do not know, excellency. His chances for Heaven are small in any event." I had no quarrel with Espinosa's soul, granting the possibility that his soul existed and was not so small as to be overlooked in the hereafter. But it would be only simple justice if his corpse brought me work. I needed a chance to recoup my fortunes, and time to recover my memory, and an opportunity to stay away from the barrio on the dump.

The coroner smiled. "It so happens that I am the leading mortician in the city, and your late colleague's remains are in my establishment."

I grinned. I couldn't help it. I bowed to the coroner. "I would be delighted, excellency, to leave the details to you at the fee you mentioned. A hundred and fifty munits can be repaid, I think." So I'd been sold a funeral; so I got a job. It balanced. I looked at the coroner and smiled. Thank God this was a smiling world. The grimace was ubiquitous; the crinkled eye corners, the drawn-back lips, the gleaming teeth were on video, in sollies, on posters, in magazines, on skyviews, and were mentioned constantly in song and story. The syndrome was universal. Nubile girls, old crones, handsome men, senile gaffers; all smiled—and smiled——and smiled! Not even broken or decayed teeth kept their owners from displaying them.

I said, "I will need an introduction to your friend on the docks."

"Of course. Of course." The coroner took a piece of paper, wrote briefly on it and handed it to me. "His name is Pedro Sanchez y' Vargas. He will find work for you. And now—there is much to do. Goodbye, Señor Torres. Go with God. The case is settled. I will see that Manuel Espinosa is properly buried. Inform me of your address."

Chapter Twenty-One:

The port of Santayana nestled behind a range of low hills that separated it from the ocean. The hills enclosed a roughly oval land-locked harbor fed from the East by the Eldorado and Agua Fria Rivers, and from the West by the Ocean Occidentale. The El Dorado was an anomaly. It rose in an area of the mountains rich in copper, lead and arsenic and poured its poison waters through a narrow slit in the hills to the north of town. No vegetation grew along its banks and where it emptied into the harbor no marine or shore life existed. The toxic flood was caught in a huge masonry basin big enough to hold a half a dozen ships at a time, and was used to clean marine growth off hulls too long at sea.

West of the basin a long rocky peninsula extended into the ocean. South of the basin were rows of piers, nestled against steep-walled limestone quarries where ballast rock had once been cut from the hills. The narrow beach area between the quarries and the piers were crowded with warehouses and storage areas, and the piers themselves hid the water's edge beneath forests of piling and acres of rock fill. The piers jutted out into the dead waters of the inner harbor, like so many snaggle teeth. Farther south of the docks, on the flats that marked the mouth of the Agua Fria River, lay the city center and the business district, while on the high ground to the east were the quiet rows of tile-roofed houses, whose whitewashed walls and red roofs looked oddly clean and unrelated to the smoke and noise of the harbor and the industrial district. Time and the

Aliens had not dealt gently with Santayana, but the area was recovering. The town had collapsed inward upon itself and many of the outlying districts were ruins. But the waterfront was active and gave promise that in time the city would recover its old boundaries and perhaps exceed them.

The harbor was crowded with shipping, much of which was sail, although the tall funnels of steamers and motorships could be seen among the forests of masts and spars. The dead, oily waters of the inner harbor swelled smoothly around the black hulls of the ships and splashed greasily against the rocky shoreline wherever it appeared between the docks and piling. The usual waterfront smells were overpowered by the metallic antiseptic reek from the El Dorado catchbasin, but this was characteristic of Santayana and the nose ultimately became accustomed to it. I had smelled it ever since I had come to Cantown—which lay along the banks of the El Dorado.

I walked down the Embarcadero glancing at the street signs. The street I was looking for—San Anselmo—was farther north than I expected. I had approached from the Agua Fria bridge south of the main harbor and so far I had not found it. My potential employer had offices at 107 San Anselmo, and I was looking forward to the meeting with some anxiety since I had never, as far as I could recall, worked for a longshore contractor.

I watched stevedores unloading cargo from the holds of ships and replacing it with stone ballast, or reversing the process as they loaded ships from the warehouses along the shore. I saw what could happen when an unloading crew was inefficient—a full-rigged ship, her yards cockbilled, lay half capsized against one of the piers while men swarmed over her with blocks and tackle, timbers and hawsers, and the bright flames of cutting torches ate at the steel masts and spars to lighten the load above her decks.

I wondered briefly what would become of the vessel once the overbearing load of masts and spars was gone. Probably she would be left dismasted and converted into a barge to end her life in coastal trade, hauled by smoky tugboats in an ignoble travesty of the days when she skimmed the sea under billowing sails. Never in my life had I been on a sailing ship, yet I was empathic enough to understand that essential gracelessness of the vessel's end, and to appreciate the grim bright-eyed looks of a small group of weatherbeaten men in flat cloth caps and heavy clothing who watched the salvage efforts.

I saw other things; a horde of skittering forklift trucks; piers bulging with cargo; lines of freight cars; mazes of tracks; waiting trucks and wagons, and a huge bronze statue of an idealized sailor with a basal legend extolling the courage of Santayana's seamen. I

saw everything except San Anselmo Street.

It was a strange melange. Class III cultures invariably had an odd dichotomy of modern and old-fashioned, and Segovia was typical. It was colorful, and fascinating to watch, and I did not regret the time I spent finding San Anselmo Street. I stopped, looked up at the street sign and hesitated. This was a turning point. I once more eyed the bustling port, listened to the sounds and smelled the odors of far-off places above the reek of hydrocarbons and the poison water of the El Dorado catchbasin, and the heavy odors of effluent and sweat, smoke and creosote. There was more here than met the nose than the eye, I thought wryly, but I liked the visceral sensations that were stimulated. I looked westward toward the sharp-edged junction of sea and sky that marked a line beyond which lay strange and wondrous things. My thoughts ranged out beyond the horizon and toward the stars and the worlds beyond.

For every hundred men who stayed home, there was one who wandered and these horizon-hunters gave the seaports and airports and spaceports their special flavor. The horizon was a challenge to stagnation and dragged men to seek it; stumbling, crawling, leaping, flying, they had pushed against the horizon and forced it back to the limits of the galaxy. They never stopped, and obstacles only stimulated them; opposition only hardened their purpose. Hail to the horizon—and to those who hunted it!

"Hey! You! You fella in the green coat!" a harsh voice shouted.

With a start of surprise I realized that the speaker was calling to me.

"Want a job, man?" the voice said. It belonged to a big-barrel-chested man who was so wide he looked short. From flat cap and blunt features to steel-toed shoes, he looked like a dock worker. He was probably a foreman or a dock boss.

"Doing what?"

"Loading that coaster." The big man cocked a thumb at a small vessel tied to a nearby pier. "She's due to leave on the tide this afternoon, and she ain't going to unless I get more help."

"I'm supposed to be reporting for a job," I said.

"With whom?"

"An outfit called..." I reached into my jacket pocket, "Vargas Stevedore Company," I said, reading from the card.

The man laughed. "You've come to the right place. This is it. I'm Pete Vargas."

"It says San Anselmo Street."

"That's the office. Here's where the work is. You can take off your coat and get going right now."

"Is that all there is to it?"

"Right now it is. The docks are screaming for men. Fernandez and Mendoza have most of them tied up on a few big jobs and the little operators like me can't get a full crew. Fact is, I've got feelers out clear up to City Hall."

"Oh!" I said. That coroner! I contemplated him with faint admiration. He didn't miss a bet.

"Well—you ready to go?"

"I need some clothes."

"There's some gloves and a coverall inside the Pierhead. I'll buy you a new shirt when we're done if you're worth wages."

"What's the rush?"

"A deadline, that's what. It costs me penalty if the ship ain't ready to sail on time. Now do you want to work or don't you? If you do, O.K. If you don't get outa my way. I need you now, not tomorrow. Tomorrow you'll be as useful as tits on a boar. The job'll be over."

"I didn't say I wouldn't work," I said.

"Well?"

"I want something more."

"Sure—I'll pay you a full day's wages."

"More than that."

"What? You gonna try to hold me up?"

"Not exactly. When the job's over I want your help to find a place to live."

"Oh hell! I thought you wanted something. You can stay at my boarding house. There's plenty of room. Come on."

So I went to work on the docks and not only labored like the proverbial horse, but enjoyed it. My muscles were soft from lack of use and I was going to ache more than a little tomorrow, but right now it was a pleasure to feel my body strain and sweat.

Vargas was an odd sort of boss. He went from spot to spot, helping out, working with the crews, giving directions, moving all the time. He was inefficient. He could do better if he supervised the entire activity from a point of vantage. But he did keep the crews moving and the ship did get loaded on time. I didn't do anything except keep my eyes open and learn how the job was done. It was easy enough to do, and there were at least half a dozen ways to improve the efficiency of the operation, but these could wait until I knew more about the work.

Meanwhile the ship's purser had paid Vargas and Vargas had collected his stevedores on the dock. "Okay boys," he said, "I'll pay off at the pierhead."

I watched with mild amusement. Vargas sat at the desk with a pile of money and the work roster in front of him. He checked the men's time, paid in cash and the worker signed the time sheet. It was highly inefficient. Checks would be much better and faster, and could be made out in advance. I couldn't understand the reason for such a primitive payroll unless custom had something to do with it. I wondered if all business practices on the docks were as inefficient as this one.

Finally Vargas was finished. He looked up and saw me waiting. "Oh yeah—you" he said. "I forgot. Guess it was because you're not on the sheet." He reached into his pocket and took out two bills. "Here's ten munits'—a full day's pay. And thanks. You really kept that gang moving. Want a job as gang boss? I got another ship coming in day after tomorrow."

"I'll take the job," I said, "but there was something else you were to do."

Vargas wrinkled his forehead.

"Room and board," I said.

The wrinkles smoothed. "Oh, yeah—sure—up at my place. There's another room. Ain't much, but the food's good and the joint's clean. I been living there for the past two years and I got no complaints. Yeah—and I said I'd buy you a new shirt."

I grinned. "I could use the shirt, but that's not necessary. You've already overpaid me."

Vargas shook his head. "I don't think so. You really helped get the job done. I wouldn't have made it without you. I made a fifty munit bonus on the completion time and it oughta be worth a shirt at least," he smiled. "Say—tell you what. Since you're gonna be straw boss for me, how about celebrating? We can go out to Durango and tie a can."

"That might be nice," I said doubtfully.

Vargas looked at me—"Say—you're a don, aren't you? What are you doing down on the docks?"

"What's a don?'

Vargas laughed. "You're putting me on. Hell—anyone can see you've got education. You don't talk like I do. You're real polite an' you got that damn don lisp. I shoulda noticed. No—you're a don all right. No wonder you got those clods moving. They just listened to you and that was all it took. Hell, man, what are you doing here? You belong uptown."

"I like it better here."

"Okay, suit yourself. The offer still goes."

"Eh?"

"Both ways. Durango tonight. Straw boss day after tomorrow —Okay?"

"Okay."

Vargas sighed. "I can use a guy like you. But why you wanta

work the docks is more than I c'n figure."

"I need the exercise," I said. "I've been in the hospital. I was burned."

"Well—that's my good luck. The men will work for you. They've been conditioned to jump when a don gives orders, and if you know how to act human, they'll break their backs for you."

"I can try," I said. "Now if you please, I'd like to see the room."

"We'll pick up the shirt on the way," Vargas said, "my car's just around the corner."

I sighed.

Vargas looked at me and grinned. "Tired—eh? Well—dock work ain't easy. Takes time to get used to it. You're gonna have a lot of sore muscles tomorrow. Say—what's your name? I can't go around yelling 'hey you' at you."

I told him.

"Ah—I thought so—one of the old families. Torres ain't a campesino handle."

"Maybe. I never kept a pedigree, nor did my mother. My people lived in the Archipelago. They were mostly killed by goons. I ran off before that happened." I did a quick double take. Now where did *that* piece of patently false information come from?

"Oh. I'm sorry." Vargas sounded compassionate. "That's a hell of a note."

"I was raised in a school of hard knocks as my father would call it."

"Oh hell—forget I said anything," Vargas said. He led the way to a low-slung three-wheeler, and we drove to a large stucco house clinging to the edge of the quarry cliff above the dock area. "You can see the whole operation from up here," Vargas said, waving a hand at the panorama of piers and warehouses spread below. "But that can wait. Let's get business over first." He led the way inside and shouted "Tia! Tia Carmela! Where are you?"

"I'm not down on your docks, you big lout," a woman's voice answered. "You don't need to raise the dead." A door down the hall framed the speaker, a plump young woman who glared at Vargas and then smiled at me. "All right Pedro—what is it?"

"I have a new boarder for you. José Torres—meet Tia Carmela Salazar, your landlady. She's a great cook and a fine landlady, but she should have become a nun. She doesn't like men."

Carmela grinned. "That one is a devil, señor," she said. "But I am happy that you will stay with us. It will be nice to cook for a gentleman rather than such a rowdy as Pedro Vargas."

"See?" Pedro said. "She calls you a don and you haven't even spoken!"

"Hmp! Anyone can recognize a don," Carmela said. "That takes no skill. They carry themselves differently. With pride. With grace."

"Thank you, señora," I said.

"Ah—you see?" she said, "I was right. He is a don."

"I think so, too," Vargas said, "but he denies it."

"Then that's his business. Stay out of it."

"Ah, Tia—your tongue bites like fire, but I know you have a great heart." He patted the woman on her broad bottom.

She laughed. "My heart is not there, Pedro Vargas," she said. "And now señor if you will follow me I will show you to your room."

"When you get through I will take you to the shops," Pedro said. "I imitate the Good Shepherd—perhaps it will give me grace tomorrow. Do you have enough money?"

"A hundred or so."

"Ha! A capitalist! That's more than enough."

"About the rent?"

"Pay in advance," Tia Carmela said promptly.

"No need to rush," Pedro said.

"How much?" I asked.

"Forty a month."

I paid two weeks, which brought a smile to Carmela's face. "I'll pay the rest when I get to work," I promised.

"You didn't need to be so generous. A week was plenty," Pedro said.

"I have it now. I might not next week."

"Hmm—a gambler, eh?" Carmela asked. "Maybe that's why you work the docks?" She didn't sound upset.

I smiled.

"Come on—let's go," Pedro said. We went to one of the nearby stores and Pedro bought me a shirt, despite my protests. "Look, man, I promised you a shirt, and besides I think you bring me good luck. Now we go back and you get dressed, get cleaned up, and get rested."—The man had a fine disregard for logical order, I thought—"I shall return for you at twenty hundred and show you something."

"What, and why?"

"Durango. Because I like you, that's the what and why—and because I'm curious about a don in old clothes who works on the docks."

"Durango?"

"Amusement town. Tia Madalena's town. It's about fifty kilometers southeast of here. You might like it, I think."

I shrugged. "Think what you will, friend Pedro. I will go with you, but in the meantime—go with God."

Pedro looked at me strangely. Surely, his expression seemed to say, surely this one is not a *priest*? I observed the look and went up to my room feeling a certain satisfaction.

Chapter Twenty-Two:

Pedro swept into my room gleaming and gorgeous in lavendar and white with blue fittings. "Come," he said, "Let's go! The night is waiting. There will be wine and music; women and gambling."

"It sounds active," I said.

"Obviously you have not been there. Your reactions are too neutral. But Durango will change that." He laughed and waved me toward the door.

Pedro's three wheeler wasn't the most comfortable car in this world, but it was fast and agile. It gave one the sensation of being surrounded by giant enemies bent on our destruction as he whirled through the evening traffic.

"Bigger cars are more comfortable," Pedro grunted, as he slipped between a Centaur and a truck, scooted past the truck on the outside and fitted the car between a Pegaso and a stately Aguila. I cringed a little lower in the bucket seat—"but these little jobs are more fun."

"It depends on what you call fun," I said.

"Once you get used to a bug you don't want a big car. They're too slow. Besides they're fuel wasters, take up too much space, and handle like a truck." He spurted ahead with a burst of acceleration that crushed me into the seat, and dove into a hole between two Aguilas. We whipped around corners, won races with traffic signals, braked violently, weaved and darted through impossibly tiny openings in the traffic stream, missed other equally insane drivers by inches and seemed determined to run down every pedestrian we encountered.

"Look out!" I yelled, "You almost hit that man!"

"It's his business to dodge me, not mine to dodge him," Pedro grunted. "Anyway, I missed him by at least half a meter. He did fine." We swept around a curve and onto a highway approach. Pedro fitted the bug between two other cars, punched a code into the computer panel on the dash, flipped a switch and took his hands off the steering sector. There was a click and a lurch and the little car became part of an orderly stream of traffic that flowed out of the city and into the countryside. The vehicles ahead spaced themselves about forty meters apart and moved along at a steady 100 k.p.h. We were, I noted, in one of the two inner lanes. The outer two were full of crowded jostling traffic, but on the inside all was smooth and orderly.

Pedro cocked a thumb at the outer lanes. "Whole damn highway was like that last year. Next year we'll be able to go clear to Cuidad Segovia on this kind of road. There's only a couple of hundred kilometers left to wire. We can take it easy now. That damn city traffic would give God gray hair. It's always rush hour."

I nodded. Control roads were new on Segovia, but it was high time they appeared.

"Now all we have to do is wait." Outside a fine drizzling rain began to fall and Pedro closed the windows. The headlights came on and cut twin tunnels of brightness through the soggy air. Our speed didn't slacken, and it made me a little nervous. I didn't trust Segovian technology that much. The muted howl of the turbine, the thin whistle of air past the windows, and the grumbling sussurration of the tires against the terraplast were the only sounds.

Pedro stirred, switched on the video and watched the overhead screen brighten. "We got half an hour," he said. "Might as well see a show."

"Hold it a minute," I said. "How about telling me what I'm getting into."

"You'll enjoy it more if you hit it cold," he said as he turned up the volume. We watched the program until a red light bloomed on the instrument panel, a buzzer sounded and we turned off the highway onto an exit ramp. Pedro took over control and drove down a dark unlighted road. The rain stopped, but the air was dark and heavy with clouds. The moons were hidden as we drove over a little hill and looked down on Durango. We went through a gate and a goon fence and down a road that dropped steeply towards the town below. It lay beside a lake whose waters shone dark against the night. It wasn't really a town. It was just the central part of one.

There were no suburbs, no rows of neat houses, just rows of business-type buildings beside the lake. It looked like a carnival. The lakeside buildings gleamed and glittered with colored light. By day, Durango might be tawdry, but at night—glowing in the bright hard sheen of incandescents and the crepuscular softness of vapor and tubelights it was a fairyland of jewelled splendor surrounded by a periphery of lesser gleamings from the side streets.

The main avenue—a broad treelined thoroughfare with the lakeshore park on one side and the glittering buildings on the other, was full of cars. The broad moving sidewalks were crowded with people and a cacophony of muted noise filled the air.

"It's the town brag," Pedro said as he turned into a parking building, "that it can furnish anything except peace and quiet." He found a parking slot, pulled the time tab and locked the car.

"I can believe it," I agreed as we descended to the street. "Do we start here?" I asked as I looked at the nearest glitter.

"No way. We're going to a first class joint, not some crummy tourist trap. No smart guy wastes time on the strip. It's okay for tourists, but the good spots are on the side streets."

We walked down the broad central mall of the concourse that was called Avenida la Luz, past the glittering facades of the Glass Palace, the Mirallante, the Platinos, the Las Mujeres and a half dozen other major fun houses, each as glittering as the next.

"It's odd," I said, "how sin must advertise in such gaudy trappings. One would think it would be darker and more discreet."

Pedro looked at me curiously. "What's with you?" he asked.

"I was just thinking," I said. "If a church put on a shining front like this, the brethren would scourge its priests and cast it out of the covenant."

"That they would," Pedro agreed. "Heaven needs no press agent because it has no competition, but sin is competitive."

"I'm not the only don," I said with a grin.

"Hell—it's simple reason," Pedro said, "Most of Durango's money comes from the tourists, the in-and-outers, the quickies. People like that have to be taken fast and the best advertising gets the gravy. The lights attract suckers just like they attract insects. For the regulars there are quieter places like Tia's where admission is restricted."

"Who's Tia?"

"Tia Madalena, of course. Durango's her town. She opened it during the Bluefoot riots a dozen years ago. She ran the biggest whorehouse in Santayana before that, but when the Purity League began to stamp out vice she moved out to Durango and built fun city. It was a wreck then. The goons had depopulated it in '88 and she got it for almost nothing, and she's held onto it ever since. It's a gold mine, now."

There had to be a lot of iron in her to hang onto a place like Durango, I thought. It was a typical joytown. I had been in dozens of them all over the Confederation. It wasn't unique. The only thing unusual about it was that a woman ran it—on Segovia. I thought I'd like to see this woman. She must really be something.

There was a familiar carnival rhythm to the town, punctuated from time to time by stronger notes that waxed and waned as we walked along. I heard a brief bray of laughter drowning a protesting voice, the slam of a door truncating a burst of music, the rattle of cans in a service alley, the voice of a street vendor rising shrill and repetitive above the basal noises of the street. There was a soprano of classic purity singing a bawdy song, the screech of braked wheels sliding on pavement, a wild burst of invective, the shimmer of a hidden bell counterpointing the heavy vibrations from the clock campanile in the town square, the soft hiss of steam escaping from a vent, and from overhead a duet muffled by a half-opened window; the man's voice demanding, the woman's delaying.

The melody was an old familiar score, and it made me smile. There was a place back home that was like enough to this to be its twin. Home!—the thought was oddly jarring. Home? I had no home. There was a world on which I was born, but it was not my home. Home was where I hung my hat. I was Navy. I went from here to there across parsecs of space and years of time. That world clear across this sector of the galaxy wasn't home. There was nothing there for me. Those whom I had known had gone their ways and become strangers if they weren't already dead. Lightspeed travel in threespace played hell with objective time and I had travelled many parsecs at Lume one. I shook off the feeling of loneliness that is a part of all of us who work in the Special Services and followed Pedro down the Avenue.

The bright showplaces had a garish uniformity that somewhat spoiled their effect. They reminded me of a gaggle of middle-aged harlots in fresh makeup moving lackadaisically through stylized posturings of sin so repetitive that the titillation was lost. I wondered if Segovians knew anything about the more highly developed forms of excitement and appeasement. The elemental approaches on Durango's main street were so blatantly physical that they repelled one who knew about developed stimulation.

I shuddered and tried to apply the inconceivably ancient cliché about rape, but somehow I couldn't relax and enjoy it. Something behind my eyes was struggling to come into the light and it bothered me. I was aware of something which I had forgotten and

149

try as I would I could not bring it to the forefront of my mind. I couldn't even be sure whether I had seen it, heard it, smelled it, tasted it, touched it, or sensed it. But whatever it was was beating against the prison of my mind.

How badly damaged am I? The thought was painful. I knew I was not functioning efficiently because I could remember flashes of things I had done that made my present activities seem childish, and somehow this fun city intensified those impressions.

Pedro looked at me and shook his head. I wasn't reacting as I should. We turned down an alley bordered by dark buildings. The gloom was accentuated rather than relieved by wide spaced street lights. "Is this dark and quiet enough to suit you?" he asked. There was laughter in his voice.

"Yes," I said, and after a moment's silence I added, "I see why we parked the car on the Avenida."

"It would be impractical to drive here," Pedro agreed, "even if Tia Madalena would permit cars to park about her house."

We walked down the inky street, past darkened windows and recessed doorways faintly illuminated by red fanlights that gave a peculiarly hellish cast to our faces as we passed. There was no sound from the street and the stridor from the Avenida was absorbed by the high walls on either side. It was very quiet. There were other walkers abroad; a couple appeared out of the darkness ahead and passed wordlessly into the darkness behind.

"Probably lost souls," Pedro observed, "looking for lodging. This is a funny town. For a place with so many hotels it is surprisingly difficult to find a place to sleep."

"I hope I'm not supposed to laugh," I said. "That joke dates back to the Interregnum."

"What Interregnum?" Pedro asked.

"Forget it," I said, "I was trying for a figure of speech." I kicked myself mentally. Segovians probably never heard of the Interregnum. "How far do we have to go from here?"

"Not too far." Pedro's voice was low. "We're almost there."

A dim fanlight shone into a tiny courtyard hidden beneath the loom of a building that surrounded it on three sides. It was an alien rectangle in the embrace of the encroaching walls. It held a pool, a tiny tower, a clump of dwarf trees with gnarled trunks and a redbark vine tortured into a travesty of a human hand with a long index finger pointing at a narrow opening in one of the walls. There was no explanation, just the living red finger pointing at a darker blot of an opening in the building wall in the surrounding shadows.

"Here we are," Pedro said.

"If I had any sense," I said, "I would go back to the lighted avenue."

"This way," Pedro said. He headed toward the black opening.

"It repels even as it points the way," I murmured, as I gestured at the finger-post. This Tia Madalena is a poet, but hers is the sort of poetry that should never be printed."

"I'll tell her how the guidepost made you feel," Pedro said. "She will be pleased."

The dark hole became a flight of uneven stairs between two close-set walls. The treads were outlined by glowstrips. The stairs ended at a green door lighted by a single fluorescent rosette that shed pallid light into the brick-walled cul-de-sac at the stair's end. Pedro placed his ID plaque against a reader set into the door frame. The lock clicked and the door swung silently open, revealing dimness, the sheen of polished wood, the gleam of glassware, and the dull shine of burnished leather.

"A bar!" I said. My voice was disappointed.

"Thought it would be fun to bring you in the back way." Pedro chuckled. "It was different, wasn't it?"

"It was too good a buildup," I said. "Reality is a letdown."

He laughed. "Order a drink," he said. "For awhile we will be inspected, for while I am known here, you are not. In time, if you pass, you will be invited farther than the entrance."

"I think I'd rather look around," I said. "I saw some things when we came in that could stand a second look."

"I'll wait for you at the bar." He turned away from me, sat down on one of the empty stools and beckoned to the scantily clad barmaid while I walked slowly past the polished length of the bar. There were people on the stools, formless blobs of no importance. There were other blobs at the little tables that lined the walls. There was a tiny dance floor that transmitted music made elsewhere to the dancers by some trick of sound that reached the dancer's ears but left the air quiet save for a subliminal murmur that was oddly soothing. The walls held inset cabinets containing hundreds of halo-lighted sculptured miniatures, stone carvings and ceramics. The accent was primitive, the emphasis phallic, and the collection would grace any museum in the Confederation. And not all of the objects came from Segovia, nor from ancient time.

I recognized the ancient symbolism of Palestra, the formless abstractions of the Midian culture, the harsh animism of Halsey, the Naturist efflorescence of the Terran pre-Interregnum. These things were *old*, but others were new, and each was a thing of beauty. I sighed as I admired the creative spirit that could make such things. Each artifact bore the stamp of loving workmanship, and though I neither understood nor recognized all of the exhibits, I appreciated the passion and skill that had gone into their making, and regarded them with delight. This Tia Madalena! I thought. She was not of this world! I had hit the jackpot!

And the barrier broke! I remembered! It was something I had heard on the Avenida la Luz in the complex rhythm of a squirm combo playing in one of the places we had passed, and I was hearing it now from the canned music coming from the dance floor. The complex beat hammered out by the drummer had a familiar rhythm. *Dit-dit*, it went, *dit-dit-dit, dit-dit-dit-dit, dit - dit - dit - brr, dit-brr.* ISH, VA, ISH VA—the letters leaped sharp and clear into my mind from the drumbeat and were repeated over and over as the combo ground out the music. It was code. Accidental or deliberate—it was code! And code was something that had long ago vanished from general use and was employed only by Special Service agencies. But what was ISH? VA was "end of communication"—the ancient Latin—"vale"—farewell, but the leader was a series I didn't know. SSH—one more dit in the lead series—would be Special Service Headquarters—probably Bur Pol—the policy arm of our Service. Could the drummer be a poor signalman?

If that beat was real, there was an agency here, and who would be better situated to run it than this incredible woman Madalena? Durango certainly was an ideal setup for an information-collecting center. I could hardly get my breath. Excitement was suffocating me.

Chapter Twenty-Three:

"Do you really like this junk?" a voice behind me asked. The words were soft and distinct, the tone cool and female.

I turned. She came barely to my shoulder, a shapely girl dressed in some sort of metallic cloth that clung lovingly to her painted body and gave the impression of shining scales. Artfully cut and pierced, it was more sensuous than nudity, and more bizarre than body-paint alone. Whoever selected her dress had a knowledge of male psychology. The woman, attractive enough in her own right, was transformed by the dress into a breathing symbol of sex. There wasn't much question about her job. She was a house-girl who furnished companionship to patrons for a fee or a percentage of what she could induce the customer to spend.

"What if I do like it?" I asked.

"Then you should go to the National Museum in Cuidad Segovia. People don't come here to look at pots and bottles, and dirty statues. They come to see and feel the real thing."

"And if I find it more pleasant to look at artistry—"

"Then you should be somewhere else than Tia Madalena's," she said. "What are dead things compared to something alive?"

"Like you?"

"Like me."

"I wish you hadn't said that," I said, "for the answer is not complimentary. From you I can get but one thing, or perhaps two. From these works of art, I get a delight of the senses, a feeling of time, an appreciation of the artist's message, an admiration of the delicacy of the work, the boldness of the conception, the skill of execution. I can get the feelings of joy and sadness, of pleasure, of contentment, of anger, fear and exaltation. Such works as these have an entire language of their own. You, my dear, have but two words: sex and amusement."

"I am alive," the woman said, "these things are dead."

"There, indeed, you have an advantage, but you waste it. I could pity you."

"Don't. I get along all right."

"You still miss a great deal. I suppose you work here?" Although I ended on a rising note, it was more a statement than a question.

She nodded. "What else? Freelancers are poison in this house. Couples are tolerated, but single girls work for the house."

"Entertainer?"

She smiled—"You might call me that."

"I imagine you are good at your work."

"I have few complaints."

"And you would entertain me?"

"Not necessarily. I was just checking to see if your interest in this stuff was real. I've never seen anyone really look at it before. I mean really look at it, not just stare at the dirty ones, but look at the whole crazy collection. Tia Madalena says there are people who appreciate things like this, but I've never met one. I wondered if you were as odd as your actions."

"And—?"

"I don't know," she said, "you *look* normal." The girl smiled again. "I'm Valencita," she said.

"Any other name?"

"You should know better." She touched her ears, the gold rings gleamed in the light.

"Oh," I said. The woman was indentured. From the absence of a tattoo she was a short termer. But short term or lifer made no difference. Slaves didn't have surnames. That was one thing they lost with their freedom. I shrugged mentally. This wasn't the time to worry about the merits or demerits of the Segovian system of justice. If they wanted to enslave their criminals and scabs, I could care less, as long as I wasn't classed as a criminal or a scab. But I might as well act interested. It would do no harm and might possibly give me some information about this place.

"How long have you been out of society?" I asked.

"I got five years—and I've finished two—almost." Her voice was flat. "Funny—I get slapped with a five-year stretch for soliciting—and what happens. I come up on the indenture list at the Spring

Assizes and who buys my papers?—Tia Madalena. Now wouldn't that grab you? So what am I doing?—the same thing I did when I was hustling. Only now I don't collect for it. Tia does. All I get is board, room, and working space." She smoothed her dress.

"No allowances?"

"Ha! You don't know Tia. We get what the law allows. Oh—she takes care of us all right. She feeds well, and sees that we get plenty of healthful exercise and pills and things to keep from getting pregnant. We get our regular medical checkups and hospitalization if we need it. But outside of that we don't get much. Right now there's a hundred twenty-eight of us working in this crib. We sleep in a dormitory on the top floor. It's a real snake-pit in the morning, competing for washroom and bath space and trying to get the taste of the night before out of our mouths."

"Sounds pretty grim."

"Oh it isn't too bad when you get used to it. We get laughs, and loving. Maybe more loving than we'd like and maybe not enough laughs, but it could be worse. Some of the girls down on the Avenida have it a lot rougher. After the first couple of months it doesn't bother you. The idea gets across after awhile that you aren't a person, that you exist to satisfy customers. Of course that's the job. We go to school and learn things that'll maybe reform us when we finish our stretches." She laughed, but she didn't sound amused. "We have a library upstairs, but not very many of us read. There's a gym on the roof, and a pool that gets a better play. Mostly we work, eat, sleep and exercise. Tia sees that we don't get too fat or too thin. You learn quick what's unhealthy. And now that you know all about me, are you still interested in those bottles?"

"Would you like a drink?" I asked.

"I'd love one," Valencita said, "but I won't get one. Tia doesn't approve of drinking. I get tea, but you pay for brandy. Now if you want me, I give you my ID plaque—" she touched a medallion on a chain around her neck, "and the cashier enters it and the time and assigns you my room number."

"Eh?"

"I have a real nice two-unit combo on the fifth floor—all stacked with gourmet foods," she said. "Just in case you'd like some home cooking."

"Oh."

"I'm a pretty good cook if you want food with your fun. You turn In my I.D. when you're done with me. My time is twenty munits an hour, payable in cash, check or credit card. And if you're a special friend of Tia's you can get me free."

"You're expensive."

"Not really. I'm good. You interested in finding out?"

I shook my head. "Not really."

Her mouth drooped. "Too bad. For a moment you looked interesting. Well—I guess I'd better move on. If I don't make my quota, I get my savings docked, and that isn't fun."

"Your quota?"

She nodded. "Sixty munits a night minimum. Monthly average of eighty. I should be able to get a hundred and twenty without pushing too hard, and anything above eighty is deposited to my account, which I get after I finish my term. I have a fairly sizeable bundle already, but I don't like to lose any of it by paying the house for nonperformance. We have an eight hour night and a good clientele most of the week except Monday, and a mob on weekends. We're really busy after Meeting. It's the best time of the week— except the night before." Valencita sighed. "I was rather hoping you'd buy three or four hours of my time."

I nodded. "Maybe I'm a special friend of Tia's," I said. "Would that help?"

Valencita's face brightened. "It'd get me off quota, and tonight I'm not interested in pay."

"Would you like me to try?"

"But I've never seen you before. You can't be one of Tia's friends. I know them all."

"I come from far away," I said, "and long ago." I beckoned to the bartender. "Bring me a house phone and put me through to Tia Madalena."

"I'm sorry, sir," the bartender began. She looked at Valencita with worried eyes. "Tia doesn't like to be disturbed. Can I say who is calling?"

"Yes—but it may do no good. I want to talk to her and she may not recognize me."

"And you're an old friend?" Valencita asked disbelievingly.

"It's been a long time," I said.

The barmaid brought a phone. "Just turn the switch," she said.

So I turned the switch. There was the brief hum of a carrier wave and a feminine voice said, "Yes?"

"If you are Tia Madalena—then listen. If not, then please repeat this message to her at once. Do you understand?"

"Yes, sir."

I put the phone close to my lips: "Dit-dit-dit," I said, "dit-dit-dit; dit - dit - dit - dit; dit-dit-dit-dah—dit-dah. Do you wish me to repeat?"

"No, sir. I have recorded your message."

"I am at a downstairs bar."

156

"I have your phone marked. What is your name?"

"José Torres."

"Please hang up Señor Torres. I will return your call shortly."

I handed the phone back to the barmaid. "There will be a return call," I said.

The barmaid smiled disbelievingly.

The phone rang. The barmaid answered. Her face acquired a look of surprise.

"Are you José Torres?" she asked.

I nodded.

She handed me the phone. "It's Tia and it's for you," she said.

"Tia Madalena?" I asked into the mouthpiece.

"Yes," the voice was a resonant controlled contralto that sent shivers up my spine.

"I am José Torres. I'd like to meet you."

"You shall, Señor Torres, but not now. We can meet after—oh—four hundred when we close. In the meantime accept my hospitality. Are you interested in the girl you are with?"

"I'm not disinterested."

"The please give the phone to her."

"Of course. Is there anything else?"

"Your expenses, except for gambling, will be assumed by the house."

"Thank you. I am looking forward to meeting you." I handed the phone to Valencita.

"Valencita, madam," the girl said. "Yes, madam. Yes, I understand. Anything the señor wishes. Yes, madam. Yes, madam. Thank you, madam." Valencita hung up. There was a fine beading of sweat on her upper lip.

"Señor," the barmaid said, "I think if you would ask Valencita to kiss her own nose, and would ask right now, she would break her jaw trying."

"You are so right, Serafina," Valencita said, "and I am very stupid not to recognize a friend of Tia."

Chapter Twenty-Four:

"What's the entertainment?" I asked.

"You name it. There's enhancing, drugs, swimming, dancing, drinking, gambling, shows, spectator sports, cock fighting, steam baths, and a few selected perversions. We try not to leave too much out. There are even a few old pleasure mechs in the basement. They're Imperial relics. Someone said they come from the Duke Leonardo's house, and I guess they do. We never made things like that even when we could. And since our science was destroyed during the wars with the Aliens—"

"How about music?" I asked.

"We have one of the best squirm combos in Estado Del Norte. Chi Chi Baronte's in the main ballroom. Cuerpo Valdez is down in the basement in the Casino Room, and we're breaking in a new dance act. She comes with a reputation, so I hear."

"Good! We'll go there."

"You like squirm?"

"Not to dance to. You have to be invertebrate to do it justice. I like to listen to it. Squirm rhythm only goes as far as my mind. I can't translate it to my muscles."

Valencita smiled. "Cuerpo Valdez is progressive. You heard a tape of his music in the bar."

"He's got a good drummer."

"Ferdie Alvarez? We had a thing going before the police got me." She laughed softly. "I wanted out, but he used to cry and I'm soft hearted. Anyway, he came here expecting to pick up where we left off. Poor Ferdie! He didn't know Tia any better than I did." She shrugged. "Anyway, he's a good drummer. Sometimes I think he imagines his skins are stretched over Tia the way he makes them pop."

I kissed my fingers to the absent Tia Madalena.

"She's a hell of a woman," Valencita said softly, "I hate her guts, but I'd no more cross her than I'd spit in a Guardia Civil's eye." She took a deep breath and let it out with a shiver.

Her breasts were magnificent, I thought. I felt a slow quiver of desire stir inside me.

The ballroom was big, square and dark, with tiers of tables surrounding three sides of a shining wood floor. On the fourth side Cuerpo and his men were belting out "Squiggly Squee" and the music writhed and curled around the tables and wiggled through the shimmering darkness. Chills chased each other down my spine.

"They're good," I said, "very good."

The music stopped abruptly. The lights went out. A bright yellow halo spot picked out a circle on the floor. A girl appeared, fully dressed in evening wear that looked painted on. She stepped into the lighted circle and the halo snuggled around her, leaving her illuminated in a field of darkness.

There was a spatter of applause.

"She's the new act." Valencita said. "Tia pays her! Brought her all·the way from Cuidad Segovia."

"Good artists always draw more than they are ever paid. It's good economics to pay for good performances."

"How about us?" Valencita asked.

"My dear—the performance you give comes naturally. It's an art, I'll admit, but it isn't the sort of thing that gets your name in the lights. Almost any girl with reasonable training can become an acceptable performer at your sort of game. Now—look at the act."

"I'll see it plenty of times before she moves on," Valencita said sulkily.

The girl in the spot had picked up the music which squiggled back into the theme she interrupted with her entrance, and was giving a magnificent exhibition of muscle control. The light operator loaded the halo spot with UV, which picked out fluorescent spots on the girl's dress and underlying epidermis, as the evening dress did a slow dissolve. The yellow glow dimmed and turned shell pink and the girl turned a nacreous blue in the light. The UV strengthened as she writhed through the stylized contortions of squirm, changing them subtly with a fluid reptilian motion as the colors changed and she became an inky blot in a ruddy halo.

She was completely nude now, a smooth alabaster statue, posed in a pool of light. I thought with genuine admiration that the light operator was a genius. He'd worked the frequencies so beautifully that he didn't leave even a trace of the light sensitive fabric on the floor. Now the statue moved. The music changed, became insistent and throbbing, building steadily note on note, rhythm on rhythm to a feverish tempo. The girl writhed in counterpoint to the music. Her hair—a dark cloud—swung wildly covering her to the thighs, swaying, flowing, concealing, revealing. I could feel my breath coming faster.

The lights went up, revealing a rapt audience, mesmerized by the light and movement. The gleaming figure in the halo stretched, rigid and straining, every muscle and curve drawn into hard relief—like an ancient statue with muscles delineated by the incredibly clever lighting.

She began to quiver. The music died to a sussurrant background. Slow rippling movements started at her ankles and swept upward around her body. She rotated slowly, vibrating. Her hair glinted and shimmered. A sheen of sweat gave off a light of its own. She scintillated. It was an incredible performance!

Somewhere in the half-shadows a hissing gasp punctuated the intricate rhythm that set the tempo of the girl's movements. And then abruptly the tempo changed to become slow and languorous. The girl swayed. Her body undulated, rose, fell, advanced, retreated, yet she never moved from the spot on which she stood.

A man leaped into the light. His face was flushed, his eyes staring, his breath harsh. The music stopped. He lunged forward. The girl moved—threw a hip into his belly with controlled violence. The sound of flesh impacting against flesh was heavy on the hot air. The man staggered back, the lights went out and then blinked on. The man stood alone, a ludicrous expression on his face. The dancer had vanished.

There was a dead silence. Then someone realized that the frustrated figure on the floor was part of the act, and laughed. Someone else applauded. The applause swelled. The man bowed, waved, and went back of the orchestra. The applause crescended. From the orchestra the girl appeared, wrapped in a crimson cape. She kissed her hands to the audience. Then she turned and disappeared toward the dressing rooms.

"Like it?" I asked. My voice was carefully neutral.

"She is good." Valencita said reluctantly. "Awfully good!" She was silent a moment, "And now what shall we do?" she asked. There was a hint of invitation in her voice. The dance had excited her.

"I'm thinking of those Imperial mechs you mentioned."

Her face stiffened and her eyes turned contemptuous. "They're down the hall. I'll show them to you."

"You'll do better than that," I said. "You'll demonstrate them for me."

She put her knuckles to her mouth and looked at me. Her eyes were wide. "You goddam voyeur—" she began.

I cut her off. "Come," I said softly. I pushed with all the power in my damaged mind. It was like walking through glue. *It's all wrong!* my brain screamed at me. *It can't be done the way you're doing it! Do it right!* But Valencita came to her feet as though an invisible hand had jerked her out of the chair.

Her mouth opened. Her eyes went wide with terror.

"Hush," I said.

Her face turned livid. She stared at me with utter horror. "What are you?" she asked. Her voice was murmurous.

"Curious," I said. I intended no double meaning, but I received more than I intended. She shivered uncontrollably. "Now come with me," I continued.

She came, reluctantly, like a man to his hanging. . . .

An hour later I took her back to her room. There was no resistance left in her. She came with me shivering a little with weariness, too tired to object to anything I might suggest.

"I'm sorry about what I did to you with those machines," I said. "But I needed to know how they operated, and I'm in no shape to risk exposure to severe stimulation. I should have known that they were useless for my purpose."

She sighed and looked at me with unfocused eyes. "I'd hate to be addicted to them," she said softly. "But it was not too bad, señor. It was just too long." She sprawled across the bed and was instantly asleep, tired beyond any other sensation. There was neither fear, nor anger, nor even a subliminal sense of shame. The machines had performed for her the services that they had once performed for their overwrought and overcultured Imperial owners in those anxious days before the Empire finally collapsed. They removed tensions, soothed rage, calmed fears, relieved worries, gave pleasure, and permitted sleep. They wrung one dry of sensation.

Chapter Twenty-Five:

I went to the door marked "Executive Office—No Admittance" and came face to face with a young woman enough like Valencita to be her sister. She looked at me with annoyance and gestured at the door. "Can't you read?" she asked.

"I am José Torres," I said, "I have an appointment."

"You are early. Madam does not expect you until 0400."

"Tell her I am here," I said.

She touched a communicator button. "Señor Torres is here, madam. Shall I tell him to return later?"

"No—I am not busy now. Send him in."

Valencita's look-alike pointed to the door beside her desk. "Through here," she said. Her voice was neutral.

I pushed the door open. Madalena's voice had come over the intercom metallic and cool. The intercom was a liar. It was a warm contralto rich with overtones and shadings. "Good morning, Señor Torres. Did you have a pleasant time?"

"Thank you," I said, "It was very pleasant."

"So I understand. Valencita has had no experience with either Imperial machines or Confleet officers." The voice laughed at me. She knew what I was. I wished I knew as much about her. "She won't be worth much tomorrow."

My eyes tried to pierce the gloom across the room where the voice originated and almost in answer to my efforts the darkness faded and vanished.

She was seated in a highbacked chair facing me, and she was one of the most beautiful women I had ever seen. Flawlessly groomed, impeccably dressed, perfectly poised—she made Valencita seem like an awkward school girl. She was something out of legend; one of those impossibly perfect androids that had graced Imperial orgies and presided over the refined perversions of the court. Of course, she wasn't that at all. She was a Mystic, human to four decimal places, but the fifth was utterly alien.

The Matriarchate on Myst had a long history of daughters in Public Service. Bur Pol—the Confederation's Foreign Service—liked them. There were unkind stories by the dozen about the Bureau of Policy and mysticism, but there was little truth and much envy in them. For Mystics were scrupulously honest, completely loyal, coldly intelligent, and highly efficient. Yet they seldom were outstanding mission heads and bureau chiefs and as a general rule the Navy distrusted them. They lacked imagination and empathy, and they weren't really human despite their similarity.

Their problem was that the Confederation—like the Empire before it—was essentially a human operation, and man tended to form brotherhoods and communities that resented alien life forms. Only man, in this corner of the galaxy, seemed to have any genius for big government and social organization, and while Mystics fitted well into Confederation society, they were incapable of becoming members of a community of humans. Human females resented them. They had too much. The Mystic female received all the dominant and attractive attributes. Male Mystics were nonentities; shrunken, undersized, adapted by a logical and relentless Nature to the only real usefulness of the male. It had created problems since the time of the Conquistadores. When men first came to Myst and showed the Mystic females what they lacked, the reciprocal fascination between Mystic female and human male began. It never died, despite the laws that decreed a Mystic must bear at least two offspring before she could leave her home planet. The Mystic-human cross was infertile, due to minor genetic differences, but—if anything—it added to the mutual desireability of both races.

The Empire had used Mystics by the millions, and made concubines of them.

The Barbarians had enslaved them whenever they could, but failed to find their homeworld.

The Confederation rediscovered them and welcomed them as partners, despite the fact that Mystics couldn't really understand the mystique of democratic organization. Their advantages more than compensated for their lacks. They were near-perfect bureaucrats.

I always had a mental picture of a spider connected with them. They sat in the center of their webs and watched the flies become entangled. Then they absorbed the flies. I shrugged mentally. Possibly I was unkind. Mystics had many good qualities, and possibly were mutated from human origin, but pride of species and a dislike for bureaucrats gave me a certain aversion to them despite their fascination.

It was present now.

"Is this a Special Service Headquarters?" I put a rising inflection on the "this" and managed to convey, quite clearly, the essential difference between the human male-run fleet and the Mystic female-operated Bureau of Policy.

Madalena smiled. "It is," she said. We exchanged recognition codes and formal greetings.

I said, "I am Senior Lieutenant José Torres Fleet Six Special Service. I need assistance."

"We must check, señor."

"My serial number is A27431C on the Navy List."

"A-grade, eh? That makes you one of the important ones," she said as she punched the communication button on the arm of her chair and gave the necessary instructions.

"It's standard procedure," she said gently. "And it's a bore, but it is regulation. In the meantime what sort of assistance do you need? If it is within our capabilities you may have it. Unfortunately we don't have too much. We were forced to vaporize the bulk of our equipment. It was still above ground when the reform movement caught us. We couldn't hide or run and we couldn't let that sort of hardware fall into Segovian hands."

And why not? my mind asked. Other than letting the natives know someone was interested in them—which would probably have helped their morale—Bur Pol gadgetry could have done no harm and might have done some good. There were no weapons in a Bur Pol set-up—and nothing that could conceivably be turned into a weapon.

"You are thinking narrowly, Commander," Madalena said, revealing that she was either a telepath or Sorovkin-trained. "But our cover wasn't ready to be blown, and it still isn't. I'm not telepathic," she continued, "that's a talent not possessed by my race."

I nodded. I had known that, but I had forgotten. The lapse was symptomatic of my problem.

"I have been waiting for contact for ten years. It's about time you came," she said.

"We came as quickly as we could. I was posted here—" I paused for a moment, and then laughed. "You know—I don't think Fleet Intelligence knew you were here. ConFleet and Bur Pol were working this world independently! The right hand of the Confederation wasn't letting the left know what it was doing!"

"Our message to Dibrugarh—" she began, "specifically requested Armed Forces cooperation."

"How did you send this message?"

"Subetheric—it was sent after we were forced to destroy the message torpedo during our move here."

"Oh—well don't worry. It probably hasn't arrived yet. Dibrugarh is about sixty parsecs from here and subetherics aren't fast. They have to go the long way around. You should have used the torp."

"My spatial math is weak," she said, "how long should it take?"

"Roughly about twelve years, give or take a couple, unless a Fleet vessel picked up the message and forwarded it by torpedo. You should know about subetherics. That's why the Empire fell. They couldn't communicate fast enough—or react fast enough—and they couldn't operate a federal system because they were an Imperium."

"I don't need the history. Now what do you need?"

"Neurocytograph analysis and neurosynthesis. I was either attacked or damaged in an accident. My mental functions are impaired badly enough for me to be aware of the impairment."

"That is obvious," she said.

I scowled.

"I'm sorry," she said and managed to sound not sorry at all, "Our neurocytograph went with the Embarcadero building. Besides, it was only a Mark Four, and you probably need something better than that."

"It would have been enough. It's only partial amnesia. Things keep coming back."

"Would narcosynthesis help?"

"It didn't work at the hospital. I'm conditioned against it."

She shrugged. "We can try," she said. "However, that's all we have. I sincerely wish we could help more, if that's any comfort to you."

"That's nice, but I have a nagging feeling that if I wait much longer, it is going to be too late. I feel that something is about to happen. It was about to happen before my brains were scrambled. Too much time has elapsed since I was hurt."

"Your reasoning?"

"I came here to survey and report, but my orders were open-ended. I remember this. I also remember when I arrived. That was two years ago. I remember a sequence that has to do with hydrogen fusion reaction. As far as I know such a thing can only be in Alien hands."

"Can you recall where it was?'

"It was mountain country. An upland valley north of here. The name eludes me."

"Hmm—that could be La Cienega. It, and the Ring were destroyed a year ago. We thought it was a blowup."

I nodded. "That's the name," I said. "The important thing is to fix the date. I was hurt *after* the explosion, but not long after. I know my capabilities. The damage I suffered *could* have been an accident. But I have a feeling of urgency. It is *important* that I recover my functional totality. I don't know why it is important, but I feel it is tied with the safety of this world."

"Could it be connected with the Aliens?"

"Perhaps. I can't recall much about them except that the ruin of Segovian civilization is because of their presence."

"You state it exactly—their presence. They merely responded to Segovian activities—but their response was violent enough to kill eighty percent of the population, and contributed in a major way to the formation of the present government that rules this world."

"What are the Aliens doing here?"

"Check our files. The story's there. I never can begin to tell you. The Aliens are the real reason Bur Pol is here. We want to contact them. Segovia isn't important to us. There's a rampant xenophobia here that will take at least a generation of therapy to correct, and it will be even longer before the planet can be eligible for Confederation status. But the Aliens are something else. They have an enormous biochemical capability and a good physical technology. The Confederation needs them—but they seem to be as xenophobic as the Segovians. We have tried to contact them, but at the slightest pressure they withdraw. It's almost as though they came from another reality."

I chuckled. "You're a romantic. They're probably not empire builders like humans, and inhabit only a single planet. In a wilderness of worlds like our galaxy, their home world could be undiscovered for centuries. Take your own situation for example. Your people are found throughout the Confederation and another civilization couldn't possibly miss either the Confederation or your presence in it; but it could easily overlook your homeworld. A civilization like Myst could well remain hidden for centuries if it didn't want to show itself. After all, the Barbarians bypassed your homeworld even though they would have loved to capture it."

"That is true."

"I wish," I said, "that your branch and mine would cooperate better. You've apparently known about the Aliens for years. You even knew about Segovia. Yet we were not informed."

"We don't like the military crashing about, stepping on things we try to nurture."

"So you play footsie with a first-rate civilization, one that shows its potential destructive capability by what it has casually done on this world—which was at least late Class III before their arrival, and you don't even alert us to the danger."

"So you could come in with your battleships and frighten them away—"

"If they run, they have a reason."

"They're xenophobic."

"That's what you say. What do they say?"

"I don't know. We've had no direct contact with them."

"How long have you been here?"

"Almost twenty years."

"And no direct contact?"

"You don't realize the difficulties. We have to work through the scabs. The Segovians have a pathological hatred for both scabs and Aliens. We were only indirectly connected with the Aliens when Headquarters was in Santayana and the citizenry nearly destroyed us completely. We were lucky to save our lives."

"Why not infiltrate?"

"We tried. It didn't work. If the Segovians didn't kill our people, the scabs did. You can't imagine what sort of a spy system has been developed over the years. Segovians and scabs know each other far better than you can possibly imagine, but in general they leave each other alone on official levels. It's too dangerous to mess around in the other's back yard. At lower echelons they vent their hatred, but at the top there's a hands-off policy. When we learned this we managed to place one of our people in a Ring. He came back babbling of gods. We had to give him complete reorientation after we milked him."

"He was a Sensitive, I suppose."

"Of course—what else could we use to penetrate a culture whose attributes are completely unknown. We don't even know their language."

"Didn't it ever occur to you that the Koalber might be telepathic?"

"Yes—afterwards. *Who* was that you said?"

"The Koalber. That's what the Aliens call themselves. They're really—" I stopped.—"Now how do I know that?" I asked wonderingly. "How do I know they're true hermaphrodites, mammalian, and carbon-oxygen biotes?"

"You could have guessed the last," she said, "but it has now become a Class—A priority to find out what you *do* know. Somehow you have gained access to information denied us." Her voice was low and controlled, but her face had lost its calm expression. "I will do everything I can to cooperate with you, and I expect, of course, that you will cooperate with me."

"I have every intention of doing so," I said. "In turn I do not expect you to cheat me. I need to know if any military or paramilitary activity is being planned. I need to know who is behind the activity."

She nodded. "That can be done. Possibly it has already been done. It could be in the files. We have small interest in military activity."

"You should have more. Military activity is the one thing that can totally destroy this world." I tried to push a little, but she held me off easily. "You must have developed a fine intelligence system with Durango under your control."

"It's better than that," Madalena said. "Every girl who has worked here is an informant. They all have microcommunicators implanted in their mastoids. The frequencies are in the subetheric spectrum so they cannot be tapped by Segovian electronics, and anything that comes to their ears comes to mine. We monitor five hundred transmitters. There are rumors of high level technology on this world other than inside the Rings. I'll have them checked out. We haven't bothered with that, either."

"Just what have you bothered with?" I asked under my breath. Overtly I bowed, placed my hands in the traditional position and spoke the classical formula. "A stranger at your gate, my lady, is grateful for the hospitality of your house."

Madalena's eyebrows rose. And then she laughed. Her laughter was silver bells; their music enfolded me. "My dear man—you are incorrigible. Yet, if you wish we can discuss this matter further another time." She eyed me appraisingly. "I can think of no one on this world who could better serve the cause of interbranch cooperation." There was gentle mockery in her voice, but I had struck precisely the right note. "It is no pleasure to build a web and catch only flies when one knows that there is a wasp about." She put her hands together and returned my bow.

Chapter Twenty-Six:

The building was being cleaned of last night's activities when I awoke in the guest room Tia had assigned to me. The indentured staff, all hundred and twenty-eight of them who functioned as check girls, bartenders, waitresses, wardrobe girls, and doxies during the evening, doubled as janitors the following morning. The paid staff was conspicuous by their absence, as the indentures, wearing nothing but a thin shine of sweat, labored with mops, dustcloths, polishers and vacuum cleaners to put the place in shape for the evening. It was perhaps a better show than the evening one, and some few privileged voyeurs were enjoying the spectacle, but I didn't linger as I went directly to Madalena's rooms. I passed Valencita operating a vacuum cleaner in the guest room hall. She looked at me and grinned.

"I see what you mean," I said.

"I want to thank you. Tia let me sleep in my room all night. She's never done that before—and those mechs aren't so bad. At least you don't dream."

I resisted the urge to stop. Valencita probably had enough to do without having me to contend with; so I smiled and walked on.

Tia Madalena was waiting for me. "Have you had breakfast?" she asked. I shook my head. "Would you like some?" I nodded. She picked up the intercom and gave swift orders. We went to a balcony that overlooked the lake and sat at a small table while a nude staffer whom I recognized as the receptionist in the office served us.

"Have you an aversion toward clothing your girls?" I asked, as the woman set our tea, hot rolls and fruit with practiced dexterity.

"Not when clothes are necessary," Madalena said. "But when they're not, I see no reason why they should be worn. Besides, there is a certain amount of psychology in it. A naked woman tends to feel helpless and subordinate. Oh—I know it's not a dominant feeling, but the fact that I can make my girls work nude reinforces my position. It also puts them all on the same level. Lola—the girl who is waiting on us—is my voice during business hours. She has my authority then—but she's just another indenture during the off-duty and cleanup period. And when we go to Meeting she wears the same house uniform as the others."

"Do you have discipline problems?"

Madalena laughed. "Of course I do. You can't have a hundred thirty indentures living together and not have problems, but I don't have many and I never let them get out of hand."

I could believe it, for I knew how Mystics operate. We finished eating, exchanged the classic compliments, and with the amenities satisfied, we went to work.

"As far as your identity is concerned," Madalena said, "we have identified you as José Torres, the matador. The identification is tentative, but it is convincing."

I nodded. If it convinced her, then it was probably right. "All right," I said. "I won't argue—but is that any use to me?"

"Your cuadrilla wanted to kill Aspromonte after the bull caught you in Sanlucar. They were mad with anger and insisted that Aspromonte jinxed you. Aspromonte had brought some of his men with him and there was a fight. When it was over and the police had calmed things you were gone."

"No bells. You're reciting someone else's history."

"There was a girl, Inez, whom you married somewhere about two months prior to your accident. According to the record her familial name prior to marriage was Corréon y' Sanmarco, and she was the daughter of the Gonsalvo Corréon I mentioned awhile ago. She was a de Sanmarco on her mother's side."

"Interesting," I said.

"Aspromonte wanted her."

"Did he get her?"

Madalena shrugged her perfect shoulders. "I think not. He's too crude to hide something like that, and if he had her there would be no more than token activity in his office directed toward finding her. However, no search orders have been rescinded. The search for her is still on. Aspromonte is still diligently beating the hustings, but without results. It may be a screen, but if it is, it's being held pretty tightly, which argues that it isn't and that the search so far hasn't been successful."

"Good for her," I said.

"No more than that?"

"Is there reason for more?"

Madalena nodded. "You were in love with her and she with you."

"It's someone else's history," I said. "Mine contains the offer of a traveller's welcome from a Mystic maiden."

Madalena smiled at me and there was a glow behind the smile. "I am pleased."

"Perhaps you have withdrawn the offer?"

"No, it is still open, but you Navy men have reputations, and I am not as resilient as when I first came here."

"You are eternally young," I said.

She inclined her head. "If you would come with me, my lord," she said, "the bath is drawn, the robes are warmed."

I laughed.

"Had you forgotten, I would have reminded you—discreetly of course." There was a hint of excitement in her voice. "For after all, I am a Mystic, and you are a man...and for the right man a Mystic can be many things...."

I didn't feel like a netted wasp when I went back to Madalena's office. She was gone when I awoke, but if I knew Mystics, she wouldn't be far away. I wondered what it would take to turn a traveller's welcome into a lover's welcome, but I didn't think that I'd be able to handle that sort of greeting. As I expected, Madalena was at work, as fresh and crisp as a newly cut blossom. I envied her.

"You have some admirable traits," I said, "and not the least of these is devotion to duty."

"Someone has to run this place. It's a constant chore. Besides, I didn't expect you to be up for another hour. You recover quickly."

"I, too, have business."

She nodded. "I know. If it were not for the fact that I was nostalgic for civilized companionship, this morning would not have happened. But I am not a machine. However, we are fortunate. The last of our problems have been cleared."

"Yes?"

"Until a moment ago, I was not certain whether I would succeed in getting you an audience or not, but my story about your arrival here was enough to trigger a favorable response."

"You told someone that I was an Outworlder?"

"Of course. It was necessary."

I groaned. "Tell a woman anything and she's sure to blab. I

should have kept my big mouth shut, but I thought you had more sense."

"Do you want your memories back?"

"Naturally—what else?"

"Then you'd better resign yourself to a blown cover. The Star-Born doesn't see everyone. In fact, not many people know she exists—and those few tend to keep their mouths closed. I learned of her existence only by chance a few years ago, and had forgotten her until your need and the mention of Imperial machinery struck the proper stimulus. Even so, it has taken the entire morning to make contact and arrange a meeting." Madalena's eyes were bright with excitement.

"I had to agree to go with you, and I have taken full responsibility for your actions," she said. "But she agreed to see you. She is interested. She's a most unusual person, Torres, and she has a working Imperial neurocytograph. If it's what she says it is, it's equivalent to one of our Mark Fours."

"That I'll believe when I see it."

"It's true. She says it's true."

"When did you take a Segovian's word for anything?" I asked.

"I'd take this Segovian's word. I checked her out, and I'm as excited to see her as you should be."

"Oh—I'm excited all right," I said, "but I have no intention of losing my head over the possibility of a thousand-year-old machine being in working order."

"She says it is."

"Do you know how complex one of those things is? I've seen Imperials in the cultural museum in Dibrugarh. It'd take years to trace circuits and test them. Neurocytographs have been robot serviced from the beginning, and it's doubtful that the service mechs have lasted, let alone the original machine."

"Don't throw the wet blanket before you see the fire," Madalena said.

"I'm trying not to jitter with hope," I replied.

Chapter Twenty-Seven:

Madalena took me up to the roof where a standard 'copter stood on the landing pad. "Do you want to drive, or shall I?" she asked.

"I'm out of practice," I said. "Anyway, I'm not really afraid of woman drivers."

Madalena looked at me, wondering if I meant it, and caught the smile on my face before I could suppress it. "This world is beginning to get to me," she murmured. "I see so much male chauvinism that I expect it anywhere."

I laughed. "I was never a good 'copter pilot," I said. "I can get along in them, but riding with me isn't fun."

We took off with Madalena at the controls and flew for three hours at cruising speed through the hills southeast of Durango. We kept below the top of the hills within radar shadow, slipping over ridges at treetop level and hugging green narrow valleys until we came to a circular valley crowned by an enormous star-shaped structure perched on an upthrust mass of granite a hundred meters above the center of the valley floor. The granite had a slight overhang and the cliffs rose past the vertical in a smooth circle that was obviously artificial. The building on top dominated the valley. It was too large for its location.

"Not even a fly could crawl up those cliffs," I said as I looked down at the fortress. "I doubt if these people ever had trouble with goons."

"They never did. The fields of fire from the fortress cover the entire valley, and the weapons are last period Imperial, which means Kellys, lasers, focussed radiation, personnel-seeking missiles and defensive fields. This place could withstand anything the Aliens could throw at it. It wasn't through poor weaponry that the Empire fell."

I nodded. She was completely right. "What is this place?" I asked. I half expected the answer and wasn't surprised when it came.

"It's a spindizzy uproot, a piece of another world carved out of the surface by a Cth converter and transported across hyperspace to this planet. It's the Source, the site of the original landing of man upon this world."

"I wonder what its removal did to the world from whence it came," I said.

Madalena shivered. "I wouldn't want to be on the same continent from where it was torn."

"I heard about this place once, but most people think it's a myth and that the original colonists came in a spaceship."

"This was a spaceship. The fortress could be sealed. It was an odd ship, but it worked. Leonardo planned it that way, but he had hoped to bring it to Palestra. Somehow he managed to get lost and ended up here."

"Lousy pilotage," I said.

"He was still a survival type," Madalena looked at the IFF light glowing on the instrument panel and flipped the switch. "This is Madalena from Durango," she said. "Have I permission to land?"

"Permission granted. A guide will be available for you and your passenger. The Star-Born is eager to see him," the dashboard speaker replied.

"Now what's this?" I asked.

"Wait," she said, "I can't tell you. You must see for yourself. Down there is something that not even the Gods have touched. They merely accept it—as I do." She brought the 'copter down on the flat roof. A couple of muscular men came over and tied the craft down, opened the door and helped us out.

"This way," one of them said. "The Star-Born awaits you." He walked quickly over to a small cubic excrescence on the roof and pushed a button. The front slid aside revealing an elevator.

"Enter, please," he said.

We went down, we stopped. The doors opened and a girl in a filmy dress met us. "This way, please, the Star-Born is impatient and we cannot follow the usual amenities. You will forgive our haste?"

"Of course," Madalena said.

We passed through a sally-port, down a hall, through doors, and down another hall, and finally stopped before a great polished portal of black basalt bound with electrum and supported on giant hinges. It was a door fit to grace the throneroom of a king. I wondered what lay behind it.

The girl touched the door. It swung smoothly open on its jewelled bearings. A short empty colonnade lay before us. It was a moment before the breathtaking beauty and exquisite workmanship registered. I drew a long breath.

"Thus it was then; thus it is today," Madalena whispered.

We walked down the colonnade, footfalls silent on the polished floor that belied its look and feel of firmness by giving forth no sound. There was a dais at the far end. On it stood a broad, deeply upholstered couch that gleamed with jewels, precious metal and ivory. On the couch was a woman.

Madalena had made Valencita look awkward and coltish, but this woman made Madalena seem ordinary.

"Welcome," she said and her voice was pure music.

Madalena went to her knees, then slid forward until her face lay against the floor and spread her arms wide. It was the ancient salute given only to an Imperial of royal blood. I recognized it from my memory of history.

"Tell your slave to rise," the woman said. She smiled mistily, "It is nice to know that the Empire is not totally vanished."

"Madalena—get up!" I said. I felt embarrassed.

She rose to her feet, blushing. "I don't know what came over me," she said.

"I do. You Mystics have always been the servants of Empire. You just reaffirmed your original loyalty."

"You could be right," Madalena said. Her voice was shaken.

"I am Irina de Sanmarco the ninetyfourth. What can I do for you," the woman said.

"For a moment, my lady," I said in Terranuevan dialect, which was as close as I could come to the melodious ancient tongue, "will you allow me the pleasure of contemplating perfection?"

"Ah! The Imperial dialect—much changed, but comprehensible. The accent is harsher, the flow less smooth," her voice was like limpid water flowing over smooth stones. "There have been hard times in the Imperium?"

"That is true, my lady." I could not take my eyes from her. The iridescent black hair laced with golden threads, the nacreous skin, the enormous sea-blue eyes in a face of surpassing delicacy gave an impression of something fey and unworldly supported by hundreds of generations of breeding for excellence. She couldn't be much over twenty, I thought, yet there was something ageless about her, something remote from humanity. She was the ultimate incarnate feminine—yet in all this quintessential perfection of face and body there was something lacking. Feminine she was, indeed, but she was not a woman. She was Madalena taken to the Nth power. She was the ultimate female, but she was neither a love object, nor a sex symbol, nor a mother image. She was an object of worship. She was as different from a woman as a star is from the moon, and between her and someone like Valencita was a gulf that staggered the imagination. Yet, I thought, there was a woman I had known whom I would not exchange for a hundred of this cool perfection. For an instant I saw Inez before me—and the memory rose in my mind and blinded me. I took half a step forward and stopped. The vision vanished, leaving me aching and empty. That was a memory I wished had waited for a more opportune time, but I knew it now and I marvelled at the resemblance.

She rose and beckoned me to her. And I was not surprised that her eyes were almost on a level with mine. Goddesses were always larger than life. She was at least two hundred centimeters tall and probably weighed in the vicinity of seventy kilograms.

She looked slender, but she was not. And by some peculiar quirk of attitude she made me feel small.

She held out her hand, but as I reached for it as Evars would have done, it slid past mine to grasp my arm at the elbow. I automatically duplicated the action. My reflexes had behaved admirably. That form of greeting was Terranuevan. It was the Imperial clasp—and except for worlds like mine the only place it was seen today was in romantic sollies dealing with the Palestran Empire. Like the handclasp it had passed into history.

"Twice welcome," she said. Her voice was lisping, liquid, remote and unreal. The Great Captains spoke that way, as did the Emperors and their minions, but it was long gone from space. Terranuevan was as close to it as any modern tongue. Even Segovian was not so close. It had become more ornate, more flowery, more affected. It was a burlesque and I did not feel that I should use it.

"Thank you," I said.

"The form has changed. Still it is better than this affected tongue my people speak."

"A long time has passed," I said. "The language has evolved as have the worlds outside. Your speech is incredibly old. I have never heard it correctly spoken until today. In the University they teach something like it, but it is a dead intonation, spoken only by scholars and it, too, is not the same."

"I myself have not spoken thus for many years. More perhaps than you are willing to believe," Irina said.

I nodded. "I can conceive the years. You are young, yet you are very old. Longevity is not unknown to us, but it is hard to believe the age that clings to you. In practice there is no such thing as perfect agelessness. My mind will not accept what my senses tell me is so."

She showed no expression. The quiet fey mask of her face remained as it had been. "Do I project such an aura?"

"To me, at least, my lady. But I am sensitive to certain things."

"Your sensitivity is correct. Physically I am twenty-two years old, but I have lived closer to two thousand. I could, perhaps, barring accident, live until the race of man dies out."

"I am curious, my lady. We have worked on longevity in our laboratories. We use cloned cell and organ transplants, rejuvenation techniques and restorative drugs. Without too much good fortune a man or woman can look forward to an active lifespan of about two hundred years. But in time, the cells of the nervous system die and these cannot be replaced. We have been unable to find a rejuvenation technique that can be applied to nerve tissue."

"Why not replace it then, as you do the body. Why not transfer the mind to a new vessel?"

"Ego transfer? Via neurosynthesis?"

"Ah—you know the technique."

"It has been tried, but it has never really worked. The conscious ego is all that can be transferred."

"Yes—that is true."

"The habits, the reactions and the subconscious—the id— remain in the recipient body. And in time the transferred conscious ego is changed until it is no longer what it was. Bit by bit the transferred ego is absorbed until in a year or two it vanishes. It is not a painful death, but it is—nevertheless—death. The technique is now a laboratory curiosity. It was abandoned many years ago, although some sections of our government use modifications of it for intelligence purposes."

"As we did," Irina said. "But ego transfer can be made to work. I am proof."

"It would seem so, my lady—unless your basics have changed and you are not aware that a change has taken place."

"I am aware of every change. I grow. I develop. I learn from year to year. I am not as I was when I started, but I am still myself. I have not lost my continuity. I am Irina, the consort of the Captain General Leonardo de Sanmarco who found this world. I am Irina, first cousin of the Emperor Honorio the twenty-fifth. My family has ruled hundreds of worlds, and this poor one on which I live in exile is among the worst of them. I remember Palestra, the jewel of Empire, the perfect world. No—I do not forget. I do not lose continuity as you call it. There is still the ache and the hunger in me to return to the world of my birth.

"Once—as you say—ego transfer did not work. The soul became diluted and slipped away. I knew this, but it occurred to me that if a child of my cells, raised from birth in a controlled environment, conditioned so that all habits and reactions were as mine, whose thinking was as mine, who cell for cell, idea for idea, habit for habit was my own mirror—such a one could receive my ego and I would continue."

"That would seem to answer most of the objections," I said, "and if the recipient's tissue were a genetic mirror there would be no conflict at the cellular level.'

She nodded.

"You thought it out very well, but how was this miracle accomplished?"

"It was accomplished because I am a woman. In my day, we had a technique. You no doubt know of the Imperial slaves—all so alike that men could not tell them apart."

"The androids?"

"They were not androids. They were clones. There was—and is—a method of diploid asexual fertilization that produced living daughter cells precisely the same in chromosome content as their mothers'. Slave breeders used this technique to produce look-alikes. It was very ancient; developed on Earth, but suppressed. It was once used in the early days of colonization, particularly to increase the numbers of food animals."

"The knowledge has been lost," I said. "Or at least it is not used today."

"I can supply the details if you wish. It is not particularly complicated, but of course it would be of no use to you since you are male."

"Which may be why the knowledge has been lost," I said with a wry grimace. "We are a male oriented society."

"In Segovia, too," Irina said in a quick and bitter aside. "At any rate I ordered that the technique be used on me." She smiled at the memory. "It scandalized my physician. Poor man—he never really understood. He couldn't appreciate why I, of royal blood, should want to be fertilized in a manner only employed in slaves.

"I bore a daughter, and since I was her only parent, her genetic pattern was identical with mine. I raised her in absolute security to young adulthood. She was conditioned from birth to react as I did, and was exposed through her early life to neurosynthesizer sessions that reinforced all habit patterns and mental processes that were mine. I was preparing a body to receive my soul."

"And what of her?"

"I transferred her ego to my body." Irina's face clouded. "It would have been better had I not been so merciful. You see, by the time she was sixteen, I was nearly sixty, and the shock of the young ego awakening in so ancient a body—"

"Sixty isn't so old."

"It is to an ego of sixteen. The child went violently insane and had to be shut away until she died. Treatment was of no avail. It was a pity." Irina's face twisted briefly. "I still remember the pain, and I still am not happy over the outcome of that transfer."

"But I learned. I fertilized my new body and produced a daughter. When the girl was sixteen I transferred her ego into my thirty-two-year-old body and my ego into her. This time my child withstood the shock of transfer and was brought out into the world where I arranged a marriage for her. I immediately fertilized my new body and produced a child—you see how it goes?"

"Of course," I said. "With each transfer you gain sixteen years. But you do not transfer your radiance. There are none like you whom I have seen—or heard about."

"It is an ancient ego," she said. "There is also a little plastic surgery and memory erasure. In no case are my daughter egos truly aware that a transfer has taken place. I marry them into outside families." She smiled. "There is a great deal of my blood in this world. I can claim with some justice to be the mother of my people."

"In my society are those who would not approve," I said.

"Of how I use my own flesh? How odd. I use only what is mine. No man goes into the making of my children, and my daughters are provided with a dowry and a husband, and I stay forever young."

"You take sixteen years."

"But I give a life to that which otherwise would not have existed." Irina shrugged. "I think it balances."

"It is a moot question," I said, "but you seem to have solved the problem of immortality."

She sighed. "Do not think it has been easy. I love life but I do not like to see my friends and helpers die. I have buried far too many friends—and at times I think I would like to die with the others. But I am a coward and remain alive and make new friends. Yet I try not to harm my children. Except for the first, I have seen to it that they live normal lives. I have many children and grandchildren. My blood is good and it has leavened this world, although in primary ego I never adventure into motherhood beyond the child necessary to keep the succession alive."

"You have adjusted well."

"After over a thousand years and a hundred children what else could I do? I would have died otherwise. I have never allowed the technique to become public for too many old women in young bodies would destroy the world," she paused and watched my face. "Is there anything else you would know of me?" she asked.

"My lady," I said. "I would like the true story of how you came here. I have heard the rumors and the myths of this world but the truth is something that will be needed for my report."

"We fled from Valladolid during the time of the Barbarian attacks," she said.

I remembered no world called Valladolid, but I could look it up in the catalogue once I got back to Garon. Perhaps it was one of the dead ones.

"There were almost ten thousand of us; soldiers, administrators, slaves and commoners—all that was left of a hopelessly outnumbered colony that had struggled to hold back the outlaws. We were driven back to the Imperial fortress and penned in by a circle of Barbarians. We resolved to sell our lives so dearly that the scum around us would think twice before ever again attacking an Imperial colony.

"The enemy gathered, swarming for the kill. We huddled in the great star-shaped fort with our weapons ready and our ports sealed, waiting for the attack that was certain to come and which would terminate with our death or enslavement. We watched the Barbarian hordes swell around us, heard their mustering orders on our communicators, rejected their insulting terms for surrender, and as their troops poised for the assault, my husband, Leonardo, energized the huge spindizzy he had installed in the fort in anticipation of this moment.

"Over a cubic mile of Valladolid's surface went into hyperspace with us, and the enormous disruption undoubtedly killed most of the attacking Barbarians, for there was no pursuit."

"There wouldn't be," I said. My mind recoiled from the awesome destruction that must have followed the ablation. The planet was undoubtedly shaken to its core. If anything had remained alive within two hundred kilometers of that maneuver it would have been a miracle.

"We sped through hyperspace. We could not navigate. Many went mad from the distortions. We went where chance directed us. Finally we broke out near a solar system and our surviving engineers managed a landing. We established Segovia in the name of the Empire. We weren't well equipped for colonization and this world was hostile, and many of us died. It was a dreadful time at first, but eventually we subdued the local area and gradually our people scattered over the world.

"In time Segovia was tamed, and there was no more hatred between this world and men. We kept the faith that the Empire would someday find us. Then the Aliens came. Faith in the Empire almost vanished, but now—once more—our people look to the stars for help." She spread her hands in a sweeping gesture that emcompassed the room, the valley and the world beyond.

"I knew the Empire would return if I waited long enough."

Madalena sent me a warning glance.

I nodded. "You have waited long enough," I said.

"Have I not done well?" There was an anxious note in her voice. "I have influence. I have kept the Imperium alive."

"You have done excellently. Like a mother—like a bird on the nest—you have preserved and hatched the eggs from which the world has come—and you have preserved the nest."

She smiled and I thought wryly that the left-handed compliment went better than it should. Some day my tongue was going to get me into trouble. Sure—she had preserved the nest. This valley hadn't changed appreciably since the Imperium and the Imperium was dead and buried these past two thousand years. And this incredible woman didn't know it was dead.

Well—I wasn't going to disillusion her—not yet at any rate. She had too much to give, and she obviously had a neurocytograph with neurosynthesis in working condition. She had to have the machine or she would not still be alive.

"I have had a dream," Irina said. Her voice was soft, like honey dripping, I thought. "I have had a dream of Palestra, which I have cherished for two thousand years. I want to return to my birth-world, to wear flame-silk again and stand in the Court of the Imperium with the worlds of Empire circling overhead on their pencils of force. I want to move like water across the golden floor in the train of the Emperor. I want to see him shining in his jewels like a star among the planets. I want to breathe the scented air, watch the Guards parade, walk the garden paths, visit the pleasure palaces, make love to a beautiful man in the moonlight while the nightbirds sing. I want to join in the rush of people, move through the great cities of State. I want to drive a ground car in the silent rush of traffic. I want to live again with the clean beautiful people who rule the Imperium." Her face twisted with longing. "Oh sir! " she said, "I want to go home!"

I felt a rush of pity for her. She had endured so long—and for what? A dream that was ashes. Palestra was long ago sacked and gutted, her people worn out and spiritless; a world notable only for the gigantic ruins that intrigue scholars and romantics; but which contribute nothing to the bustling Confederation. Palestra was dead.

"When your ship appeared on my instruments, I could hardly believe it," Irina went on. She was talking compulsively, her face strained, her eyes bright with longing. "Above Segovia in orbit was an Imperial ship! I had almost lost hope of ever seeing one again, but I could never mistake its shape."

"It's a scout," I said. "A two-seater. I came alone."

"No matter. To me it looked as big as a dreadnaught. We had been found. The Empire would gather us in."

"I ordered a search, but it was fruitless. I knew you had landed but my men could not find you. I was desolate. But then I remembered you would not fail to recognize the Imperial Spacefleet Headquarters code sign—ISH; so I had it incorporated into places where I had agents, knowing that sooner or later you would hear and understand. It has been hard to be patient, but you had to come to me. It was my will that you do so." There was something oddly regal in her voice and something in me responded.

"My lady," I said, "I am yours to command—when my mission here is done."

"Then finish it quickly and take me home," she said, "I am the only one left. I want to leave. This world wearies me. My friends, my husband—all are long dead, and every year has added to my loneliness. I want to return to my own kind."

"I shall do my best," I said, "but I must have help. I have been injured. I am partially aphasic. I need to be brought to realization of myself."

"You need much."

"You have a neurocytograph and synthesis techniques. They are enough. They can compress years of healing and re-cognition into a few hours. I need my full ability if I am to leave."

"You shall have everything you need as long as I can leave with you."

"I swear it," I said, "on my honor as a Navy officer."

"I am content."

"Yet there is a problem, my lady. Things have changed beyond this world. You may not like what you find out there."

"I can always return here. But I must see. I must know how it goes with the Empire and the Eternal Imperium."

The irony, I thought, was bitter-sweet. *"Look on my works ye mighty—and despair!"* The epitaph was as apt for Palestra as it had been for that long dead Pharaoh and the poet who immortalized him.

Madalena, I noticed, had finally drawn a normal breath. She

was smiling and her expression was tender toward Irina, and kind toward me. The all-mother, I thought. This is her real function. Irina represents something she needed, something to protect, something to cherish. There had always been stories about Myst, and the Imperials were excellent biological engineers. I wondered if there were truth to the tales that the Mystics were really androids. The Empire *did* have androids, and they *were* honest, loyal, and incredibly efficient. I shrugged. What difference did it make? It was a new galaxy and a new society. Whether it was better or not was a question for philosophers and not for soldiers or bureaucrats.

Chapter Twenty-Eight:

"Come with me," Irina said. "There is no need for you to wait, and I have waited too long." She led the way into the depths of the building, moving with a dancer's grace, until we finally came to a vault. On the way we picked up an entourage; a doctor, two technicians and a couple of men whose only apparent function was to open doors and push buttons.

"The machines are kept in a nitrogen atmosphere to prevent deterioration," Irina said. "They are, so I am assured, as good as they were when they were installed in the palace." She turned to the technicians. "Please unseal the vault," she said.

The men went to work and presently the thick metal door swung back. In the center of the stark gray room stood the machines. They were functionally and artistically beautiful in a way that modern machinery could not duplicate. The Imperials had been artists as well as engineers, I thought.

I put on a dustfree coverall one of the technicians held for me and went in to inspect the machines. Irina, similarly clad, went with me, together with the technicians.

I felt a momentary surge of disappointment. There was no area mockup. The controls, instead of being spatial were planar with row after row of dials and meters. The rationale of the panels evaded me.

I shook my head. "I'm sorry," I said. "The controls on today's machines are different." I shrugged. "In any event I could not operate it."

"But you would not have to do that. My technicians are highly skilled."

"I still would like to know what is being done."

"I am afraid you will have to take our skill on faith. It is impossible to teach you the procedure of this machine in any reasonable length of time."

"Have you processed any other egos except you own in them?"

"Of course. We have mental disease here, and we treat our people. The machines are used for other things then to preserve me."

"And they work all right?"

"Of course, why shouldn't they?"

"I like to know the rationale."

"Alfredo—" she said.

"Yes, Star-Born," one of the technicians said.

"Are you competent to explain the machines to my guest?"

"Of course, Star-Born. I was raised with them."

"Then tell him, show him, explain to him how they work. He has a need to know."

"Yes, Star-Born. I can do this."

"How long will it take?" I asked.

"That depends upon your comprehension señor. At the shortest, I would say a day to go over the various regional groups. Then perhaps another day for the major linkages and the coarse synaptical connections. Then several more days for the major details. A complete resumé of basic function would take perhaps two weeks, but that, of course, would cover only the superficial aspects. The deeper connections and relationships—ah—there would be a problem." The man shrugged and raised his eyes toward heaven as though to call for divine assistance. "I know these things, Señor, but to explain them—"

Irina laughed. "Now, Torres, do you wish to go on?"

"No—I merely wanted to know if your people knew what they are doing," I said. I smiled. "They do. They give precisely the answers that our technicians give laymen. And as far as this device is concerned, I am a layman." I turned to the technician. "Alfredo," I said, "how soon could you run a brain scan and identify damaged areas?"

"If I had your normal EEG tapes, perhaps an hour. Without them, perhaps never. It depends on the damage."

"All areas have, or should have, comparable efficiency," I said.

"*All* areas? Sir, do you know what you are saying?"

I nodded. "I think I do," I said. "I had total capability."

"That is only a term, sir. One man's capability is not another's. The good God gave us many more cells than we use. If all of them were operative, one would either understand the Universe, or be mad." He shrugged, "Or perhaps both," he added.

"If I outlined my problem, and told you where my defects lie, do you think you could correct the damage?"

"I could open the paths, stimulate the cells, resynthesize damage, repair synapses, reestablish conduction paths, if the matrices are still present. Yes, I could do those things. Providing there has been no irreversible damage, your mind can be restored."

"There was trauma."

"Then there will be some permanent changes, but we can hope they are not extensive. Generally they are not, and if it is some simple thing, a substitute pathway can be formed and placed in an unused section and connected to the main communication trunks by opening unused neural channels."

"Well, let's see what can be done."

"Am I needed here?" Irina asked.

I shook my head.

"Very good. I will be available if you need me." Irina turned and went out of the portal, followed by her attendants.

"Señor," the technician said, "you are a very lucky man. If the Lady Irina takes an interest in your case you are cured. There is no one with her skill and experience. In her long life she has come to know the human mind like no other person could. Conceivably, if one lived—" he stopped. He was talking to emptiness. I had already gone.

I caught her in the hall before she had gone ten meters from the door. "My lady," I said. "I apologize."

Irina laughed. "It is always hard for you lordly males to accept the fact that women might know something. It was so in the days of my childhood. It is so today. But you realized faster than most."

"My lady—women on today's worlds run major divisions of industry and government. I know better. But I have been here long enough to absorb some of this world's culture and attitudes. Nevertheless I should have used my brain. I am ashamed."

"Don't worry about it. I intended to take charge of you once you were in the machine. I thought perhaps you might be too proud to accept help from a woman. Your customs are strange, and perhaps there is more damage than you suspect. We shall see. Now shall we really get to work?"

"By all means," I said.

Time passed. I did not know how long, nor did I care. There were interminable questions and answers that went on tape for analysis. There were physical examinations, reflex examinations,

EEG scans, area checks, synaptical resistance checks, and a hundred other things, most of which I dimly understood if at all.

Irina presided over the examination like a seeress over the auguries, and I felt like the haruspex itself by the time it was over; stripped bare and laid open as I had never been before in my life.

"To assemble you properly," Irina said in answer to my questions why such detail was necessary, "I have to know you intimately. I must know your smallest thoughts and motivations in order to assemble the pattern of ego that is you. We finished with the superficial layers of your ego, and from here we can explore more deeply—trace other paths down to the basic cells. This, of course, must be done under the neurocytograph. That is the reason for the tests.

"To work from effect to cause is difficult. To discriminate between correct and incorrect response is harder. So much depends upon the judgment of the operator in the evaluation of sets and patterns—so much depends on what I believe you must have been and what I can deduce from your responses. Some of these decisions must be made while the scan is in progress. Therefore I must know everything that can be known before I put you into the machine."

She watches me as a cat would watch a mouse, I thought. "I understand," I said. "At home would be easier. They have my record."

"Have you ever been in love?" she asked abruptly. "I mean love—not mere physical attraction. Men are easily attracted, but are seldom in love. If you do not know the difference, do not answer."

"I believe I am in love, my lady," I said. "The memory came to me when I first saw you. She is much like you in features. Her name was Inez Corréon y' Sanmarco before we were wed." I wondered why she had saved this question for the last. There was a reason, but she gave me no answer.

"I think I shall proceed under the assumption that you love," she said. "You are certainly old enough and you have romantic attitudes. We can see what comes of it. If you are left in love with a figment of imagination, it can do no great harm—but if your love is genuine your entire mental set can be affected."

She rose and stretched. "It is now time for the machine," she said. "I think we might as well keep going. The data won't change, but your reaction to them might. This business of mental engineering is a difficult thing. It seldom pays to wait once a pattern has been developed."

Alfredo put me into the machine, adjusted the cups, the cap, and the electrodes. Irina seated herself in the operator's chair. "Well, Sénor Torres—are you ready?"

"Go ahead," I said.

A soundless nova exploded in my skull. Monsters pursued me. I died of thirst. I starved. I made love to a series of lovely women, and to a series of hags. I fought, I was hurt. I screamed from the pain of strange tortures. I relaxed in ineffable bliss. I knew nothing. I knew everything. I examined the universe and rejected it as imperfect and created a better one. I saw sound and heard color. I smelled the tactile sensations of my fingertips and saw the sweet odors of corruption. I was disoriented, turned inside out, sifted, examined, laid organ by quivering organ on a dissection tray, stirred and reassembled into something that looked like me but wasn't because it had no soul. I was an embryo, a child, an adult, an innocent, a cynic, a sadist, a compassionate, a sentimentalist—the pure states and intangibles of my being were separated from each other, analyzed, proportioned and distributed. I loved and was in love. I tasted life and death and respected them both. I was a kaleidoscope, changing, turning, presenting ever shifting facets of ego to be examined. I moved outward and upward, inward and downward. My ego concentrated to a flaming point and vanished. I slid down a long black tunnel with nothing at the end. My velocity increased beyond that of light and I went hurtling off into a trans-einsteinian universe where there was neither day or night and the uncontrolled distortions of Cth space were child's illusions compared to the new reality. For a while I was mad with a madness at once hellish and divine.

Reality pulsed, wavered, coalesced, united, fragmented, reunited, and held—a flame burning clear and beautiful in the surrounding darkness. I felt whole, complete.

I was aware. I understood my mission and realized my purpose in being here. Things were as they should be. Then something wiped out the lights. My self-realization vanished. My awareness vanished. Everything dissolved and I realized, as I rushed into warm velvet blackness, that I had been treated and must now rest in darkness until it was time for me to be reborn.

Chapter Twenty-Nine:

I awoke. I was lying naked in a bed in a large opulently furnished room. I was weak, drained, and spent, but my mind was clear. I knew who I was, what I was, where I was, and why I was here. My perception was brilliant. I could visualize the man called Alberto who was outside the door of my room waiting for me to recover consciousness. He had a broken fastener on his jacket pocket and was holding a handful of raisins which he was eating slowly one by one.

My memory ran easily back through time past Madalena and Valencita, past Vargas and Espinosa, to Sanlucar, the corrida and—Inez—Inez!—she was larger than life, more than a woman. What had become of her? Had Aspromonte found her?

Aspromonte! I must know more about the man. What had he done? What was he doing? What did he plan? Even in my damaged state I had recognized his capacity for harm, but now it was tremendous. For he was in Cuidad Segovia, at the hub of power, and that was the one place he should never be. He was a menace to all human life upon this world.

I thought of the Imperial spacer at the bottom of Laguna Estrella. Was the contrary bitch still there or did Aspromonte's effort to raise her send her into orbit? I had thought Evars was an old woman for selecting defense fields over armament, but maybe he was right.

Evars! Good God! How could I possibly have ignored the Old

Man!—and for two years! The original damage had been worse than I had dreamed. Had those surgeons in Santayana not removed the depressed fracture I could still be chasing bulls around the arenas of Segovia in a burlesque of childhood games! I thought back to the landing on Segovia—could I possibly have been such a child as my memory recalled? Did I really run around this world killing bulls and imitating Don Quixote by destroying the Alien Ring? Where was my mind? What had I done? What a fool—fool—fool! I shuddered.

I scanned the landing of the Imperial scout, pinpointed the damage and swore. I *knew* that computer was defective! That flying object which had knocked me out had done the original damage when it had cracked my skull. It was just blind luck that the bull at Sanlucar finished the job....

I lay quietly, letting my mind correlate, considering what I must do, where I must begin to avoid the danger toward which we were heading. One thing was certain; this situation demanded force. Evars was a vital link in the chain if the problems of Segovia were to be brought down to their proper proportions. And with force should be the wisdom and experience that I still lacked. I was here as Evars' eyes and ears—to identify the problem, but not necessarily to solve it. Hell! I should have done that inside a month, but I had been gone *two years!* I hoped I was not written off as dead.

"Alfredo." I said. I didn't speak loudly, but the door to my room opened instantly, framing the muscular figure of the technician.

"You called, señor?"

I swung my legs over the edge of the bed and stood up. I swayed, and the floor felt oddly unsteady, but the feeling passed.

"Señor!" Alfredo's voice was anxious as he crossed the room and supported me. "You should rest, señor. You had a long and difficult session. The Star-Born was exhausted when it ended. There was much damage and your mind is most complex."

"It does not matter now, Alfredo. I am in control of myself. I must do what I should have done years ago. I have been idle too long. Get my clothes."

"But señor—"

"Enough! My clothes, Alfredo." My voice was peremptory. Alfredo wilted. Few ordinary men can withstand the inherent force behind an A-class demand, backed as it is by training and development in the art of being obeyed. He went to the closet and came back with a complete outfit, and helped me dress.

"Is the lady Madalena here?" I asked.

"Yes, señor."

"Take me to her, please."

Alfredo guided me from the room through the maze of corridors to an elevator that bore us swiftly upward and stopped with a hiss of displaced air at an upper level.

There was a hanging garden, a balcony and a broad railing jutting out over the sheer drop to the ground some two hundred meters below. A couple of men were tending the plants and shrubbery. Madalena was leaning on the rail looking across the valley. She turned toward me and the frown disappeared from her face.

"Torres! Are you whole again?"

I nodded.

"Good. I need to get back to work. This idleness is killing me, but the Star-Born will not let me leave. Are you aware of the situation? It grows critical. Aspromonte has been appointed defense minister. I do not think there is much more time."

"He still has to train his army," I said.

"Not as much as you think. He has brought his people from Industrial Protection. They're combat trained. We do not have much time."

I nodded. "We shall have to return to Durango," I said. "I need your intelligence net."

She nodded. "You are indeed restored, señor. I can feel the power. You are now one to be obeyed. I do not think that even I could oppose you."

"You couldn't. This is a military emergency."

Her face stiffened. "So you say—" she began.

I cut her off. "Does the military *ever* interfere with Bur Pol or the diplomatic component unless force is necessary?"

"No—it does not."

"The situation will probably require force. You are superseded."

"Yes sir. What are your wishes?"

"Take me to Irina. We'll have to get cleared from here."

I followed Madalena with Afredo bringing up the rear. "What is all this hurry?" she asked as we went down the corridor.

"The Aliens are probably planning to sterilize this world."

"Are you serious?"

"Completely. As of now, if they were equipped properly. The Segovians can destroy every Ring on this planet. We cannot assume that the Aliens are not aware of this. Indeed, it would be stupid to assume that they are not."

"There has been increased activity around the Rings lately. My contacts in Cuidad Segovia have commented on it."

"They are not as individualistic as Segovians would like to believe," I went on. "Individualists could not produce such technology."

"I saw the fallacy of that years ago," Madalena said, "but they never contact each other."

"Correction. They are in constant contact with each other."

"But we have detected no etheric or subetheric radiation."

"They're telepathic."

Madalena's face whitened. "So that's why the Sensitives—" she began.

"Of course. They ran into developed telepathy and it blew their minds. But, being telepathic, the Aliens look upon us as inferior animals—clever perhaps, but not on a level that they could class us as equals. It was their good luck, of course, to run into a fairly stagnant backwater of civilization. Segovia had gone just about as far as it could go with its sexual dichotomy and its ideas of male predominance. The cooperation of both sexes is essential to move into Class IV."

"But the Confederation is still male dominant—"

"However, it is not female repressive. Any woman who has the skills and wishes to use them can rise to the top. And many do. Here, females have been actively suppressed into the mother-housekeeper -sex object role that ultimately causes stasis. Any race that doesn't use all its potential will always stop short of its possibilities."

"Is that why—on Myst—" she said.

I nodded. "You have to leave your world to realize your full potential. But enough of this. You can extrapolate as well as I can. Koalber, by their biological nature, have no sex dichotomies. They're hermaphroditic."

"Where did you learn all this?"

"From Inez," I said, and realized even as I said it that I had never told her about Inez Corréon. So I began, but by that time we were in Irina's reception room.

I was in no mood for formalities and Irina recognized it. "We shall have to leave you for awhile, my lady," I said. "There are things I must do."

"Tell me," Irina said.

So I did. I told her of the Aliens and what they thought of humans. I told her how the goons could be interpreted and what I thought would be their next step if Aspromonte was permitted to continue. I told her what I thought must be done and how I would do it.

I had feedback from both Irina and Madalena. Irina agreed to have her friends in Cuidad Segovia come to the valley and Madalena offered her help. The Segovians were always eager for such invitations. "We shall have a series of parties," Irina said. "Like none we have had for years. There will be food and wine and Imperial delicacies." She smiled a tight Mona Lisa smile. "And when they return to Cuidad Segovia they will oppose this Aspromonte in whatever way they can."

"The neurocytograph?" I asked.

She nodded.

"Tie them to you more strongly," I advised. "Segovia will need an autocrat for awhile, and you're the logical candidate."

"I was one once, but in the past few years I have no longer cared," Irina said. "It would not be too hard to try to guide them again."

"With a harder hand, perhaps," Madalena said. "I think you were too soft, too easy, too feminine before. You must become an angry mother, my lady, not a gentle one. I run a town, and in its little way it is like the world. There must be a hard hand in the soft glove."

Irina nodded.

"I must have information about Aspromonte," I said. "I must inform Evars. I must find Inez and open communication with the Aliens. And we must have force to back up this activity. How many people do you control, my lady?"

"Do you wish the exact figure?"

I shook my head.

"About ten thousand, I would guess."

"So few?"

"I need very little. Most of what I want I have."

"How many could be trained for war?—and remember a woman can press a firing stud as well as a man."

"Perhaps half."

"In my mind was a complete emergency training manual," I said. "You undoubtedly have it in your scan records."

Irina nodded. "If you have such a memory, the record will be on file."

"Pull it and use it. Build me two regiments of combat trained troops. Start at once."

"Yes, my lord," Irina said.

I hadn't realized I had used the command mode, and for a moment I was embarrassed, but that didn't last. There was too much to be done.

Chapter Thirty:

"Do you think we can swing it?" Madalena asked as we sat in her office in Durango.

I nodded. "It will be close, but if Irina does her part we can delay Aspromonte long enough to get our power into action."

"She's only a woman in a male dominant society," Madalena said.

"She's more than that. She's a world symbol. She's the lineal contact with Duke Leonardo. If she uses her status properly, she can do more than you think. Forget that 'only a woman' line. She's royal. And what about you—you're only a woman, but look at what you've done."

"I'm chief of a mission. I have a staff."

"So does Irina. Now stop going female on me and get to work."

"Yes, master," Madalena said, and for the life of me I wasn't sure whether she meant it or not. Ever since I recovered my lost talents she had relegated herself to an advisory role, and I wasn't sure that was necessary or advisable. She waited for me to make the decisions rather than moving out on her own initiative.

"Madalena," I said, "don't play games with me. There is no peck order here. We have to cooperate or we will fail."

"I can't help it," she said. "You have become so dominant that I must await your word."

"Then it's time I got out of here and let you work. You know your job better than I ever could, and I can't hold you back. I have to find

Inez and get word to Evars. I'm not needed around here; so I'll leave."

"No—" Madalena said, and then shrugged. "You're right, of course, but I shall miss you. It has been nice to lean on someone else, if only for a moment. You will, of course, need money and a car. Take my Pegaso. It's new. And tell Lola to give you what you need in the way of cash. And when you find Inez, tell her that I envy her." She turned from me and left the room.

A half hour later I was on my way to Santayana, sound asleep in the front seat of Madalena's car while the control road took me back to the city.

I awoke with the alarm ringing. I was stopped on the #2 exit ramp in one of the parking slots. I turned off the alarm, left the car, went down to the exit service stop and after a trip through the refresher and a quick meal, I felt ready to meet Pedro Vargas. I found him down on the waterfront bossing a stevedore gang that was unloading a coastal freighter. He eyed me with delighted recognition.

"Hey! Don José! Where the hell you been? Haven't seen you since that night at Durango. Where'd you get those fancy clothes and fine car? What you been doing? Robbing banks? You owe me a hundred and fifty munits. I had to pay the coroner to keep the old bastard off your neck with a debt warrant. Ah—you dons, you have the damndest ways of doing things. I keep telling Carmela you'll be back to collect on the rent you never used, but she won't believe me—"

"Shut up Pedro," I said, "and let me talk." I expect my grin was as big as his, but I liked the big fellow. I'd known him only a few hours, but I would have trusted him farther than some men I have known for years.

"Okay, Don José—what you want?"

"I need your help."

He nodded. "I figured that. Well, tell me what you want."

"A scuba outfit."

"Scuba?"

"Self contained underwater breathing apparatus."

"Oh—you mean free dive gear. Where in hell did you hear that word scuba?"

I shrugged. "Somewhere," I said, "I don't remember."

"What you gonna do? Go spearfishing?"

"Something like that."

"How soon you want the rig?"

"Now."

"Give me an hour."

He was as good as his word. I went back to the dock office with him. He made one call and in slightly less than an hour later a man came with a box of underwater gear.

"You know how to use this stuff?" Pedro asked.

"Check me out," I said.

Ten minutes later I was in my car with the diving gear in the back seat. I drove to the Segovia Union Bank on the Avenida Irina de Sanmarco. I looked at the street sign and grinned. It was a good omen.

I found the vice president with whom I had arranged for a safe deposit box two years ago when I was starting my career as a matador. He, of course, didn't recognize me but I knew the numerical code of the box lock and gave the right password. Besides, my signature was correct.

"I can tell you the contents of the box, if you doubt me," I said.

"No señor. You know the name and numbers and your signature matches. That is all that is needed."

Five minutes later I had my Alpharzian Kelly, a half dozen fresh charges for it, and a sackful of gold coins. Whoever had furnished me with these back on Garon had known the Segovian mentality, for I had found that hard money—silver or gold—did twice as much as equivalent amounts of paper, and I might need a harder bribe than the wad of currency in my pocket.

I took Highway 25 to La Cienega and Pontecorvo. It felt strange driving alone. The last time I had been surrounded with half my cuadrilla. I laughed. Lord God! What a fool I had been, but after all, I couldn't be blamed. That damned Imperial computer on the scoutship wasn't programmed to be more than a superficial medimech. It had checked me out and to its limited abilities I had been A-OK. I wasn't, of course, but the computer had no way of knowing that. People in my profession weren't in existence when that machine was built. It was a miracle that I wasn't killed, but of course I had the reflexes of a Special Service officer even though I had lost most of the other attributes. Still, it was surprising how far a good set of reflexes can carry one.

I reached the fork in the road that led to the Camino Monosabio before sunset. There was a sign blocking the left hand fork that led to La Cienega. "Danger of death," it read, "Radiation—No Entry—Trespassing Forbidden." Below the sign was the clasped hands seal of the Guardia and the ducal coronet of the Central Government. I ignored the sign and drove up into the hills towards the caldera that rimmed Lake Estrella.

I didn't waste time driving down to the lake through the still-raw slash of an emergency road that had been cut through the woods. Instead I went airborne and dropped the Pegaso on the gravel beach where I had come ashore two years ago.

I cursed softly under my breath as I donned the scuba gear. I could have settled this mess within six months if I had half the brains I was supposed to possess. Instead, I went happily off like some modern Don Quixote tilting at windmills and slaying bulls while the planetary situation deteriorated toward a stupid extermination campaign that would probably fail, and at best would only result in exacerbating the hatreds already present. I wasn't too worried about human or Alien survival. Evars would get here in time to stop any all-out effort. For, unless I was badly mistaken, the Aliens didn't have the power to exterminate the Segovians. It would be too big a job and they were too few to do it. However, the Segovians were in no better case. With hardened defenses, the Aliens would be completely safe from Segovian attacks. It would be another bloody impasse with the Segovians taking the brunt of the casualties. And I didn't want that to happen.

I swam out to where my ship lay in the deep spot under the loom of the ringwall. The sun had set and the fast moon was rising as I dove. The ship was still there, outlined in the faint halo of a standby screen. I touched the screen. It flared briefly and then died. I shook my tingling fingers as I went to the airlock which swung open to greet me. Air purged the lock as I entered and within moments I was in the control room.

Despite my damaged appearance, the computer recognized me instantly. "You are back" it breathed seductively. "Your facial lineaments have been altered. Your original ones were better."

I ignored the comment.

"Did anything happen while I was gone?" I asked.

"Someone tried to enter, but I hardened the fields and they went away. They came back with machines, but the machines were crude. I fired on one and vaporized it. They went away and have not come back. I energized the engine and restored reserve power in case of attack."

"Have we any message torpedos aboard?"

"No sir. A message torpedo is almost as large as I am."

"Then you will have to do. You have the coordinates in your tank. You will go into space, compute as short as possible Distorter shift to Garon, check in with the orbital forts, and deliver the message which I will give you to Admiral A. Evars if he is still in command. If he is not in command you will deliver the message to the ranking officer of Fleet Base Six. When this is done you will place yourself at the disposal of the Commanding officer of Fleet Base Six."

"Yes sir."

"Any questions?"

"Yes sir. Are you coming with me?"

"No, I have business here." I took out the message I had written during the drive from Santayana and read it to the computer. Then I taped it to the pilot's chair where it wouldn't be overlooked. I took a handful of charges, a new service Kelly, a personal protection shield and my dress uniform, packed them into a waterproof gear sack, and left the ship. As I went through the water to the surface I could feel the rising whine of the atomics as the computer energized the drive. The thought occurred to me that I hadn't told the ship to delay until I reached shore. Obviously something was still wrong with my head. I shrugged. If I swam fast I'd probably be out of harm's way before the computer energized the drive. I swam like hell.

I was out of the water and in the Pegaso when the scout broke the surface, flashed upward and disappeared into the high thin overcast with a crack of riven air. She went so fast I hardly knew she was gone before she vanished. If I'd been aboard I'd be pulp now since the ship had no acceleration dampers.

Yet, fast as she was, she was barely fast enough to avoid the sunburst that bloomed on her trail and turned the night to brief white day. I wondered for a moment if she had escaped, until I saw the characteristic vortex of a Distorter hole in normal space. The fast moon passed through it and assumed an oddly helical shape as I watched. It was an optical illusion, of course, but it was the prettiest thing that I'd seen in weeks. I hoped, when Confleet came, that they would be alert; for the Aliens were not only alert, they were as touchy as a wounded sleeth. It was going to be no easy task to quell their suspicions. They were ready for whatever the Segovians planned.

I hoped that they would not change their traditional pattern of responding to Segovian attacks. In my book that was asking a lot, but I asked it anyway. I even prayed a little as I started the Pegaso's engine.

Chapter Thirty-One

I stuffed the service Kelly I had brought from the scoutship into the cleft between the front seats and put the box of extra charges in the storage compartment under the dash. Regulations be damned, I thought. This time I wasn't going naked into the snake pit of Segovia. I was going as a representative of the Confederation in Navy uniform, with body shield and a Kelly capable of blowing a hole through ten centimeters of durilium. No one was going to misunderstand who I was and what I was.

I had a bad time getting the Pegaso out of the caldera. I didn't have room enough to go airborne and the road Aspromonte had bulldozed through the low point of the lake bowl in his abortive attempt to raise my ship was a horrid mess suitable only for tracklaying vehicles, yet by some miracle of driving skill which I never imagined I possessed, I brought the car to the rim of the caldera and the easy trail down to the Camino Monosabio.

I stopped at the junction long enough to change into Confederation uniform and weaponry. Then I drove on down the road I had walked two years ago.

As I rolled toward La Cienega, disregarding the warning signs, I thought about Aspromonte and the leader mystique. He had the brains to look farther once his men found my spacesuit; so he had discovered the ship. But then he became impatient. He tried to raise the scout despite the obvious warning of the standby screens. Had he been patient he would have eventually caught me with no defense except an Alpharzian Kelly and he'd have gotten into the ship. But he'd been too eager to destroy the Ring and take the ship and in consequence he lost both La Cienega and the ship. But eagerness was his major fault.

I found the road I wanted and turned off into the hills a few kilometers past the major highway junction where Camino Monosabio intersected the highway between Santayana and Pontecorvo. If I was right, it would not be long before I saw Inez again.

I stopped the car at the corral area at the foot of the talus slope, and after putting my Kelly in its holster and turning on my body shield, I began the ascent to Carlos Ramirez' village. I was halfway up the slope when the rifleman on guard challenged me. I ignored him, and the coruscating blaze of lights as my shield dispersed the bullets he fired at me.

Seeing that his fire was ineffective, the guard sounded the alarm, which brought every able-bodied man to the defense of the village.

In the center of a blinding display of pyrotechnics I walked on toward the village wall. Someone brought up a quick firer which was fairly heavy ordnance. I let them fire two rounds at me and then melted the gun with a needle beam from my Kelly. After that, the alarm signalling retreat sounded and I walked into a deserted village.

I stopped in the center of the street, knowing that the villagers were watching me from their underground retreat.

"Carlos Ramirez," I said. "Come out. I wish to talk to you. I will do you no harm."

"Damn right you won't," Carlos' amplified voice came from the nearest building. "You're right on top of a low yield nuke. Make a move and I'll incinerate you."

"And destroy yourselves," I said.

"That's immaterial."

"But it's a poor exchange."

There was a silence. "Okay," the speaker said, "I'll come out." And come he did, dressed in his work clothes, his floppy hat pushed back on his head, his chin jutting like the prow of an ancient ship. "Just what in hell is this?" he asked.

"A demonstration," I said. "You won't recognize me—"

"Hell I won't. You're that fellow Torres, Inez' man."

"How—" I began.

"Your voice. Sure, you don't look like Torres, but you talk like him, and you knew too much about how to get here to be anyone else. We don't have that many visitors. And besides, you're from Outside.

I think I knew you were an Outsider from the beginning, and from what Inez tells me I've been certain of it ever since your man Robles brought her here. She'll be glad to see you, I think. Or maybe she'll put a knife in you. I don't know which would be best." He looked at me with a quizzical expression. "Your new face sure is no improvement," he said. "You looked better before."

"I'll go into that later," I said. "Is Inez here?"

"Sure—where else could she be that'd be safe from Aspromonte?" He peered at me again and grinned. "The eyes—they are yours as I remember them. So is the voice. Maybe they will be enough to convince her. They convince me, and I'm not in love with you."

I turned off my shield. "Now let us go someplace and talk. I had to show you what you are facing. That is why I came as I did. This, I think, is what the Aliens will use next—goons with defensive shields. They have the technology and if the goons were invulnerable to hand weapons they could decimate the world again."

He nodded. "They almost can do it now. We don't have that much edge."

There was an explosion of movement at the door of the stone house and Inez came running down the street. She stopped, eyed me disapprovingly, muttered something about plastic surgery not changing a man's soul, and was in my arms. The world stopped for a brief golden moment as I recognized just how much I had missed her. And then the three of us went up to the stone house as the villagers began to emerge. They eyed me curiously but with the innate courtesy of their kind they left the three of us alone. And presently the three of us became five as Juanito and Vittorio joined us.

They all had questions as they ushered me into the common room of the house, found me a comfortable chair and a bottle of brandy. I told them everything, and gave a few demonstrations to show I wasn't lying. They watched me with round eyes in which pride mingled with a touch of fear.

"Are all Outsiders like you, José?" Juanito asked.

I shook my head. "Only a few—too few."

"That is good."

"And will our José be like you?" Inez asked.

"Our José?"

"Oh my God!" she said. "I forgot you could not know. I have borne you a son. He is two months old."

"A find healthy boy," Carlos said, "and he is big for his age."

That did it. For awhile everything stopped as Inez brought our child and I felt the odd wonderment of fatherhood. There was a lot of talk, some laughter, a few tears, but nothing consequential until the baby took hold of my finger with a surprisingly firm grip and tried to convey it to his mouth.

"I expect he needs food," I said.

"He always does," Inez said in a curiously self-satisfied tone. "But I expect that we can go into that in private."

"I expect we can," I said.

"I was certain you were from the Outside from the very beginning," Carlos said. "I knew someday that men would come to free us from the Aliens."

"That's not why I am here. I'm here to keep the Aliens from killing you, and to offer them a place in the Confederation."

"But when your fleet comes—"

"Nothing will happen, I hope," I said. "We will make contact with the Aliens. A commission will study your claims and theirs and make a judgment. And we will enforce that judgment."

"But—"

"I told you once, Carlos, that things might not be as you would wish."

"But you are a man—"

"True—but I am also a citizen of the Confederation and an officer in Confleet. I have sworn oaths and I keep my word. I have sworn to protect all intelligent friendly races, and I have sworn to be a true citizen of the Confederation and obey her laws."

"Still—"

"The laws of the Confederation are not the laws of Segovia."

He nodded. "But you will bring us justice?"

"Yes," I said, "but you may not like it."

"As long as it is just—no man can complain."

"But many will." I shrugged. "There is no way my people can keep yours perfectly happy. You will hate us. You cannot help but hate us, for we cannot possibly avoid violating some of your beliefs and customs."

"You can get rid of the Aliens."

"Perhaps we can."

"Then you will have friends on Segovia."

I shrugged. "It isn't that simple, but you'll learn about that from others."

"From others I may not take it as well as I would from you. But that, I think, is not the reason you are here. You came for another purpose."

I nodded. "I came for Inez, but our child makes this impossible."

He shook his head. "Not really. Vittorio's woman has just borne a child and she has plenty of milk. We can care for your son while you are gone."

"But Inez won't like this—"

"On Segovia it is the wishes of the father that count. The wife does as she is told."

I smiled. It sounded good, but Inez was not the average Segovian wife. Yet to my surprise, when I told her what I wanted to do she agreed at once.

"Joselito won't mind. He's too young to know the difference, and I can stand the discomfort until we return. I want to be with you, my husband. We have been too long apart."

Chapter Thirty-Two:

The appointment of Aspromonte as minister of defense had caught him off balance. Although he was not the most powerful single man in the government, he no longer headed the small, well-trained security force that would have done his bidding. Now he had to revise the operations of the ministry to develop the private army he would need to destroy the aliens.

Madalena had worked out a tentative timetable, basing her extrapolations on what she could glean from her agents and her customers. I had more time than I expected. I had been confident that I would have to go into action immediately upon my return to Durango. Instead, I had time enough to work with Inez in an attempt to contact the Aliens. We used the Ring near a place called Paso Leone and tried regularly without success, to make contact.

"They hear me," Inez said bitterly, "but they ignore me. One of the Pair condescended to tell me that they do not talk to animals. They continue to strengthen their defenses and experiment with a new type goon."

"They don't have much originality," I said.

"They don't need much. The goon is still a pretty good homicidal agent. With modifications in brain power and a body shield to turn bullets, the new model should be much more deadly than the old."

"You gave us the anti-goon scent."

"But I have no idea whether it will work on the new model, and they're almost ready to go into production."

"Evars is due anytime," I said hopefully.

"I hope he isn't as slow returning to you as you were to me. He just might have a Mystic in his life." Inez, with a certain amount of justice, disliked and distrusted Madalena, for she saw things which I did not, and with sure feminine instinct realized that the Mystic had been more than my co-worker in the affairs of the Confederation.

I was impatient with sex-based jealousy even though I realized that it could be important on Segovia. After all, I didn't love Madalena; she wasn't the mother of my child; she wasn't truly human; there was no species affinity, and in no way did she have a special place in my heart. Yet I had to agree with Inez that she was thoroughly attractive and desirable. Coming as I did from a civilization that had long since discarded sexual possession, I found it hard to rationalize Inez' attitude, for I always turned to my wife for love, even though I often turned to the Mystic for knowledge.

I would presently have to go to the capitol if I were to follow my plan, and I didn't think it was advisable to leave Inez and Madalena together in Durango. That would be asking for trouble, and I already had enough; so before I left I took Inez to the Valle de Sanmarco and introduced her to her grandmother. The two, somewhat to my surprise, got along beautifully. Indeed, Irina sent for her great grandson and spoiled him shamefully between parties for government officials, and sessions with the neurocytograph after the parties were over. We were rapidly depriving Aspromonte of his support in the capitol, and for awhile we had the hope that he might accept one of the invitations to Irina's parties, but he never did. I didn't think he was suspicious. He was simply too busy reorganizing the ministry of defense. I think he recognized that this office would be the lever that would let him move the world.

Inez was perhaps safer in the Valle de Sanmarco than she was with Ramirez, for the loyalty of Irina's retainers couldn't be suborned by Aspromonte or anyone else. They were tied to her by mental sets reinforced by neurosynthesizing. I didn't think much of the tactic, but I wasn't ready to argue as long as Inez' safety was at stake.

Inez and Irina worked on trying to improve Inez' telepathic ability whenever there was time. Irina was fascinated with tales of life on a ganaderia and of the domestic life of the wife of a matador de toros. Once I heard a portion of one of Inez' tales and was hard put to recognize myself. I was, I suspected, the husband of a congenital—but flattering—liar.

I think Irina treated me with more respect after Inez got through with me. For despite my aura of command, and despite the honor of being a Special Service officer in the Navy, it was much more important that last season I was the number one torero. And despite my belief that bullfighting is a game for mental adolescents, I couldn't help a certain pride in the admiration of the women. I suspect this is one of my greater failings.

Meanwhile I went on with my plans for Aspromonte. I learned that he had known I was in Cantown and had left me in that death in life since it kept me out of his way. I do not ordinarily let personal feelings influence my actions, but with Aspromote I couldn't help but feel there was a certain poetic justice in what I had in mind for him. Actually, I wanted nothing more from Aspromonte than he had wanted from me. I wanted him out of the way until Evars came. Inez, I decided, would be the bait to tempt him into a personal visit to the Valle de Sanmarco. And I let him know by devious means that Inez was with Irina.

He didn't have a chance. Irina's people took him and his guards before they realized what was happening. We took them down to the neurocytograph. We left Aspromonte perfectly normal except for complete aphasia, but a man who can neither speak nor comprehend written symbols is not capable of being a leader. As for his bodyguards, we wiped out their memory of what happened on landing and substituted a pleasant time at the fortress, with a formal reception, a dinner, a long interview between Aspromonte and Irina, and an uneventful trip back to Cuidad Segovia. Then we took them all back to where they came from, and for awhile, at least, Aspromonte was immobilized. I didn't know how long the treatment would last, and Irina couldn't tell me, since she had never tried this technique before.

"It could be a week, Don José; it could be forever," she said.

I shrugged. "It makes little difference. We are committed, now, and if we cannot do what must be done within a week, we will never do it."

"Won't Aspromonte's condition stop them?"

I shook my head. "For a time, perhaps, but not forever. I expect his people will wait to see if he recovers. If he doesn't someone in his organization will take his place. When affairs have advanced as far as they have, they tend to run their course. Killing the commanding general in the middle of a battle does not stop the fighting."

She nodded. "I understand," she said. "Therefore we must continue."

"The thing that bothers me, my lady," I said, "is why you ever allowed yourself to become shorn of power when you had in your hand the ideal means for holding people to you."

"I didn't care," she said softly. "I only wanted to go back to

Palestra. I was living in a dream, and I didn't want to be awakened."

"But you are awake now?"

"The Empire has changed. This I understand. I learned a great deal when I restored your powers, Don José. People like you did not exist in my time."

"They were an outgrowth of the Interregnum," I said. "The Empire is dead. The Barbarians won. Palestra is in ruins. The successor to the Empire is the Confederation, and it exists as much by trickery and compromise as it does by power. The Empire was too simple. It was based on power and human domination. The Brotherhood of Man ruled this sector of the galaxy. And it fell because it had too many intelligent enemies who were not men. They did not know how to rule, but they knew how to destroy a mature political unit that did not have sufficiently rapid communication to concentrate its power.

"The Empire was nibbled to death until its foes had reduced it to its core and the lawless elements organized for the final offensive that brought it down."

She nodded. "I know," she said. "You could not withhold that knowledge from me. Yet I still wish to see Palestra."

"And so you shall. You shall also see Dibrugarh and the worlds of the Confederation. And you will also become the ruler of this world. Not overtly, of course, but your will shall prevail where it does not prevail now. We shall tie these politicians to you with bonds they cannot break, since they will not know they exist."

"And if I become a tyrant?"

"Why should you? You have no reason. A dozen years should be enough to redirect this world, and you can again retire to your valley—to live forever if you wish."

"And what of the Aliens?"

"Inez and I are leaving today to try again. With what you have done for her with neurosynthesis, she thinks she can force the Koalber to listen. If she can, I can convince them."

But we didn't have to. Scarcely an hour later an out-of-breath technician burst into the garden where we were.

"Star-Born," he gasped. "The skies are full of ships!"

Evars had come at last.

Chapter Thirty-Three:

"It was well done, Torres," Admiral Evars said. "The board of inquiry could find no fault in your actions and recommendations once you were restored to full efficiency."

"Thank you, sir," I said.

"Your recommendations, however, have proposed a problem, and one that has been exacerbated during the month you and your family have been on Dibrugarh."

"Yes sir?"

"The Lady Irina de Sanmarco has concluded the series of state banquets and receptions which you started, and Bur Pol informs us that she is now the *de facto* ruler of Segovia."

"That's good. That world needs a single titular head. It still has the Imperial mentality."

"But the Lady Irina does not think she is competent to rule."

"That's bad. For Segovia needs a single head. With someone to make command decisions the Aliens will not be nearly the problem they now are."

"They won't be a problem in any event. They have left."

"Why—?"

"Because they came here and endured the unpleasant conditions only to mine thorium from the planet's mantle. When we showed them that we could deliver the metal to their world cheaper than they could process and ship it, there was no reason for the Rings to remain. They have been dismantled and abandoned. We, meanwhile, have added the Koalber to the Confederation." He grimaced. "They're going to be difficult to assimilate, since they have such a godawful superiority complex, but they're learning that in many ways they aren't as superior as they thought. It was a chastening experience for them when our troops walked straight into their Rings in spite of all their technology. And it was even more chastening when your wife told them what we could have done." Evars built a tent with his fingers. "And now, Torres, I have a new assignment for you."

My heart sank. The past month had been wonderful. Inez, Joselito and I had been having the grandfather of Grand Tours. Special Service rewards successful agents with a lavish hand, and we had made the most of it. I had discovered that there was a streak of conservatism in me that appreciated family life, and I had enjoyed every minute. But now it was over. Inez would be erased from my memory—and I suppose I would be erased from hers. Joselito, being too young to remember, would probably be left alone.

I would go somewhere else on Confederation business, and all this would be as though it had never been. But that is the way it is. The matador does not remain after a corrida. There are other bulls in other towns. And on a larger scale I was still a matador. There were other problems on other worlds. Yet I couldn't help feeling the pain I would soon forget.

Evars shrugged. "We have a problem," he said. "We have been forced to contact a world that was not ready for contact. It is filled with divergent groups that are at loggerheads. Some want isolation. Others want to leap into the Confederation. Others simply want to be left alone. We have managed to get them talking, but they have private armies and hot tempers."

I eyed the prospect with distaste. It was as bad as Segovia. "We've got them talking," Evars said, as if that was an answer. Possibly it was, as far as he was concerned. He had that half kind, half cruel introspective smile on his face. It was the mark of the man and for a moment it repelled me. "And how many lives will be lost before they come to agreement?" I asked.

He looked at me. "Who knows?" he said. "That will be your responsibility. The important thing is to keep them talking and hope that they will some day start listening to each other."

I understood him well enough. The future was his dream. The future was the important thing. I didn't feel that way. To me the present was paramount, but then I'm not Evars, nor will I ever be.

"You will prepare to leave at once, Commodore," Evars said.

"Commodore?"

"The advance in rank is mandatory. The Navy has been

requested to supply a viceroy for the world and viceregal rank is that of Commodore. It is a request we cannot deny, and since you have had experience with developing cultures—" the introspective smile became a grin—"we have decided to send you and your family to Segovia for an indefinite term to represent the Confederation."

About the Author:

J.F. Bone was born in Tacoma, Washington in 1916. A liberal arts graduate from The State College of Washington, he spent nine years in the U.S. Army. During World War II, while in William Beaumont Army Hospital in El Paso, Texas, he learned about corridas de toros, matadors and aficionados. In 1950, he became a doctor of Veterinary Medicine. His first story was published in 1957, and since that time he has published over 40 short stories and five novels, including *The Lani People* (1962), *Legacy* (1976), *The Meddlers* (1976) and *Gift of the Manti* (1977). He now lives with his wife Faye in Corvallis, Oregon.